PENGUIN BOOKS

2122

UNCONDITIONAL SURRENDER

EVELYN WAUGH

Evelyn Waugh was born in Hampstead in 1903, second son of the late Arthur Waugh, publisher and literary critic, and brother of Alec Waugh, the popular novelist. He was educated at Lancing and Hertford College, Oxford, where he read Modern History. In 1927 he published his first work, a life of Dante Gabriel Rossetti, and in 1928 his first novel, *Decline and Fall*, which was soon followed by *Vile Bodies* (1930), *Black Mischief* (1932), *A Handful of Dust* (1934), and *Scoop* (1938). During these years he travelled extensively in most parts of Europe, the Near East, Africa, and tropical America. In 1939 he was commissioned in the Royal Marines and later transferred to the Royal Horse Guards, serving in the Middle East and in Yugoslavia. In 1942 he published *Put Out More Flags* and then, in 1945, *Brideshead Revisited*. *When the Going Was Good* and *The Loved One* were followed by *Helena* (1950), his historical novel. *Men at Arms*, which came out in 1952, is the first volume in a trilogy of war memoirs, and won the James Tait Black Prize; the other volumes, *Officers and Gentlemen* and *Unconditional Surrender*, were published in 1955 and 1961. Evelyn Waugh was received into the Roman Catholic Church in 1930 and his earlier biography of the Elizabethan Jesuit martyr, *Edmund Campion*, was awarded the Hawthornden Prize in 1936. In 1959 he published the official *Life of Ronald Knox*. He is married and has six children. Since 1937 he and his family have lived in the West Country.

EVELYN WAUGH

UNCONDITIONAL SURRENDER

The conclusion of *Men at Arms and Officers and Gentlemen*

PENGUIN BOOKS

Penguin Books Ltd, Harmondsworth, Middlesex, England
Penguin Books Pty Ltd, Ringwood, Victoria, Australia

—

First published by Chapman & Hall 1961
Published by Penguin Books 1964

—

Copyright © Evelyn Waugh, 1961

—

Made and printed in Great Britain
by Hazell Watson & Viney Ltd
Aylesbury, Bucks
Set in Linotype Times

To my daughter
MARGARET
Child of the Locust Years

CONTENTS

Synopsis of Preceding Volumes

'THE enemy at last was in plain view, huge and hateful, all disguise cast off. It was the Modern Age in arms. Whatever the outcome there was a place for him in that battle.'

This was the belief of Guy Crouchback in 1939 when he heard the news of the Molotov–Ribbentrop Treaty. What follows is the story of his attempt to find his 'place in that battle'.

He is 35 years old, rising 36, the only surviving son of his father, Gervase. For some years he has lived alone in Italy in the villa built by his grandfather. Of his brothers one was killed in the war, the other died insane. He had a sister Angela married to an MP, Arthur Box-Bender. The Crouchbacks are a family of old-established, west-country, Catholic gentry allied to most of the other historic recusant families of the country. One of them was martyred under Elizabeth I. Their estates have been sold. The family house, Broome, remains in their possession but is let to a convent. Gervase Crouchback lives in a small seaside hotel at Matchet. He has a bachelor brother, Peregrine, a notorious bore.

Guy married a wife named Virginia who quickly deserted him for a soldier, Tommy Blackhouse. At the time the story opens, she is in process of separation from a third husband, an American named Troy. For eight years she has lived in the world of rich, gay, cosmopolitan society. Guy has grown lonely and joyless. His Church does not allow him to seek a second wife. He sees the war as an opportunity to re-establish his interest in his fellow men and to serve them.

After many difficulties he is commissioned in the Royal Corps of Halberdiers, an unfashionable regiment of infantry, proud of its achievements and peculiarities; he proves himself a reasonably efficient officer. In the Halberdiers he serves under Ritchie-Hook, a ferocious hero of the first war. Among his batch of officers in training are De Souza, a cynic, and Trimmer, a former hairdresser, whose probationary commission is speedly terminated.

Virginia has returned to England at the moment when many are leaving it. One evening on leave Guy attempts to make love to her in Claridge's Hotel but is repulsed with mild ridicule.

He sails on the Dakar expedition, comes under official disapprobation for an escapade arranged by Ritchie-Hook and is indirectly responsible for the death of another officer, by the injudicious gift of a bottle of whisky when he is down with fever. All this time he has ludicrously aroused the suspicions of a secret department of counter-espionage presided over by Grace-Groundling-Marchpole. He returns to England, and becomes attached to the newly formed Commandos, one of which is commanded by Blackhouse. Here he makes friends with Ivor Clare, a dandy. 'Jumbo' Trotter, an ancient Halberdier, deeply versed in service lore, is also temporarily attached to the commando. Clare has a Corporal of Horse named Ludovic, a mysterious reservist recalled to the regiment, who keeps a volume of *pensées*. Ludovic rises to be Brigade Corporal Major. The commando, as part of 'Hookforce', sails to Egypt. Here a brigade-major is attached to them from the staff pool named 'Fido' Hound. Mrs Stitch, a beauty, is in Alexandria with her husband, who holds a cabinet appointment in the Middle East.

Hookforce – without Blackhouse, who has broken his leg – goes to Crete at the moment when the defence is falling. 'Fido' Hound and Ludovic severally desert and meet in a cave on the south coast where an irregular body of Spanish refugees have taken shelter. Nothing more is ever heard of Hound. It is to be supposed that Ludovic perpetrated or connived at his murder. Blackhouse's commando is ordered to provide the rearguard for the disembarkation and surrender on the following morning. That night Clare deserts his troop and insinuates himself into the disembarkation. On the morning of the surrender Guy meets Ludovic on the beach. They join a small party escaping by boat. They suffer acutely from privation and exposure. Ludovic alone remains capable. The delirious sapper officer who was originally in command, disappears overboard during the night. It is to be supposed that Ludovic precipitated him. Finally they reach the African coast. Ludovic carries Guy ashore, and while he is half-conscious in hospital, is sent back to England to be decorated and commissioned. Ludovic believes that Guy knows the truth of the disappearance of 'Fido' Hound. He does know, and has the proof in the written orders to the rearguard, the full culpability of Clare's desertion. Mrs Stitch, in order to save Clare's reputation, gets Guy sent back to England by slow convoy to rejoin the Halberdier Depot.

Virginia meanwhile is in difficulties. Troy no longer remits her allowance. Trimmer is used by Lord Kilbannock, who is Press Officer in Hazardous Offensive Operations HQ, an organization which from small beginnings becomes one of the busiest departments of war, to carry out a raid for publicity purposes. He becomes a national hero and falls deeply in love with Virginia, whom he knew professionally, and with whom he had a brief affair in Glasgow. At Kilbannock's instigation, in order to keep Trimmer in heart for his public appearances, Virginia falls into a prolonged and, to her, distasteful liaison with Trimmer.

As Guy, in the late autumn of 1941, rejoins his regiment he believes that the just cause of going to war has been forfeited in the Russian alliance. Personal honour alone remains.

'The hallucination was dissolved, like the whales and turtles on the voyage from Crete, and he was back after less than two years' pilgrimage in a Holy Land of Illusion in the old ambiguous world, where priests were spies and gallant friends proved traitors and his country was led blundering into dishonour.'

PROLOGUE

Locust Years

WHEN Guy Crouchback returned to his regiment in the autumn of 1941 his position was in many ways anomalous. He had been trained in the first batch of temporary officers, had commanded a company, had been detached for special duties, had been in action and acquitted himself with credit; he had twice put up captain's stars and twice removed them; their scars were plainly visible on his shoulder straps. He had been invalided home on an order direct from GHQ ME and the medical authorities could find nothing wrong with him. There were rumours that he had 'blotted his copybook' in West Africa. When he was commissioned in 1939 his comparative old age had earned him the sobriquet of 'uncle'. Now he was two years older and the second batch of officers in training were younger than those who had joined with him. To them he seemed a patriarch; to him they seemed a generation divided by an impassable barrier. Once he had made the transition, had thrown himself into the mêlée on the ante-room floor, had said 'cheerioh' when he drank with them, and had been accepted as one of themselves. He could not do it a second time. Nor were there any longer mêlées and guest nights, nor much drinking. The new young officers were conscripts who liked to spend their leisure listening to jazz on the wireless. The first battalion, his battalion, followed Ritchie-Hook, biffing across the sands of North Africa. A draft of reinforcements were sent out to them. Guy was not posted with them. Hookforce, all save four, had been taken prisoner in Crete. He had no comrades in arms in England except Tommy Blackhouse who returned to raise another Special Service Force. They met Tommy in Bellamy's and he offered him a post on his staff, but the shadow of Ivor Clare lay dark and long over Commandos, and Guy answered that he was content to soldier on with the Halberdiers.

This he did for two blank years. A Second Brigade was formed, and Guy followed its fortunes in training, with periodic changes of quarters from Penkirk in Scotland to

Brook Park in Cornwall. Homes Forces no longer experienced the shocks, counter-orders, and disorders of the first two years of war. The army in the Far East now suffered as they had done. In Europe the initiative was now with the allies. They were laboriously assembled and equipped and trained. Guy rose to be second-in-command of his battalion with the acting rank of major.

Then in August 1943 there fell on him the blow that had crushed Jumbo at Mugg: 'I'm sorry, uncle, but I'm afraid we shan't be taking you with us when we go to foreign parts. You've been invaluable in training. Don't know what I should have done without you. But I can't risk taking a chap of your age into action.'

'Am I much older than you, colonel?'

'Not much, I suppose, but I've spent my life in this job. If I get hit, the second-in-command will have to take over. Can't risk it.'

'I'd gladly come down in rank. Couldn't I have a company? Or a platoon?'

'Be your age, uncle. No can do. This is an order from brigade.'

The new brigadier, lately arrived from the Eighth Army, was the man to whom, briefly, Guy had been attached in West Africa when he encompassed the death of Apthorpe. On that occasion the brigadier had said: 'I don't want to see you again ever.' He had fought long and hard since then and won a DSO, but throughout the dust of war he remembered Guy. Apthorpe, that brother-uncle, that ghost, laid, Guy had thought, on the island of Mugg, walked still in his porpoise boots to haunt him; the defeated lord of the thunder-box still worked his jungle magic. When a Halberdier said: 'No can do', it was final.

'We shall need you for the embarkation, of course. When you've seen us off, take a spot of leave. After that you're old enough to find yourself something to do. There's always "barrack duties", of course, or you might report to the War House to the pool of unemployed officers. There's plenty of jobs going begging for chaps in your position.'

Guy took his leave and was at Matchet when Italy surrendered. News of the king's flight came on the day the brigade

14

landed at Salerno. It brought Guy some momentary exhilaration.

'That looks like the end of the Piedmontese usurpation,' he said to his father. 'What a mistake the Lateran Treaty was. It seemed masterly at the time – how long? Fifteen years ago? What are fifteen years in the history of Rome? How much better it would have been if the Popes had sat it out and then emerged saying: "What was all that? Risorgimento? Garibaldi? Cavour? the House of Savoy? Mussolini? Just some hooligans from out of town causing a disturbance. Come to think of it wasn't there once a poor little boy whom they called King of Rome?" That's what the Pope ought to be saying today.'

Mr Crouchback regarded his son sadly. 'My dear boy,' he said, 'you're really talking the most terrible nonsense, you know. That isn't at all what the Church is like. It isn't what she's *for*.'

They were walking along the cliffs returning at dusk to the Marine Hotel with Mr Crouchback's retriever, ageing now, not gambolling as he used but loping behind them. Mr Crouchback had aged too, and for the first time showed concern with his own health. They fell silent, Guy disconcerted by his father's rebuke, Mr Crouchback still, it seemed, pondering the question he had raised; for when at length he spoke it was to say: 'Of course it's reasonable for a soldier to rejoice in victory.'

'I don't think I'm interested in victory now,' said Guy.

'Then you've no business to be a soldier.'

'Oh, I want to stay in the war. I should like to do some fighting. But it doesn't seem to matter now who wins. When we declared war on Finland . . .'

He left the sentence unfinished, and his father said: 'That sort of question isn't for soldiers.'

As they came into sight of the hotel, he added: 'I suppose I'm getting like a schoolmaster. Forgive me. We mustn't quarrel. I used often to get angry with poor Ivo; and with Angela. She was rather a tiresome girl the year she came out. But I don't think I've ever been angry with you.'

Matchet had changed in the last two years. The army unit for whom Monte Rosa had been cleared, had gone as quickly as they came, leaving the boarding-house empty. Its blank windows and carpetless floors stood as a symbol of the little town's brief popularity. Refugees from bombing returned to their former homes. Mrs Tickeridge moved to be near a school for Jennifer. The days when the Cuthberts could 'let every room twice over' were ended and they reluctantly found themselves obliged to be agreeable. It was not literally true, as Miss Vavasour claimed, that they 'went down on their knees' to keep their residents, but they did offer Mr Crouchback his former sitting room at its former price.

'No, thank you very much,' he had said. 'You'll remember I promised to take it again *after* the war, and unless things change very much for the worse I shall do that. Meanwhile my few sticks are in store and I don't feel like getting them out again.'

'Oh, we will furnish it for you, Mr Crouchback.'

'It wouldn't be quite the same. You make me very comfortable as I am.'

His former rent was now being paid as a weekly allowance to an unfrocked priest.

The Cuthberts were glad enough to accommodate parents visiting their sons at Our Lady of Victories and obscurely supposed that if they antagonized Mr Crouchback, he would somehow stop their coming.

Guy left next day and reported to the Halberdier barracks. He had little appetite for leave now.

Three days later a letter came from his father:

Marine Hotel
Matchet
20 September 1943

My Dear Guy,

I haven't been happy about our conversation on your last evening. I said too much or too little. Now I must say more.

Of course in the 1870s and 80s every decent Roman disliked the Piedmontese, just as the decent French now hate the Germans. They had been invaded. And, of course, most of the Romans we know kept it up, sulking. But that isn't the Church. The Mystical Body doesn't strike attitudes and stand on its dignity. It accepts suffering and injustice. It is ready to forgive at the first hint of compunction.

When you spoke of the Lateran Treaty did you consider how many souls may have been reconciled and have died at peace as the result of it? How many children may have been brought up in the faith who might have lived in ignorance? Quantitative judgements don't apply. If only one soul was saved that is full compensation for any amount of loss of 'face'.

I write like this because I am worried about you and I gather I may not live very much longer. I saw the doctor yesterday and he seemed to think I have something pretty bad the matter.

As I say, I'm worried about you. You seemed so much enlivened when you first joined the army. I know you are cut up at being left behind in England. But you mustn't sulk.

It was not a good thing living alone and abroad. Have you thought at all about what you will do after the war? There's the house at Broome the village calls 'Little Hall' – quite incorrectly. All the records refer to it simply as the 'Lesser House'. You'll have to live somewhere and I doubt if you'll want to go back to the Castello even if it survives, which doesn't seem likely the way they are bombing everything in Italy.

You see I am thinking a lot about death at the moment. Well that's quite suitable at my age and condition.

> Ever your affec. father,
> G. Crouchback

2

WHEN Hookforce sailed without him, Jumbo Trotter abandoned all hope of active service. He became commandant of No. 6 Transit Camp, London District, a post which required good nature, sobriety, and little else except friends of influence – in all of which qualities Jumbo was rich. He no longer bore resentment against Ben Ritchie-Hook. He accepted the fact that he was on the shelf. The threat of just such a surrender of his own condition overcast Guy.

Jumbo often took a drive to the Halberdier barracks to see what was on. There in late September he found Guy disconsolately installed as PAD officer and assistant adjutant.

'Put in to see the Captain Commandant,' he advised. 'Say

there is something coming through for you any day but you have to be in London. Get posted to the "unemployed pool" and come and stay at my little place. I can make you quite comfortable.'

So Guy moved to Jumbo's little place – Little Hall? Lesser House? – No. 6 Transit Camp, London District, and for a few days looked into the depths of the military underworld. There was a waiting-room in an outlying dependency of the War Office where daily congregated officers of all ages whose regiments and corps had no use for them.

There had been a 'Man-power Directive' from the highest source which enjoined that everyone in the country should be immediately employed in the 'war-effort'. Guy was interviewed by a legless major who said: 'You seem to have done all right. I don't know why they've sent you to this outfit. First Halberdier I've had through my hands. What have you been up to?'

He studied the file in which was recorded all Guy's official biography of the last four years.

'Age,' said Guy.

'Thirty-nine, just rising forty. Yes, that's old for your rank. You're back to captain now of course. Well all I can offer at the moment is a security job at Aden and almoner at a civilian hospital. I don't suppose either particularly appeals to you?'

'No.'

'Well, stick around. I may find something better. But they don't look for good fellows in my office. Look about outside and see what you can find.'

And, sure enough, one evening early in October, after his third attendance on the legless major (who offered him, with undisguised irony, an administrative post in Wales at a school of air photography interpretation) he met Tommy Blackhouse once more in Bellamy's. Tommy now had a brigade of Commandos. He was under orders to sail shortly for Italy to rehearse the Anzio landings and was keeping dead quiet about his movements. He only said, 'Wish you'd decided to come to me, Guy.'

'Too late now?'

'Far too late.'

Guy explained his predicament.

'That's the hell of a mess.'

'The fellow at the War Office has been very civil.'

'Yes, but you'll find he'll get impatient soon. There's a flap about man-power. They'll suddenly pitch you into something awful. Wish I could help.'

Later that evening he said: 'I've thought of something that might do as a stop-gap. I keep a liaison officer at HOO HQ. God knows what he does. Anyway I'm taking him away somewhere else. There are a few odd bodies that have got attached to me. They came under HOO. You could liaise with them for a bit if you liked.'

When Jumbo heard of it, he said: 'Strictly speaking I suppose you aren't "in transit" any more.'

'I hope I am.'

'Well, anyway, stay on here as long as you like. We'll find a way of covering you in the returns. London District is never much trouble. All stock-brokers and wine-merchants from the Foot Guards. Awfully easy fellows to deal with.'

But it was not for this that he had dedicated himself on the sword of Roger of Waybroke that hopeful morning four years back.

BOOK ONE

State Sword

1

IN all the hosts of effigies that throng the aisles of Westminster Abbey one man only, and he a sailor, strikes a martial attitude. The men of the middle ages have sheathed their swords and composed their hands in prayer; the men of the age of reason have donned the toga. A Captain Montagu alone, in Flaxman's posthumous statue, firmly grips his hilt, and, because they had so many greater treasures to protect, the chapter left him to stand there throughout the war unencumbered by sand bags, gazing across the lower nave as he had gazed at the ships of revolutionary France in the waters of Ushant on the day of victory and death.

His name is not well remembered and his portrait, larger than life and portly for his years, has seldom attracted the notice of sightseers. It was not his sword but another which on Friday, 29 October 1943, drew the column of fours which slowly shuffled forward from Millbank, up Great College Street, under a scarred brick wall, on which during the hours of darkness in the preceding spring a zealous, arthritic communist had emblazoned the words, SECOND FRONT NOW, until they reached the door under the blasted and bombed west window. The people of England were long habituated to queues; some had joined the procession ignorant of its end – hoping perhaps for cigarettes or shoes – but most were in a mood of devotion. In the street a few words were exchanged; no laughter.

The day was overcast, damp, misty, and still. Winter overcoats had not yet appeared. Each member of the crowd carried a respirator – valueless now, the experts secretly admitted, against any gas the enemy was likely to employ, but still the badge of a people in arms. Women predominated; here and there a service man – British, American, Polish, Dutch, French – displayed some pride of appearance; the civilians were

21

shabby and grubby. Some, for it was their lunch hour, munched 'Woolton Pies'; others sucked cigarettes made of the sweepings of canteen floors. Bombing had ceased for the time being but the livery of air-raid shelter remained the national dress. As they reached the abbey church, which many were entering for the first time in their lives, all fell quite silent as though they were approaching a corpse lying in state.

The sword they had come to see stood upright between two candles, on a table counterfeiting an altar. Policemen guarded it on either side. It had been made at the King's command as a gift to 'the steel-hearted people of Stalingrad'. An octogenarian, who had made ceremonial swords for five sovereigns, rose from his bed to forge it; silver, gold, rock-crystal, and enamel had gone to its embellishment. In this year of the Sten gun it was a notable weapon and was first exhibited as a feat of craftsmanship at Goldsmith's Hall and at the Victoria and Albert Museum. Some few took comfort at this evidence that ancient skills survived behind the shoddy improvisation of the present. It was not thus that it affected the hearts of the people. Every day the wireless announced great Russian victories while the British advance in Italy was coming to a halt. The people were suffused with gratitude to their remote allies and they venerated the sword as the symbol of their own generous and spontaneous emotion.

The newspapers and the Ministry of Information caught on. *The Times* 'dropped into poetry'.

> ... I saw the Sword of Stalingrad,
> Then bow'd down my head from the Light of it,
> Spirit to my spirit, the Might of it
> Silently whispered – O Mortal, Behold ...
> I am the Life of Stalingrad,
> You and its people shall unite in me,
> Men yet unborn, in the great Light in me
> Triumphs shall sing when my Story is told.

The gossip-writer of the *Daily Express* suggested it should be sent round the kingdom. Cardiff, Birmingham, Sheffield, Manchester, Glasgow, and Edinburgh paid it secular honours in their Art Galleries and Guild Halls. Now, back from its tour, it reached its apotheosis, exposed for adoration hard by the shrine of St Edward the Confessor and the sacring place of the kings of England.

Guy Crouchback drove past the line of devotees on his way to luncheon. Unmoved by the popular enthusiasm for the triumphs of 'Joe' Stalin, who now qualified for the name of 'uncle', as Guy had done and Apthorpe, he was not tempted to join them in their piety. 29 October 1943, had another and more sombre significance for him. It was his fortieth birthday and to celebrate the occasion he had asked Jumbo Trotter to luncheon.

It was through Jumbo's offices that he now sat at ease behind a FANNY driver instead of travelling by bus. After four years of war Jumbo preserved his immunity to sumptuary regulations. As also did Ruben. In a famine-stricken world the little fish-restaurant dispensed in their seasons Colchester oysters, Scotch salmon, lobsters, prawns, gulls' eggs, which rare foods were specifically exempt from the law which limited the price of hotel meals to five shillings, and often caviar, obtained, only Ruben knew how, through diplomatic channels. Most surprising of all there sometimes appeared cheeses from France, collected by intrepid parachutists and conveyed home by submarine. There was an abundance of good wine, enormously costly, at a time when the cellars of the hotels were empty and wine merchants dealt out meagre monthly parcels only to their oldest customers. Ruben had for some years enjoyed a small and appreciative clientèle. Once he had served in Bellamy's and there were always tables for its members. There was also an increasing dilution of odd-looking men who called the proprietor 'Mr Ruben' and carried large quantities of bank notes in their hip pockets. That restaurant was a rare candle in a dark and naughty world. Kerstei Kilbannock, who had made noxious experiments with custard powder and condiments, once asked: 'Do tell me, Ruben, how do you make your mayonnaise?' and received the grave reply: 'Quite simply, my lady, fresh eggs and olive oil.'

Guy led Jumbo to a corner table. He had spent little time in London since his return from Egypt and he could seldom

23

afford to feast, but Ruben was loyal to old faces and familiar names.

'Rather a change from the Senior,' Jumbo remarked as he surveyed the company. 'A *great* change,' he added as he read the menu. They consumed great quantities of oysters. As they rose surfeited from their table, it was seized by a couple who had just come in; Kerstei Kilbannock and an American soldier. As though playing musical chairs, she was in Jumbo's warm place before he had taken his cap from the peg above him.

'Guy, how are you?'

'Forty.'

'We've been lunching with Ruby at the Dorchester and are so hungry we had to pop in here and fill up. You know the Lootenant?'

'Yes, indeed. How are you, Loot?'

Everyone knew Lieutenant Padfield; even Guy who knew so few people. He was a portent of the Grand Alliance. London was full of American soldiers, tall, slouching, friendly, woefully homesick young men who seemed always in search of somewhere to sit down. In the summer they had filled the parks and sat on the pavements round the once august mansions which had been assigned to them. For their comfort there swarmed out of the slums and across the bridges multitudes of drab, ill-favoured adolescent girls and their aunts and mothers, never before seen in the squares of Mayfair and Belgravia. These they passionately and publicly embraced, in the blackout and at high noon, and rewarded with chewing-gum, razor-blades, and other rare trade-goods from their PX stores. Lieutenant Padfield was a horse of a different colour; not precisely, for his face, too, was the colour of putty; he too slouched; he, too, was a sedentary by habit. But he was not at all homesick; when not in a chair he must have been in rapid motion, for he was ubiquitous. He was twenty-five years old and in England for the first time. He had been one in the advanced party of the American army and there was no corner of the still intricate social world where he was not familiar.

Guy first met him when on leave he went reluctantly to call on his uncle Peregrine. This was during the Loot's first days in England.

'. . . Brought a letter from a fellow who used to come to Cowes. Wants to see my miniatures. . . .'

Then during the same week Guy was asked to dinner at the House of Commons by his brother-in-law Arthur Box-Bender. '. . . Told we ought to do something about some of these Americans. They're interested in the House, naturally. Do come along and give a hand. . . .' There were six young American officers, the Loot among them.

Very soon he had ceased to be a mere member of the occupying forces to whom kindness should be shown. Two or three widows survived from the years of hospitality and still tried meagrely to entertain. The Lieutenant was at all their little parties. Two or three young married women were staking claims to replace them as hostesses. The Loot knew them all. He was in every picture gallery, every bookshop, every club, every hotel. He was also in every inaccessible castle in Scotland, at the sick bed of every veteran artist and politician, in the dressing-room of every leading actress and in every university common-room, and he expressed his thanks to his hosts and hostesses not with the products of the PX stores but with the publications of Sylvia Beach and sketches by Fuseli.

When Guy went to have his hair cut the Loot seemed always to be in the next chair. One of the few places where he was never seen was HOO HQ. He had no apparent military function. In the years of peace he had been the junior member of an important firm of Boston lawyers. It was said that the Loot's duties were still legal. Either the American army was exceptionally law-abiding or they had a glut of advocates. The Loot was never known to serve on a court-martial.

Now he said: 'I was at Broome yesterday.'

'Broome? You mean our Broome? What on earth took you there, Loot?'

'Sally Sackville-Strutt has a daughter at the school. We went to see her play hockey. She's captain of "Crouchback". You knew the school was divided into two houses called "Crouchback" and the "Holy Family"?'

'The invidious distinction has been remarked on.'

' "Crouchback" won.' He began beckoning to Ruben. 'Do we meet tonight at the Glenobans?'

'No.'

'Did you go to see the Sword of Stalingrad? I went when it was first on view at the Goldsmiths' Hall. I think it is a very lovely gesture of your king's but there was a feature no one could explain to me – the escutcheon on the scabbard will be upside down when it is worn on a baldric.'

'I don't suppose Stalin will wear it on a baldric.'

'Maybe not. But I was certainly surprised at your College of Arms passing it. Well I'll be seeing you around.'

'Around' was the right word.

'Pretty fair cheek that young American finding fault with the sword,' said Jumbo as they left the restaurant. 'What's more *he* didn't discover the mistake. There was a letter about it in *The Times* weeks ago. I'll drop you back at your office. Can't have you using public transport on your birthday. I haven't anything much on this afternoon. That was the best lunch I've had for three years. I may take a little nap.'

In the autumn of 1943 Hazardous Offensive Operations Headquarters was a very different organization from the modest offices which Guy had visited in the winter of 1940. The original three flats remained part of their property – an important part, for they housed Ian Kilbannock's busy Press service – as did numerous mansions from Hendon to Clapham in which small bands of experts in untroubled privacy made researches into fortifying drugs, invisible maps, noiseless explosives, and other projects near to the heart of the healthy schoolboy. There was a Swahili witch-doctor in rooms off the Edgware Road who had been engaged to cast spells on the Nazi leaders.

'D'you know, Charles, I sometimes think that black fellow's something of a charlatan,' General Whale once remarked to Major Albright in a moment of confidence. 'He indents for the most extraordinary stores. But we know Hitler's superstitions and there's a good deal of evidence that with superstitious people these curses do sometimes work.'

Even Dr Glendening-Rees, fully recovered from the privations of Mugg, had a dietary team in Upper Norwood, from whose experiments batches of emaciated 'conscientious objectors' were from time to time removed to hospital. But the ostensible authority of these activities resided in the Venetian-Gothic brick edifice of the Royal Victorian Institute, a museum nobly planned but little frequented in the parish of Brompton. Its few valuable exhibits had been removed to safe storage. Other less portable objects had been left to the risks of bombardment and still stood amid the labyrinth of ply-board partitions with which the halls were divided.

The compartment assigned to the Special Service Forces Liaison Office – Guy's – was larger than most but there was little floor space for he shared it with the plaster reconstruction of a megalosaurus, under whose huge flanks his trestle table was invisible from the door. This table carried three wire trays 'In', 'Out', and 'Pending', all empty that afternoon – a telephone, and a jig-saw puzzle. For the first few days of his occupancy he had had an AT secretary but she had been removed by a newly installed civilian efficiency-expert. Guy did not repine, but to fill his time, he prosecuted a controversy on the subject. Tommy had said he did not know what the liaison office was supposed to do; nor did Guy.

A captain of Marines peered round the giant carnivore and presented him with a file marked: *Operation Hoopla. Most Secret. By Hand of Officer only*.

'Will you minute this and pass it on to "Beaches"?'

'I thought "Hoopla" had been cancelled.'

'Postponed,' said the Marine. 'The party we had in training was sent to Burma. But we're still working on it.'

The intention of 'Hoopla' was to attack some prodigious bomb-proof submarine-pens in Brittany. A peremptory demand for Immediate Action against these strongholds had been received from the War Cabinet. 'If the Air Force can't destroy the ships, we can kill the crews,' General Whale had suggested. Twelve men were to perform this massacre after landing in a Breton fishing boat.

The latest minute read:

In view of Intelligence Report C/806/RT/12 that occupied France is being supplied with ersatz motor fuel which gives an easily recognizable character to exhaust fumes, it is recommended that samples of this fuel should be procured through

appropriate agency, analysed, reproduced, and issued to
Hoopla Force for use in auxiliary engine of fishing boat.

Someone before Guy had added the minute: *Could not a*
substance be introduced into standard fuel which would pro-
vide a characteristic odour of ersatz?

Someone else, an admiral, had added: *It was decided (see*
attached minute) that auxiliary engine should be used only
under a strong offshore wind. I consider risk of detection of
odour negligible in such circumstances.

Guy more modestly wrote: *Noted and approved. Guy*
Crouchback, Capt. for Brig. Commander S.S. Forces, and
squeezed past the megalosaurus to carry the file on its
way.

'Beaches' was rather a jovial room. It housed an early Victorian locomotive engine, six sailors, and a library of naval
charts. The reappearance of 'Hoopla' was here greeted with
ironic applause. Some time back General Whale had forfeited
the kindly sobriquet of 'Sprat' and was now known in the lower
and more active regions of his command as 'Brides-in-thebath'; for the reason that all the operations he sponsored
seemed to require the extermination of all involved.

Next door to 'Beaches' there lived three RAF sergeants in
what was called 'the studio'. Here beaches were constructed in
miniature, yards and yards of them, reproducing from air-
photographs miles and miles of the coast of occupied Europe.
The studio was fully of tools and odd scraps of material,
woods, metals, pastes, gums, pigments, feathers, fibres, plasters,
and oils many of them strongly aromatic. The tone was egali-
tarian in an antiquated, folky way distantly derived from the
disciples of William Morris. Two of the sergeants were mature
craftsmen; one, much younger, wore abundant golden curls
such as the army would have cropped. He was addressed as
'Susie' and like his predecessors in the Arts and Crafts movement professed communism.

In their ample spare time these ingenious men were building
a model of the Royal Victorian Institute. Guy took every
opportunity to visit them and admire their work, as it daily
grew in perfection. He paused there now.

'Been to see the Stalingrad sword?' Susie asked. 'Nice bit

of work. But I reckon a few machine guns would be more to the point.'

He was addressing a tall, grey civilian dandy who stood nonchalantly posed beside him twirling a single eye-glass on its black cord. This was Sir Ralph Brompton, the diplomatic adviser to HOO HQ. He seemed a figure of obsolescent light comedy rather than of total war.

'It affords the People an opportunity for self-expression,' said Sir Ralph.

He was a retired ambassador who daily patrolled the building in the self-imposed task of 'political indoctrination'; an old man with a mission, but in no hurry.

He had called on Guy and after a very few words had despaired of him as a sympathetic subject. He did not now disguise his annoyance at being found with Susie.

'I just dropped in,' he said, half to Guy, half to the senior sergeant, 'to see if you were getting the *Foreign Affairs Summary* regularly.'

'I don't know' said the senior sergeant. 'Are we, Sam?' He looked vaguely round the littered work-benches. 'We don't get bothered with much paper work here.'

'But you *should*,' said Sir Ralph. 'I make a special point of it being circulated to *all* ranks. Much devoted labour went into the last issue. You have to read between the lines sometimes. I'm at a disadvantage in saying quite all that needs saying in black and white. There is still a certain amount of prejudice to be cleared up – not in the highest quarters, of course, or among the People. But *half way down*,' he said, gazing at Guy through his single eyeglass, without animosity seeing him with his back to a wall, facing a firing squad. 'One learns a certain amount of professional discretion in my absurd occupation. There will be no need for that after the war. Meanwhile one can only hint. I can tell you the main points: Tito's the friend, not Mihajlovic. We're backing the wrong horse in Malaya. And in China too. Chiang is a collaborationist. We have proof. The only real resistance is in the northern provinces – Russian trained and Russian armed, of course. They are the men who are going to drive out the Japs. It's all in the *Summary* if you read it attentively. I'll get you a copy. Don't forget this evening, Susie. I'm afraid I can't be there myself, but they are counting on you.'

He sauntered out twirling his eyeglass.

'What are you and that old geezer up to?' asked Sam.

'Party meeting,' said Suzie.

'I know better things to do in the blackout than meetings.'

'So does the old geezer, it seems,' said the third sergeant.

'He's a bit of a bourgeois at heart for all his fine talk,' Susie admitted. All the time he spoke he was concentrating on his small lathe, turning tiny spiral columns with exquisite precision.

'You'll soon have that finished,' said Guy to the senior sergeant.

'Yes, barring interruptions. You can never tell when they'll come asking for more beaches. There isn't the same satisfaction in beaches.'

'They ought to have landed on them this summer,' said Susie. 'That's what was promised.'

'I didn't give no promises,' said Sam, busy with the fretsaw cutting little mahogany flagstones.

Guy left these happy, industrious men and paused in his progress at the room of Mr Oates, the civilian efficiency expert.

No one could be reasonably described as 'out of place' in HOO HQ, but Mr Oates, despite his unobtrusive appearance (or by reason of it), seemed bizarre to Guy. He was a plump, taciturn little man and he alone among all his heterogeneous colleagues proclaimed confidence. Of the others some toiled mindlessly, passing files from tray to tray, some took their ease, some were plotting, some hiding, some grousing; all quite baffled. But Mr Oates believed he was in his own way helping to win the war. He was a profoundly peaceful man and his way seemed clear before him.

'Any result of my application for the return of my typist?'

'Negative,' said Mr Oates.

'Kilbannock has three typists.'

'Not now. I have just withdrawn two of them. There is another, Mrs Troy, who is officially attached to him but her work seems mainly extramural. In fact her position is somewhat anomalous in this headquarters. I shall raise it at the next man-power conference.'

There had been a showy addition to Mr Oates's furniture since Guy's last visit; an elaborate machine of more modern construction than any permanent exhibit in the museum.

'What have you got there?'

Mr Oates made a little grimace of gratification.

'Ah! You have found my tender spot. You might call it my pet. Absolutely new. It's just been flown in from America. It took 560 man hours to install. The mechanics came from America, too. There isn't another like it in the country.'

'But what is it?'

'An Electronic Personnel Selector.'

'Have we any electronic personnel?'

'It covers every contingency. For example, suppose I want to find a lieutenant-colonel who is a long-distance swimmer, qualified as a barrister, with experience in catering in tropical countries, instead of going through all the records I just press these buttons, one, two, three, four, and ...' there was a whirring noise from the depths of the engine a series of clicks as though from a slot-machine telling fortunes on a pier, a card shot up. 'You see – totally blank – that means negative.'

'I think I could have guessed that.'

'Yes, I was illustrating an extreme example. Now here' – he picked up a chit from his tray – 'is a genuine inquiry. I've been asked to find an officer for special employment; under forty, with a university degree, who has lived in Italy, and had Commando training – one, two, three, four, five –' whirr, click, click, click, click, click. 'Here we are. Now that *is* a remarkable coincidence.'

The card he held bore the name of A/Ty. Captain Crouchbank, G., RC, att. HOO HQ.

Guy did not attempt to correct the machine on the point of his age, or of the extent of his Commando training.

'I seem the only one.'

'Yes. I don't know what it's for, of course, but I will send your name in at once.'

2

THIRTY-SEVEN years old, six foot two in height, upright, powerful, heavier than he had been in the Middle East and paler, with a hint of flabbiness in the cheeks, wearing service dress, a well-kept Sam Browne belt, the ribbon of the MM and the badges of a Major in the Intelligence Corps; noticeable, if at all, for the pink-grey irises of his eyes; the man whom Hookforce had known as Corporal Major Ludovic paused reminiscently by the railings of St Margaret's, Westminster.

This was the place where he and others of his regiment had paraded twelve years and a few months ago, in King's Guard order as guard of honour for the wedding of one of their officers. Ludovic was a corporal then. The crowds had been enormous, less orderly and lighter of heart than those who now shuffled forward towards the Abbey, for the bride was a fashionable beauty and the bridegroom's name was familiar on advertisement hoardings and the labels of beer bottles.

They had lined the aisle; then while the register was being signed, had formed up along this path which led from the door to the motor car. Their finery had excited cries of admiration. As the organ sounded the first notes of the Wedding March they had drawn their swords and held them in a posture for which no drill-book has a name, forming an arch over the wedded couple. The bride had smiled right and left looking up at each of them in the eyes, thanking them. The bridegroom held his top hat in his hand and greeted by name those of his squadron he recognized. Two manikins carried the train clothed at enormous cost in replicas of Ludovic's own uniform; then the bridesmaids, plumper and plainer than the bride but flowery in full June. Then they had lowered their swords to the 'carry'; a royal party had passed between them smiling also; then parents, and after them a long stream of guests; scarcely visible under the peak of the helmet behind and all round them were reporters and photographers and a cheering, laughing London crowd.

It was after that wedding, in the tented yard behind a house in St James's Square (now demolished by a bomb), that Sir Ralph Brompton had first accosted Ludovic. The royal party sat in the ballroom on the first floor, where the young couple received their guests. A temporary wooden stair had been built from the ballroom balcony to the tent (for it was a rule that no member of the royal family should be in a room without an alternative egress) and the guests, after they had made their salutations, went below, leaving that still little pool of humble duty for the noisier celebrations under the canvas. Later, when they discussed the question, as they often did, neither Sir Ralph nor Ludovic was able to explain what distinguished the young corporal from his fellows, except that he stood a little apart from them. He did not like beer, and great jugs of special brew, made by the bridegroom's father for the occasion, were being pressed on the guard of honour, the tenants, and fore-men and old servants who segregated themselves in their own corner of the marquee. Sir Ralph, as tall as any trooper and almost as splendid in grey tail suit and full cravat, had joined the convivial, plebeian group and said: 'You're much better off with the ale. The champagne is poison,' and so had begun an association which developed richly.

Sir Ralph was then doing a spell at the Foreign Office. When the time came for him to go abroad on post, he arranged for Ludovic's release from the regiment, who were sorry to lose him; he had lately been promoted corporal of horse at an early age. Then had begun five years' life abroad in Sir Ralph's company, as 'valet' at the embassy, as 'secretary' when they travelled on leave. Sir Ralph discreetly attended to his protégé's education, lending him books on psychology which he relished and on Marxist economics which he found tedious; giving him tickets for concerts and the opera, leading him, when they were on holiday, through galleries and cathedrals.

The marriage did not last long. There was an unusually early divorce. Ludovic, as he now was, constituted the sole progeny of that union.

It was 5 o'clock. At 5.30 the Abbey had to be shut for the night. Already the police were turning away the extremity of the queue saying: 'You won't get in today. Come back to-morrow morning – early,' and the people obediently drifted into the dusk to join other queues elsewhere.

Major Ludovic went straight to the Abbey entrance, laid his blank oyster gaze on the policeman and raised his gloved hand to acknowledge a salute that had not been given.

' 'Ere, just a moment, sir, where are you going?'

'The – er – King's present to the – er – Russians – they tell me it's on show here.'

'Got to wait your turn. There's others before you, sir.'

Ludovic spoke with two voices. He had tried as an officer; now he reverted to the tones of the barrack-room. 'That's all right, cock. I'm here on duty same as yourself,' and the puzzled man stood back to let him by.

Inside the Abbey it seemed already night. The windows gave no light. The two candles led the people forward, who, as they were admitted in twenties, broke their column of fours, advanced in a group and then fell into single file as they reached the sword. They knew no formal act of veneration. They paused, gazed, breathed, and passed on. Ludovic was the tallest of them. He could see the bright streak from above their heads. He held his cap and his cane behind his back and peered intently. He had a special interest there, but when he came to the sword and tried to linger he was pressed silently on, not jostled resentfully, but silently conscripted into that unseeing, inarticulate procession who were asserting their right to the fair share of everything which they believed the weapon symbolized. He had no time to study the detail. He glimpsed the keen edge, the sober ornament, the more luxurious scabbard, and then was borne on and out. It was not five minutes before he found himself once more alone, in the deeping fog.

Ludovic had an appointment with Sir Ralph for 5.30. He had to meet by appointment in these days. They were no longer on the old easy terms, but Ludovic did not lose touch. In his altered and exalted status he did not look for money, but there were other uses to which their old association could be put. Whenever he came to London he let Sir Ralph know and they had tea together. Sir Ralph had other companions for dinner. They met at their old place of assignation. Once Sir Ralph had a house in Hanover Terrace, and his retreat in Ebury Street – rooms over a shop, which had something of the air of expensive undergraduate digs – had been a secret known to barely fifty men. Now these rooms were his home; he had moved the smaller pieces of his furniture there; but not many more people – fewer perhaps – knew the way there than in the old days.

Ludovic walked down Victoria Street, crossed the shapeless expanse at the bottom and reached the familiar doorstep at the same moment as his host. Sir Ralph opened the door and stood back for Ludovic to enter. He had never lacked devoted servants. 'Mrs Embury,' he called, 'Mrs Embury,' and his housekeeper appeared above them on the half landing. She had known Ludovic in other days.

'Tea,' he said, handing her a little parcel 'Lapsang Suchong – half a pound of it. Bartered in what strange eastern markets, I know not. But the genuine article. I have a friend at our headquarters who gets me some from time to time. We must go easy with it, Mrs Embury, but I think we might "brew up" for "the Major".'

They went upstairs and sat in the drawing-room.

'No doubt you want to hear my opinion of your "*Pensées*".'

'I want to hear Everard Spruce's.'

'Yes, of course, I deserved that little snub. Well, prepare yourself for good news – Everard is *delighted* with them and wants to publish them in *Survival*. He is quite content to leave them anonymous. The only thing he doesn't quite like is the title.'

'*Pensées*,' said Ludovic. 'D'you know what they call our badge?' He tapped the floral device on the lapel of his tunic. ' "A pansy sitting on its laurels".'

'Yes, yes. Very good. I have heard the witticism before. No; Everard thinks it dated. He suggests "Notes in Transit" or something of the sort.'

'I don't see it matters.'

'No. But he's definitely interested in you. Wants to meet. In fact I tentatively accepted an invitation for you this evening. I shan't, alas, be able to introduce you. But you're expected. I'll give you the address. I am expecting another visitor here.'

'Curly?'

'They call him "Susie" at the headquarters. No, not Susie. He's a dear boy and a stalwart party member but a little earnest for the long blackout. I am packing him off to a meeting. No I expect a very intelligent young American named Padfield – an officer, *like you*.'

Mrs Embury brought in the tea, and the little, over-furnished room was full of its fragrance.

'I can't offer you anything to eat I'm afraid.'

'I know better than come to London for food,' said Ludovic. 'We do all right at my billet.' He had learned his officer's voice from Sir Ralph but seldom used it when they were alone. 'Mrs Embury isn't very matey these days?'

'It's your high rank. She doesn't know how to take it. And you, what have you been up to?'

'I went to the Abbey before I came here – to see the sword.'

'Yes, I suppose like everyone else you are coming to appreciate the Soviet achievement. You usen't to have much share in my "red" sympathies. We nearly had a tiff once, remember? about Spain.'

'There were Spaniards in the Middle East – proper bastards.' Ludovic stopped short remembering what he resolutely strove to forget. 'It wasn't anything to do with politics. That sword is the subject of this week's literary competition in *Time and Tide* – a sonnet. I thought if I went to see it, I might get some ideas.'

'Oh dear, don't tell Everard Spruce about that. I'm afraid he would look down his nose at literary competitions in *Time and Tide*.'

'I just like writing,' said Ludovic. 'In different ways about different things. Nothing wrong with that, I suppose?'

'No, indeed. The literary instinct. But don't tell Everard. *Did* you get any ideas?'

'Not what I could use in a sonnet. But it set me thinking – about swords.'

'That wasn't quite their idea; not, as they say now, the object of the exercise. You were meant to think about tanks and bombers and the People's Army driving out the Nazis.'

'I thought of *my* sword,' said Ludovic stubbornly. 'Technically, I suppose, it was a sabre. *We* called them "swords" – "state swords". Never saw it again after I left the regiment. They weren't reissued when we were recalled. Took a lot of looking after, a sword. Every now and then the armourer had them in and buffed them; ordinary days it was Bluebell and the chain-burnisher. Mustn't leave a spot on it. You could always tell a good officer. On a wet day he didn't give the order "Return swords" but "With drawn swords, prepare to dismount". You took it half way up the blade in your left hand and transferred to the near side of the withers. That way you didn't get water into the scabbard. Some officers didn't think of that; the good ones did.'

'Yes, yes, most picturesque,' said Sir Ralph. 'Not much bearing on the conditions at Stalingrad.'

Then Ludovic suddenly assumed his officer's voice and said 'After all, it was the uniform first attracted you, don't you remember?'

Only a preternaturally astute reader of Ludovic's aphorisms could discern that their author had once been at heart – or rather in some vestigial repository of his mind – a romantic. Most of those who volunteered for Commandos in the spring of 1940 had other motives besides the desire to serve their country. A few merely sought release from regimental routine; more wished to cut a gallant figure before women; others had led lives of particular softness and were moved to re-establish their honour in the eyes of the heroes of their youth – legendary, historical, fictitious – that still haunted their manhood. Nothing in Ludovic's shortly to be published work made clear how he had seen himself. His early schooling had furnished few models of chivalry. His original enlistment in the Blues, so near the body of the king, so flamboyantly accoutred, had certainly not been prompted by any familiarity or affection for the horse. Ludovic was a townsman. The smell of stables brought no memories of farm or hunt. In his years with Sir Ralph Brompton he had lived soft; any instinct for expiation of which he was conscious, was unexpressed. Yet he had volunteered for special service at the first opportunity. His fellow volunteers now had ample leisure in their various prison camps to examine their motives and strip themselves of illusion. As also had Ludovic, at liberty; but his disillusionment (if he ever suffered from illusion) had preceded the débâcle at Crete. There was a week in the mountains, two days in a cave, a particular night in an open boat during the exploit that had earned him his MM and his commission, of which he never spoke. When questioned, as he had been on his return to Africa, he confessed that his memory of those events was almost blank; a very common condition, sympathetic doctors assured him, after a feat of extreme endurance.

His last two years had been as uneventful as Guy's.

After his rapid discharge from hospital he had been posted to the United Kingdom to be trained as an officer. At the board who interviewed him, he had expressed no preference for any arm of the service. He had no mechanical bent. They had posted him to the Intelligence Corps, then in process of formation and expansion. He had attended courses, learned to interpret air-photographs, to recognize enemy uniform, and compute an order of battle, to mark maps, to collate and sum-marize progress-reports from the field; all the rudimentary skills. At the end his early peace-time training as a trooper impressed the selection-board that he was a 'quartermaster type' and an appointment was found for him far from the battle, far from the arcane departments whose existence was barely hinted at in the lecture room; in a secret place, indeed, but one where no secrets were disclosed to Ludovic. He was made commandant of a little establishment where men, and sometimes women, of all ages and nations, military and civilian, many with obviously assumed names, were trained at a neighbouring aerodrome to jump in parachutes.

Thus whatever romantic image of himself Ludovic had ever set up was finally defaced.

In his lonely condition he found more than solace, positive excitement, in the art of writing. The further he removed from human society and the less he attended to human speech, the more did words, printed and written, occupy his mind. The books he read were books about words. As he lay unshriven, his sleep was never troubled by the monstrous memories which might have been supposed to lie in wait for him in the dark. He dreamed of words and woke repeating them as though memorizing a foreign vocabulary. Ludovic had become an addict of that potent intoxicant, the English language.

Not laboriously, luxuriously rather, Ludovic worked over his note-books, curtailing, expanding, polishing; often consulting Fowler, not disdaining Roget; writing and rewriting in his small clerkly hand on the lined sheets of paper which the army supplied; telling no one what he was up to, until at length there were fifty foolscap pages, which he sent to Sir Ralph, not asking his opinion, but instructing him to find a publisher.

It was in miniature a golden age for the book-trade; anything sold; the supply of paper alone determined a writer's popularity. But publishers had obligations to old clients and an eye to the future. Ludovic's *pensées* stirred no hopes of a sequel of best-selling novels. The established firms were on the look out for promise rather than accomplishment. Sir Ralph therefore sent the manuscript to Everard Spruce, the founder and editor of *Survival*; a man who cherished no ambitions for the future, believing, despite the title of his monthly review, that the human race was destined to dissolve in chaos.

The war had raised Spruce, who in the years preceding it had not been the most esteemed of his coterie of youngish, socialist writers, to unrivalled eminence. Those of his friends who had not fled to Ireland or to America had joined the Fire Brigade. Spruce by contrast had stood out for himself and in that disorderly period when Guy had sat in Bellamy's writing so many fruitless appeals for military employment, had announced the birth of a magazine devoted 'to the Survival of Values'. The Ministry of Information gave it protection, exempted its staff from other duties, granted it a generous allowance of paper, and exported it in bulk to whatever countries were still open to British shipping. Copies were even scattered from aeroplanes in regions under German domination and patiently construed by partisans with the aid of dictionaries. A member who complained in the House of Commons that so far as its contents were intelligible to him, they were pessimistic in tone and unconnected in subject with the war effort, was told at some length by the Minister that free expression in the arts was an essential of democracy. 'I personally have no doubt,' he said, 'and I am confirmed in my opinion by many reports, that great encouragement is given to our allies and sympathizers throughout the world by the survival' (laughter) 'in this country of what is almost unique in present conditions, a periodical entirely independent of official direction.'

Spruce lived in a fine house in Cheyne Walk cared for by secretaries to the number of four. It was there that Ludovic was directed by Sir Ralph. He went on foot through the lightless streets, smelling the river before him in the deepening fog.

He was not entirely unacquainted with men of letters. Several had been habitués of Ebury Street; he has sat at café tables with them on the Mediterranean coast; but always in those days he had been an appendage of Sir Ralph's, sometimes ignored, sometimes punctiliously brought into the conversation, often impertinently studied; never regarded as a possible confrère. This was the first time that Ludovic had gone among them in his own right. He was not the least nervous but he was proudly conscious of a change of status far more gratifying than any conferred by military rank.

Spruce was in his middle thirties. Time was, he cultivated a proletarian, youthful, aspect; not successfully; now, perhaps without design, he looked older than his years and presented the negligent elegance of a fashionable don. One of his friends, on joining the Fire Brigade, had left a trunk under Spruce's protection and when he was buried by a falling chimney Spruce had appropriated his wardrobe; the secretaries had adjusted the Charvet shirts and pyjamas; the suits were beyond their skill; Spruce was, thus, often seen abroad in a voluminous furlined overcoat, while at home, whenever the temperature allowed, he dispensed with a jacket. Tonight he wore a heavy silk, heavily striped shirt and a bow tie above noncommittal trousers. The secretaries were dressed rather like him though in commoner materials; they wore their hair long and enveloping, in a style which fifteen years later was to be associated by the newspapers with the King's Road. One went bare-footed as though to emphasize her servile condition. They were sometimes spoken of as 'Spruce's veiled ladies'. They gave him their full devotion; also their rations of butter, meat, and sugar.

One of these opened the door to Ludovic and without asking

his name said through a curtain of hair: 'Do come in quick. The blackout's not very efficient. They're all upstairs.'

There was a party in the drawing-room on the first floor.

'Which is Mr Spruce?'

'Don't you know? Over there, of course, talking to the Smart Woman.'

Ludovic looked round the room where, in a company of twenty or so, women predominated, but none appeared notably dressy, but the host identified himself by coming forward with an expression of sharp inquiry.

'I am Ludovic,' said Ludovic. 'Ralph Brompton said you were expecting me.'

'Yes, of course. Don't go until we have had the chance of a talk. I must apologize for the crowd. Two anti-fascist neutrals have been wished on me by the Ministry of Information. They asked me to collect some interesting people. Not easy these days. Do you speak Turkish or Portuguése?'

'No.'

'That's a pity. They are both professors of English Literature but not very fluent in conversation. Come and talk to Lady Perdita.'

He led Ludovic to the woman with whom he had been standing. She was wearing the uniform of an air-raid warden and had smudges of soot on her face. 'Smart', Ludovic perceived denoted rank rather than chic in this milieu.

'I was at your wedding,' said Ludovic.

'Surely not? No one was.'

'Your first wedding.'

'Oh, yes, of course, everyone was *there*.'

'I held my sword over your head when you left the church.'

'That was a long time ago,' said Lady Perdita. 'Think of it; *swords*.'

The bare-footed secretary approached with a jug and a glass.

'Will you have a drink?'

'What is it?'

'There's nothing else,' she said. 'I made it. Half South African Sherry and half something called "Olde Falstaffe Gin".'

'I don't think I will, thank you,' said Ludovic.

'Snob,' said Lady Perdita. 'Fill me up, Frankie, there's a dear.'

'There's hardly enough to go round.'

'I'll have this chap's ration.'

The host interrupted: 'Perdita, I want you to meet Dr Iago from Coimbra. He talks a bit of French.'

Ludovic was left with the secretary, who kept custody of her eyes. Addressing her bare toes she said: 'One thing about a party, it does warm the room. Who are you?' she asked.

'Ludovic. Mr Spruce has accepted something I wrote for *Survival*.'

'Yes, of course,' she said. 'I know all about you now. I read your manuscript too. Everard is awfully impressed with it. He said it was as though Logan Pearsall Smith had written Kafka. Do you know Logan?'

'Only by his writing.'

'You must meet him. He's not here tonight. He doesn't go out now. I say, what a relief to meet a real writer instead of all these smarties Everard wastes his time on' (this with a dark glance from her feet to the air-raid warden). 'Look; there *is* some whisky. We've only got one bottle so we have to be rather careful with it. Come next door and I'll give you some.'

'Next door' was the office, a smaller room austerely, even meanly furnished. Back-numbers of *Survival* were piled on the bare floorboards, manuscripts and photographs on the bare table; a black sheet was secured by drawing-pins to cover the window. Here, when they were not engaged on domestic tasks – cooking, queueing, or darning – the four secretaries stoked the cultural beacon which blazed from Iceland to Adelaide; here the girl who could type answered Spruce's numerous 'fan letters' and the girl who could spell corrected proofs. Here it seemed some of them slept for there were divan beds covered with blankets only and a large, much undenticulated, comb.

Frankie went to the cupboard and revealed a bottle. Many strange concoctions of the 'Olde Falstaffe' kind circulated in those days. This was not one of them.

'Not opened yet,' she said.

Ludovic was not fond of spirits nor was whisky any rarity

at his well-found station; nevertheless he accepted the offered drink with a solemnity which verged on reverence. This was no mere clandestine treat. Frankie was initiating him into the occult company of Logan and Kafka. He would find time in the days to come to learn who Kafka was. Now he drained the glass swallowing almost without repugnance the highly valued distillation.

'You seemed to want that,' said Frankie. 'I daren't offer you another yet I'm afraid. Perhaps later. It depends who else turns up.'

'It was just what I wanted,' said Ludovic; '*all* that I wanted,' repressing a momentary inclination to retch.

3

THE Kilbannocks' house in Eaton Terrace had suffered no direct damage from bombing; not a pane of glass had been broken, not a chimney-pot thrown down; but four years of war had left their marks on the once gay interior. Kerstie did her best, but paint, wallpapers, chintzes, and carpets were stained and shabby. Despite these appearances the Kilbannocks had in fact recovered from the comparative penury of 1939. Kerstie no longer took lodgers. She had moved from the canteen of the Transit Camp to a well paid job as cipher clerk; Ian's pay rose with the rings on his cuff; an aunt had died leaving him a modest legacy. And there was nothing in those days to tempt anyone to extravagance. Kerstie had had Ian's evening clothes cleverly adapted into a serviceable coat and skirt. The children were still confined to their grandmother in Scotland and came to London only on occasions.

On this October evening they were expecting Virginia Troy, once an inmate, now rather a rare visitor.

'You'd better go out to Bellamy's or somewhere,' said Kerstie, 'I gathered on the telephone that Virginia wants a heart-to-hearter.'

'Trimmer?'

'I suppose so.'

'I'm thinking of shipping him to America.'

'It will be much the best thing.'

'We've done pretty well all we can with him in this country. We've finished the film. The BBC don't want to renew "The Voice of Trimmer" Sunday evening postscripts.'

'I should think not.'

'It seemed a good idea. Somehow it didn't catch on. Trimmer has to be seen as well as heard. Besides, there are a lot of rival heroes with rather better credentials.'

'You think the Americans will swallow him?'

'He'll be something new. They're sick of fighter pilots. By the way, do you realize it was Trimmer who gave the monarch the idea for this Sword of Stalingrad? Indirectly, of course. In the big scene of Trimmer's landing I gave him a "commando dagger" to brandish, I don't suppose you've even seen the things. They were an idea of Brides-in-theBath's early on. A few hundred were issued. To my certain knowledge none was ever used in action. A Glasgow policeman got a nasty poke with one. They were mostly given away to tarts. But they were beautifully made little things. Well, you know how sharp the royal eye is for any detail of equipment. He was given a preview of the Trimmer film and spotted the dagger at once. Had one sent round to him. Then the royal mind brooded a bit and the final result was that thing in the Abbey. An odd item of contemporary history.'

'Are you going to Bellamy's?'

'Everard Spruce asked us to a party. I might look in.'

The bell of the front door sounded through the little house.

'Virginia, I expect.'

Ian let her in. She kissed with cold detestation and came upstairs.

'I thought you were sending him out,' she said to Kerstie.

'I am. Run along, Ian, we have things to talk about.'

'Do I have to remind you that I am your direct superior officer?'

'Oh God, how that joke bores me.'

'I see you've brought luggage.'

'Yes, can I stay for a bit, Kerstie?'

'Yes, for a bit.'

'Until Trimmer's out of the country. He says he's had a

warning order to stand by for a trip – somewhere where he can't take me, thank God.'

'I always hoped,' said Ian, 'you might come to like him.'

'I've done two years.'

'Yes, you've been jolly good. You deserve a holiday. Well, I'll leave you two. I expect I'll be pretty late home.'

Neither woman showed any regret at this announcement. Ian went downstairs and out into the darkness.

'There's nothing in the house to drink,' said Kerstie. 'We could go out somewhere.'

'Coffee?'

'Yes, I can manage that.'

'Let's stay in then.'

'Nothing much to eat either. I've got some cod.'

'No cod, thanks.'

'I say, Virginia, you're pretty low.'

'Dead flat. What's happened to everyone? London used to be full of chums. Now I don't seem to know anyone. Do you realize that since my brother was killed I haven't a single living relation?'

'My dear, I am sorry. I hadn't heard. In fact I didn't know you had a brother.'

'He was called Tim – five years younger than me. We never got on. He was killed three years ago. You've such hundreds of children and parents and cousins, Kerstie. You can't imagine what it feels like to be quite alone. There's my step-mother in Switzerland. She never approved of me and I can't get at her now anyway. I'm scared, Kerstie.'

'Tell.'

Virginia was never one whose confidences needed drawing out.

'Money,' she said. 'I've never known what it was like to have *no* money. It's a very odd sensation indeed. Tim made a will leaving all he had to some girl. Papa never left me anything. He thought I was well provided for.'

'Surely Mr Troy will have to cough up eventually. Americans are great ones for alimony.'

'That's what I thought. It's what my bank manager and lawyer said. At first they thought it was just some difficulty of exchange control. They wrote him a lot of letters polite at first, then firm, then threatening. Finally, about six months ago they hired a lawyer in New York to serve a writ. A fine move that turned out to be. Mr Troy has divorced me.'

'Surely he can't do that?'

'He's done it. All signed and sealed. Apparently he's had a man watching me and taking affidavits.'

'How absolutely disgusting.'

'It's just like Mr Troy. I ought to have suspected when he lay so low. We've sent for copies of the evidence in case there is any sort of appeal possible. But it doesn't sound likely. After all, I haven't been strictly faithful to Mr Troy all this time.'

'He could hardly expect that.',

'So not only no alimony, but an overdraft and a huge lawyer's bill. I did the only thing I could and sold jewels. The beasts gave me half what they cost; said no one was buying at the moment.'

'Just what they said to Brenda.'

'Then this morning a very awkward thing happened. One of the things I sold was a pair of clips Augustus gave me. I'd quite forgotten about them till they turned up in an old bag. What's more I'd forgotten that when I lost them years ago I had reported it to the insurance company and been paid. Apparently I've committed a criminal offence. They've been fairly decent about that. They aren't going to the police or anything but I've got to refund the money – £250. It doesn't sound much but I haven't got it. So this afternoon I've been hawking furs around. They say no one's buying *them* either, though I should have thought it's just what everyone *will* want with winter coming on and no coal.'

'I always envied your furs,' said Kerstie.

'Yours for £250.'

'What's the best offer you got?'

'Believe it or not, £75.'

'I happen to have a little money in the bank at the moment,' said Kerstie thoughtfully. 'I could go a bit higher than that.'

'I need three times as much.'

'You must have *some* other things left.'

'All I possess in the world is downstairs in your hall.'

'Let's go through it, Virginia. You always had so many things. I'm sure we can find something. There's that cigarette case you're using now.'

'It's badly knocked about.'

'But it was good once.'

'Mr Troy, Cannes, 1936.'

'I'm sure we can find enough to make up £250.'

'Oh Kerstie, you are a comfort to a girl.'

So the two of them, who had 'come out' the same year and led such different lives, the one so prodigal, the other so circumspect and sparing, spread out Virginia's possessions over the grubby sofa and spent all that evening like gypsy hucksters examining and pricing those few surviving trophies of a decade of desirable womanhood, and in the end went off to bed comforted, each in her way, and contented with their traffic.

4

GUY felt that he had been given a birthday present; the first for how many years? The card that had come popping out of the Electronic Personnel Selector bearing his name, like a 'fortune' from a seaside slot-machine, like a fortune indeed in a more real sense – the luck of the draw in a lottery or sweepstake – brought an unfamiliar stir of exhilaration, such as he had felt in his first days in the Halberdiers, in his first minutes on enemy soil at Dakar; a sense of liberation such as he had felt when he had handed over Apthorpe's legacy to Chatty Corner and when he broke his long silence in the hospital in Alexandria. These had been the memorable occasions of his army life; all had been during the first two years of war; of late he had ceased to look for a renewal. Now there was hope. There was still a place for him somewhere outside the futile routine of HOO HQ.

He came off duty at six and, at the Transit Camp, on an impulse, did what he had seldom done lately, changed into blue patrols. He then took the tube railway, where the refugees were already making up their beds, to Green Park Station and walked under the arcade of the Ritz towards St James's Street and Bellamy's. American soldiers leant against the walls every few paces hugging their drabs, and an American soldier of another kind greeted him in the front hall of the club.

'Good evening, Loot.'

'Are you going to Everard Spruce's party?'

'Haven't been asked. Don't know him really. I thought you were expected at the Glenobans'.'

'I shall visit them later. First I am taking dinner with Ralph Brompton. But I thought I should look in on Everard on the way.'

He returned to his task of letter writing at the table opposite Job's box, which Guy had never before seen used.

In the back hall Guy found Arthur Box-Bender.

'Just slipped away from the House for a breather. Everything is going merrily on the eastern front.'

'Merrily?'

'Wait for the nine o'clock news. You'll hear something then. Uncle Joe's fairly got them on the run. I shouldn't much care to be one of his prisoners.'

By a natural connexion of thought Guy asked: 'Have you heard from Tony?'

Gloom descended on Box-Bender. 'Yes, as a matter of fact, last week. He's still got that tom-fool idea in his head about being a monk. He'll snap out of it, I'm sure, as soon as he gets back to normal life, but it's worrying. Angela doesn't seem to mind awfully. She's worried about your father.'

'So am I.'

'She's at Matchet now. As you know he's stopped working at that school, which is something gained. He never ought to have taken it on at his age. He's got this clot you know. It might become serious any moment.'

'I know. I saw him last month. He seemed all right then but he wrote to me afterwards.'

'There's nothing one can do about it,' said Box-Bender. 'Angela thought she should be handy in case anything happened.'

Guy went on to the bar where he found Ian Kilbannock talking to an elderly Grenadier.

'... You know how sharp the royal eye is for any detail of

equipment,' he was saying. 'The monarch sent for one of those daggers. That's what set the royal mind brooding about cutlery.'

'It's been a great success.'

'Yes I claim a little indirect credit for it myself. Evening, Guy. Who do you think has just turned me out of my house? – Virginia.'

'How was she?'

'On the rocks. I only saw her for a second but she was palpably on the rocks. I'd heard some loose talk about her affairs before.'

'I'll give you a drink,' said Guy, 'it's my birthday. Two glasses of wine, Parsons.'

Guy did not speak about the Electronic Selector but the thought of it warmed him as they talked of other things. When their glasses were empty the Grenadier said: 'Did someone say it was his birthday? Three glasses of wine, Parsons.'

When it would have been Ian's turn to order, he said: 'They've put up the prices. Ten bob a glass for this champagne now and it's not good. Why don't you come to Everard Spruce's and drink free?'

'Will he have champagne?'

'Sure to. He enjoys heavy official backing and tonight he's got two distinguished foreigners to impress. It's pleasant to get into a completely civilian circle once in a while. D'you read his paper?'

'No.'

'Nor do I. But it's highly thought of. Winston reads it.'

'I don't believe you.'

'Well perhaps not personally. But a copy goes to the Cabinet Offices I happen to know.'

'I hardly know Spruce. The Loot's going.'

'Then anyone can. He'll be able to get a cab. They always stop for Americans.'

Lieutenant Padfield was still at work on his correspondence; he wrote rather laboriously; the pen did not come readily to him; in youth he had typed; in earliest manhood dictated. Ian sent him up to Piccadilly and, sure enough, he returned in a quarter of an hour with a taxi.

'Glad to have you come with me,' he said. 'I thought you were not acquainted with Spruce.'

'I changed my mind.'

'*Survival* is a very significant organ of opinion.'

'Signifying what, Loot?'

'The survival of values.'

'You think I need special coaching in that subject?'

'Pardon me.'

'You think I should read this paper?'

'You will find it very significant.'

It was nearly eight o'clock when they reached Cheyne Walk. Some of the party, including the neutral guests, had already sickened of Frankie's cocktail and taken their leave.

'The party's really over,' said one of the secretaries, not Frankie; she wore espadrilles and the hair through which she spoke was black. 'I think Everard wants to go out.'

Lieutenant Padfield was engaged in over-paying the taxi; he still, after his long sojourn, found English currency confusing and the driver sought to confuse him further. On hearing these mumbled words he said: 'My, is it that late? I ought to be in Ebury Street. If you don't mind I'll take the taxi on.'

Guy and Ian did not mind. The Lieutenant had fulfilled his manifest destiny in bringing them here.

Strengthened in her resolution by this defection the secretary, Coney by name, said: 'I don't believe there's anything left to drink.'

'I was promised champagne,' said Guy.

'Champagne,' said Coney, taken aback, not knowing who he was, not knowing either of these uniformed figures looming out of the lightless mist, but knowing that Spruce had, in fact, a few bottles of that wine laid down. 'I don't know anything about champagne.'

'Well, we'll come up and see,' said Ian.

Coney led them upstairs.

Though depleted the company was still numerous enough to provide a solid screen between the entrance and the far corner in which Ludovic was seated. For two minutes now he had been in enjoyment of what he had come for, the attention of his host.

'The arrangement is haphazard or planned?' Spruce was asking.

'Planned.'

'The plan is not immediately apparent. There are the more or less generalized aphorisms, there are the particular observations – which I thought, if I may say so, extremely acute and funny. I wondered: are they in any cases libellous? And besides these there seemed to me two poetic themes which occur again and again. There is the Drowned Sailor motif – an echo of the *Waste Land* perhaps? Had you Eliot consciously in mind?'

'Not Eliot,' said Ludovic. 'I don't think he was called Eliot.'

'Very interesting. And then there was the Cave image. You must have read a lot of Freudian psychology.'

'Not a lot. There was nothing psychological about the cave.'

'Very interesting – a spontaneous liberation of the unconscious.'

At this moment Coney infiltrated the throng and stood beside them.

'Everard, there are two men in uniform asking for champagne.'

'Good heavens, not the police?'

'One might be. He's wearing an odd sort of blue uniform. The other's an airman. I've never seen them before. They had an American with them but he ran away.'

'How very odd. You haven't given them champagne?'

'Oh no, Everard.'

'I'd better go and see who they are.'

At the door Ian had collided with the Smart Woman and kissed her warmly on each dusty cheek.

'Drinks have run out here,' she said, 'and I am due at my Warden's Post. Why don't you two come there? It's only round the corner and there's always a bottle.'

Spruce greeted them.

'I'm afraid we're a little late. I brought Guy. You remember him?'

'Yes, yes, I suppose so. Somewhere,' said Spruce. 'Everything is over here. I was just having a few words with a very interesting New Writer. We always particularly welcome contributions from service men. It's part of our policy.'

The central knot of guests opened and revealed Ludovic, his appetite for appreciation whetted but far from satisfied, gazing resentfully towards Spruce's back.

'Ludovic,' said Guy.

'That is the man I was speaking of. You know him?'

'He saved my life,' said Guy.

'How very odd.'

'I've never had a chance to thank him.'

'Well, do so now. But don't take him away. I was in the middle of a fascinating conversation.'

'I think I'll go off with Per.'

'Yes, do.'

The gap had closed again. Guy passed through and held out his hand to Ludovic who raised his oyster eyes with an expression of unmitigated horror. He took the hand limply and looked away.

'Ludovic, surely you remember me?'

'It is most unexpected.'

'Hookforce. Crete.'

'Oh yes, I remember.'

'I've always been hoping to run into you again. There's so much to say. They told me you saved my life.' Ludovic mutely raised his hand to the ribbon of the MM. It was as though he were beating his breast in penitence. 'You don't seem very pleased to see me.'

'It's the shock,' said Ludovic, resuming his barrack-room speech, 'not looking to find you here, not at Mr Spruce's. You of all people, here of all places.'

Guy took the chair where Spruce had sat.

'My memory's awfully vague of those last days in Crete and in the boat.'

'Best forgotten,' said Ludovic. 'Things happen that're best forgotten.'

'Oh, come. Aren't you rather overdoing the modest hero? Besides I'm curious. What happened to Major Hound?'

'I understand he was reported missing.'

'Not a prisoner?'

'Forgive me Mr – Captain Crouchback. I am not in Records.'

'And the sapper who got the boat going. I was awfully ill – so was he – delirious.'

'You were delirious too.'

'Yes. Did you rescue the sapper too?'

'I understand he was reported lost at sea.'

'Look,' said Guy, 'are you doing anything for dinner?'

It was as though Banquo had turned host.

'No,' said Ludovic. 'No,' and without apology or a word of farewell to Guy or Spruce or Frankie, he made precipitately for the stairs, the front door and the sheltering blackout.

'What on earth happened to him?' asked Spruce. 'He can't have been drunk. What did you say to him?'

'Nothing. I asked him about old times.'

'You knew him well?'

'Not exactly. We always thought him odd.'

'He has talent,' said Spruce. 'Perhaps a hint of genius. It's most annoying his disappearing like that. Well, the party's over. Will you girls shoo the guests away and then clear up? I have to go.'

Guy spent the remaining hours of his fortieth birthday at Bellamy's playing 'slosh'. When he returned to his room at the Transit Camp his thoughts were less on the past than on the future.

Unheard in Bellamy's the sirens sounded an alert at eleven o'clock and an 'all clear' before midnight.

Unheard too in Westminster Abbey where the Sword of Stalingrad stood unattended. The doors were locked, the lights all extinguished. Next day the queue would form again in the street and the act of homage would be renewed.

Ludovic was not successful in the *Time and Tide* literary competition. His sonnet was not even commended. He studied the winning entry:

> . . . Here lies the sword. Ah, but the work is rare,
> Precious the symbol. Who has understood
> How close the evil or how dread the good
> Who scorns the vestures that the angels wear?

He could make no sense of it. Was the second 'who' a relative pronoun with 'good' as its antecedent? He compared his own lucid sonnet:

> Stele of my past on which engravéd are
> The pleadings of that long divorce of steel,
> In which was stolen that directive star,
> By which I sailed, expunged be. No spar,
> No mast, no halyard, bowsprit, boom or keel
> Survives my wreck . . .

Perhaps, he reflected, the lines were not strictly appropriate to the occasion. He had failed to reflect the popular mood. It was too personal for *Time and Tide*. He would send it to *Survival*.

BOOK TWO

Fin de Ligne

1

VIRGINIA TROY had not been in his house ten days before Ian Kilbannock began to ask: 'When is she going?'

'I don't mind having her,' said Kerstie. 'She's not costing us much.'

'But she isn't contributing anything.'

'I couldn't ask Virginia to do that. She was awfully decent to us when she was rich.'

'That's a long time ago. I've had Trimmer shipped to America. I just don't understand why she has to stay here. The other girls used to pay their share.'

'I might suggest it to her.'

'As soon as you can.'

But when Virginia returned that evening she brought news which put other thoughts out of Kerstie's head.

'I've just been to my lawyers,' she said. 'They've got the copy of all Mr Troy's divorce evidence. Who do you think collected it?'

'Who?'

'Three guesses.'

'I can't think of anyone.'

'That disgusting Loot.'

'It's not possible.'

'Apparently he's a member of the firm who works for Mr Troy. He still does odd jobs for them in his spare time.'

'After we've all been so kind to him! Are you going to give him away?'

'I don't know.'

'People ought to be warned.'

'It's all our own fault for taking him up. He always gave me the creeps.'

'A thing like this,' said Kerstie, 'destroys one's faith in human nature.'

'Oh, the Loot isn't human.'

'No, I suppose not really.'

'He made a change from Trimmer.'

'Would you say Trimmer was human?'

They fell back on this problem, which in one form or another had been fully debated between them for three years.

'D'you miss him at all?'

'Pure joy and relief. Every morning for the last four days I've woken up to the thought "Trimmer's gone".'

At length after an hour's discussion Kerstie said: 'I suppose you'll be looking for somewhere else to live now.'

'Not unless you want to get rid of me.'

'Of course it isn't that, darling, only Ian ...'

But Virginia was not listening. Instead she interrupted with: 'Have you got a family doctor?'

'We always go to an old boy in Sloane Street called Puttock. He's very good with the children.'

'I've never had a doctor,' said Virginia, 'not one I could call *my* doctor. It comes of moving about so much and being so healthy. I've sometimes been to a little man in Newport to get him to sign for sleeping pills, and there was a rather beastly Englishman in Venice who patched me up that time I fell downstairs at the Palazzo Corombona. But mostly I've relied on chemists. There is a magician in Monte Carlo. You just go to him and say you have a pain and he gives you a *cachet* which stops it at once. I think perhaps I'll go and see your man in Sloane Street.'

'Not ill?'

'No. I just feel I ought to have what Mr Troy calls a "check-up".'

'There's a most luxurious sick-bay in HOO HQ. Every sort of apparatus and nothing to pay. General Whale goes there for "sun-rays" every afternoon. The top man is called Sir Somebody Something – a great swell in peacetime.'

'I think I'd prefer your man. Not expensive?'

'A guinea a visit I think.'

'I might afford that.'

'Virginia, talking of money: you remember Brenda and Zita used to pay rent when they lived here?'

'Yes, indeed. It's awfully sweet of you to take me in free.'

'I adore having you. It's only Ian; he was saying tonight he wondered if you wouldn't feel more comfortable if you paid something . . .'

'I couldn't be more comfortable as I am, darling, and anyway I·couldn't possibly afford to. Talk him round, Kerstie. Explain to him that I'm broke.'

'Oh, he knows that.'

'*Really* broke. That's what no one understands. I'd talk to Ian myself only I think you'd do it better.'

'I'll *try*. . . .'

2

THE processes of army postings were not yet adapted to the speed of the Electronic Personnel Selector. It was a week before Guy received any notification that his services might be needed by anyone for any purpose. Then a letter appeared in his 'In' tray addressed to him by name. It contained a summons to present himself for an interview with an officer who described himself as 'G I Liberation of Italy'. He was not surprised to learn that this man inhabited the same building as himself, and when he presented himself he met a nondescript lieutenant-colonel whom he had seen off and on in the corridors of the building; with whom indeed he had on occasions exchanged words at the bar of the canteen.

The Liberator gave no sign of recognition. Instead he said: 'Entrate e s'accomode.'

The noises thus issuing from him were so strange that Guy stood momentarily disconcerted, not knowing in what tongue he was being addressed.

'Come in and sit down,' said the colonel in English. 'I thought you were supposed to speak Italian.'

'I do.'

'Looks as though you needed a refresher. Say something in Italian.'

Guy said rapidly and with slightly exaggerated accent: 'Sono più abituato al dialetto genovese, ma di solito posso capire e farmi capire dapertutto in Italia fuori Sicilia.'

The colonel caught only the last word and asked desperately and fatuously: 'Siciliano lei?'

'Ah, no, no, no.' Guy gave a lively impersonation of an Italian gesture of dissent. 'Ho visitato Sicilia, poi ho abitato per un bel pezzo sulla costa ligure. Ho viaggiato in quasi ogni parte d'Italia.'

The colonel resumed his native tongue. 'That sounds all right. You wouldn't be much use to us if you only talked Sicilian. You'll be working the north, in Venetia probably.'

'Lì per me tutto andrà liscio,' said Guy.

'Yes,' said the colonel, 'yes, I see. Well let's talk English. The work we have in mind is, of course, secret. As you probably know the advance in Italy is bogged down at the moment. We can't expect much movement there till the spring. The Germans have taken over in force. Some of the wops seem to be on our side. Call themselves "partisani", pretty left wing by the sound of them. Nothing wrong with that of course. Ask Sir Ralph Brompton. We shall be putting in various small parties to keep GHQ informed about what they're up to and if possible arrange for drops of equipment in suitable areas. An intelligence officer and a signalman are the essentials of each group. You've done Commando training, I see. Did that include parachuting?'

'No, sir.'

'Well, you'd better take a course. No objection I suppose?'

'None whatever.'

'You're a bit old but you'll be surprised at the ages of some of our chaps. You may not have to jump. We have various methods of getting our men in. Any experience of small boats?'

Guy thought of the little sailing-craft he had once kept at Santa Dulcina, of his gay excursion to Dakar and the phantasmagoric crossing from Crete, and answered truthfully, 'Yes, sir.'

'Good. That may come in useful. You will be hearing from us in due course. Meanwhile the whole thing is on the secret list. You belong at Bellamy's, don't you? A lot of loose talk gets reported from there. Keep quiet.'

'Very good, sir.'

'A rivederci, eh?'

Guy saluted and left the office.

When he returned to the Transit Camp he found a telegram from his sister, Angela, announcing that his father had died suddenly and peacefully at Matchet.

3

ALL the railway stations in the kingdom displayed the challenge: IS YOUR JOURNEY REALLY NECESSARY?

Guy and his brother-in-law caught the early, crowded train from Paddington on the morning of the funeral.

Guy had a black arm band attached to his tunic. Box-Bender wore a black tie with a subfusc suit of clothes and a bowler.

'As you see, I'm not wearing a top hat,' said Box-Bender. 'Seems out of place these days. I don't suppose there'll be many people there. Peregrine went down the day before yesterday. He'll have fixed everything up. Have you brought sandwiches?'

'No.'

'I don't know where we'll get lunch. Can't expect the convent to do anything about us. I hope Peregrine and Angela have arranged something at the pub.'

It was barely light when they steamed out of the shuttered and patched station. The corridor was full of standing sailors travelling to Plymouth. The little bulbs over the seats had been disconnected. It was difficult to read the flimsy newspapers they carried.

'I always had a great respect for your father,' said Box-Bender. Then he fell asleep. Guy remained open-eyed throughout the three-hour journey to the junction at Taunton.

Uncle Peregrine had arranged for a special tram-like coach to be attached to the local train. Here were assembled Miss Vavasour, the priest from Matchet and the headmaster of the school of Our Lady of Victory. There were many others wearing mourning of various degrees of depth, whom Guy knew he should recognize, but could not. They greeted him with murmured words of condolence, and seeing it was necessary, reminded him of their names – Tresham, Bigod, Englefield,

Arundell, Hornyold, Plessington, Jerningham, and Dacre – a muster of recusant names – all nearly or remotely cousins of his. Their journey was really necessary.

Out of his hearing Miss Vavasour said of Guy, sighing: *'Fin de ligne.'*

Noon was the hour appointed for the beginning of the Requiem Mass. The local train was due at Broome at half-past eleven and arrived almost on time.

There is no scarcity of places of worship in this small village.

In penal times Mass had been said regularly in the house and a succession of chaplains employed there in the guise of tutors. This little chapel is preserved as a place of occasional pilgrimage in honour of the Blessed Gervase Crouchback.

The Catholic parish church is visible from the little station yard; a Puginesque structure erected by Guy's great-grandfather in the early 1860's at the nearer extremity of the village street. At the further end stands the medieval church of which the nave and chancel are in Anglican use while the north aisle and adjoining burying ground are the property of the lord of the manor. It was in this plot that Mr Crouchback's grave had been dug and in this aisle that his memorial would later stand among the clustered effigies and brasses of his forebears.

After the Act of Emancipation a wall had been built to divide the aisle from the rest of the church and for a generation it had served the Catholic parish. But the monuments left little room for worshippers. It was for this reason that Guy's great-grandfather had built the church (which in the old style the Crouchbacks spoke of as 'the chapel') and the presbytery and had endowed the parish with what was then an adequate stipend. Most of the village of Broome is Catholic, an isolated community of the kind that is found in many parts of Lancashire and the outer islands of Scotland, but is very rare in the west of England. The Anglican benefice has long been united with two of its neighbours. It is served by a clergyman who rides over on his bicycle once a month and reads the service if he finds a quorum assembled. The former vicarage has been partitioned and let off as cottages.

Broome Hall stands behind iron gates, its drive a continuation of the village street. Mr Crouchback used often, and not quite accurately, to assert that every 'good house', by which he meant one of medieval foundation, stood on a road, a river, or a rock. Broome Hall had been on the main road to Exeter until the eighteenth century when a neighbour who sat for the county in the House of Commons obtained authority to divert it through his own property and establish a profitable toll pike. The old right of way still runs under the walls of the Hall but it carries little traffic. It is a lane which almost invisibly branches off the motor-road swells into the village street, runs for half a mile as a gravelled carriage-drive and then narrows once more amid embowering hedge-rows which, despite a rough annual cutting, encroach more and more on the little frequented track.

When the convent came to Broome they brought their own chaplain and converted one of the long, panelled galleries into their chapel. Neither they nor their girls appeared in the parish church except on special occasions. Mr Crouchback's funeral was such a one. They had met the body when it arrived from Matchet on the previous evening, had dressed the catafalque and that morning had sung the dirge. Their chaplain would assist at the Requiem.

Angela Box-Bender was on the platform to meet the train. She had an air of gravity and sorrow.

'I say, Angie,' her husband asked, 'how long is this business going to take?'

'Not more than an hour. Father Geoghegan wanted to preach a panegyric but uncle Peregrine stopped him.'

'Any chance of anything to eat? I left the flat at six this morning.'

'You're expected at the presbytery. I think you'll find something there.'

'They don't expect me to take any part, do they? I mean carry anything? I don't know the drill.'

'No,' said Angela. 'This is one of the times when no one expects anything of you.'

The little parlour of the presbytery was much crowded. Besides their host, uncle Peregrine and the chaplain from the convent, there were four other priests, one with the crimson of a monsignore.

'His lordship the Bishop was unable to come. He sent me to represent him and convey his condolences.'

There was also a layman whom Guy recognized as his father's solicitor from Taunton.

Father Geoghegan was fasting, but he dispensed hospitality in the form of whisky and cake. Uncle Peregrine edged Guy into a corner. His fatuous old face expressed a kind of bland decorum.

'The hatchment,' he said. 'There was some difficulty about the hatchment. One can't get anything done nowadays. No heraldic painters available anywhere. There are quite a collection of old hatchments in the sacristy, none in very good condition. There was your grandfather's, but of course that was impaling Wrothman so it would hardly have done. Then I had a bit of luck and turned up what must have been made for Ivo. Rather rough work, local I should think. I was abroad at the time of his death, poor boy. Anyway, it is the simple blazon without quarterings. It is the best we can do in the circumstances. You don't think I did wrong to put it up?'

'No, uncle Peregrine, I am sure you did quite right.'

'I think I'd better be going across. People are beginning to arrive. Someone will have to show them where to sit.'

The priest from Matchet said: 'I don't think your father has got long for purgatory.'

The solicitor said: 'We ought to have a word together afterwards.'

'No reading of the will?'

'No, that only happens in Victorian novels. But there are things we shall have to discuss some time and it's difficult to meet these days.'

Arthur Box-Bender was seeking to make himself agreeable to the domestic prelate '... not a member of your persuasion myself but I'm bound to say your Cardinal Hinsley did a wonderful job of work on the wireless. You could see he was an Englishman first and a Christian second; that is more than you can say of one or two of *our* bishops.'

Angela said: 'I've been dealing with letters as best I can. I've had hundreds.'

'So have I.'

'Extraordinary the number of people one's never heard of who were close friends of papa. I slept at the convent last night and shall go home tonight. The nuns are being awfully decent. Reverend Mother wants anyone to come back and have coffee afterwards. There's so many people we'll have to talk to. I had no idea so many people would get here.'

They were arriving on foot, by motor car and in pony traps. From the presbytery window Guy and Angela watched them. Angela said: 'I'm taking Felix home with me. They're keeping him at the inn at the moment.' Then the clergy withdrew to vest and uncle Peregrine came to fetch the chief mourners.

'Prie-dieus,' he said, 'on the right in front.'

They crossed the narrow strip of garden and entered under the diamond-shaped panel cut by the house carpenter for poor mad Ivo. The sable and argent cross of Crouchback had not greatly taxed his powers of draughtsmanship. It was no ornament designed by the heralds to embellish a carriage door but something rare in English armoury – a device that had been carried into battle. They walked up the aisle with their eyes on the catafalque and the tall unbleached candles which burned beside it. The smell of beeswax and chrysanthemums, later to be permeated by incense, was heavy on the brumous air.

The church had been planned on a large scale when the Crouchback family were at the height of prosperity and the conversion of England seemed something more than a remote, pious aspiration. Gervase and Hermione had built it; they who acquired the property of Santa Dulcina. It was as crowded for Mr Crouchback's funeral as for midnight Mass at Christmas. When the estate was bit by bit dispersed in the lean agricultural years, the farms had been sold on easy terms to the tenants. Some had changed hands since, but there were three pews full of farmers in black broadcloth. The village were there in force; many neighbours; the Lord Lieutenant of the county was in the front pew on the left next to a representative of the Knights of Malta. Lieutenant Padfield sat with the Anglican vicar, the family solicitor, and the headmaster of Our Lady of Victory. The nun's choir was in the organ loft. The priests, other than the three who officiated, lined the walls of the chancel. Uncle Peregrine had seen that everyone was in his proper place.

Box-Bender kept his eyes on Angela and Guy, anxious to avoid any liturgical solecism. He genuflected with them, sat, then, like them, knelt, sat again, and stood as the three priests vested in black emerged from the sacristy knelt again but missed signing himself with the cross. He was no bigot. He had been to Mass before. He wanted to do whatever was required of him. Across the aisle the Lord Lieutenant was equally undrilled, equally well disposed.

Silence at first; the Confiteor was inaudible even in the front pew. Just in time Box-Bender saw his relations cross themselves at the absolution. He hadn't been caught that time. Then the nuns sang the *Kyrie*.

Guy followed the familiar rite with his thoughts full of his father.

'*In memoria aeterna erit °justus: ab auditione mala non timebit.*' The first phrase was apt. His father had been a 'just man'; not particularly judicious, not at all judicial, but 'just' in the full sense of the psalmist – or at any rate in the sense attributed to him by later commentators. Not for the first time in his life Guy wondered what was the *auditio mala* that was not to be feared. His missal gave the meaningless rendering 'evil hearing'. Did it mean simply that the ears of the dead were closed to the discords of life? Did it mean they were immune to malicious gossip? Few people, Guy thought, had ever spoken ill of his father. Perhaps it meant 'bad news'. His father had suffered as much as most men – more perhaps – from bad news of one kind or another; never fearfully.

'Not long for purgatory,' his confessor had said of Mr Crouchback. As the nuns sang the *Dies Irae* with all its ancient deprecations of divine wrath, Guy knew that his father was joining his voice with theirs:

Ingemisco, tamquam reus:
Culpa rubet vultus meus
Supplicanti parce, Deus;

That would be his prayer, who saw, and had always seen, quite clearly the difference in kind between the goodness of the most innocent of humans and the blinding, ineffable goodness of God. 'Quantitative judgements don't apply,' his father had written. As a reasoning man Mr Crouchback had known that he was honourable, charitable and faithful; a man who by all the formularies of his faith should be confident of salvation; as a man of prayer he saw himself as totally unworthy of divine notice. To Guy his father was the best man, the only entirely good man, he had ever known.

Of all the people in the crowded church, Guy wondered how many had come as an act of courtesy, how many were there to pray that a perpetual light should shine upon Mr Crouchback? 'Well,' he reflected. ' "The Grace of God is in courtesy"; in Arthur Box-Bender glancing sidelong to be sure he did the right thing, just as in the prelate who was holding his candle in the chancel, representing the bishop; in Lieutenant Padfield, too, exercising heaven knows what prodigy of ubiquity. "Quantitative judgements don't apply." '

The temptation for Guy, which he resisted as best he could, was to brood on his own bereavement and deplore the countless occasions of his life when he had failed his father. That was not what he was here for. There would be ample time in the years to come for these selfish considerations. Now, *praesente cadavere*, he was merely one of the guard who were escorting his father to judgement and to heaven.

The altar was censed. The celebrant sang: '... *Tuis enim fidelibus, Domine, via mutatur, non tollitur* ...' 'Changed not ended' reflected Guy. It was a huge transition for the old man who had walked with Felix along the cliffs at Matchet – a huge transition, even, for the man who had knelt so rapt in prayer after his daily Communion – to the 'everlasting mansion prepared for him in heaven'.

The celebrant turned the page of his missal from the Preface to the Canon. In the hush that followed the sacring bell Guy thanked God for his father and then his thoughts strayed to his own death, that had been so near in the crossing from Crete, that might now be near in the mission proposed for him by the nondescript colonel.

'I'm worried about you,' his father had written in the letter which, though it was not his last – for he and Guy had exchanged news since; *auditiones malae* of his father's deteriorating health and his own prolonged frustration – Guy regarded as being in a special sense the conclusion of their regular, rather reserved correspondence of more than thirty years. His father had been worried, not by anything connected with his worldly progress, but by his evident apathy; he was worrying now perhaps in that mysterious transit camp through which he must pass on his way to rest and light.

Guy's prayers were directed to, rather than for, his father. For many years now in the direction in the *Garden of the Soul*, 'Put yourself in the presence of God', had for Guy come to mean a mere act of respect, like the signing of the Visitors' Book at an Embassy or Government House. He reported for duty saying to God: 'I don't ask anything from you. I am here if you want me. I don't suppose I can be any use, but if there is anything I can do, let me know,' and left it at that.

'I don't ask anything from you'; that was the deadly core of his apathy; his father had tried to tell him, was now telling him. That emptiness had been with him for years now even in his days of enthusiasm and activity in the Halberdiers. Enthusiasm and activity were not enough. God required more than that. He had commanded all men to *ask*.

In the recesses of Guy's conscience there lay the belief that somewhere, somehow, something would be required of him; that he must be attentive to the summons when it came. They also served who only stood and waited. He saw himself as one of the labourers in the parable who sat in the market-place waiting to be hired and were not called into the vineyard until late in the day. They had their reward on an equality with the men who had toiled since dawn. One day he would get the chance to do some small service which only he could perform, for which he had been created. Even he must have his function in the divine plan. He did not expect a heroic destiny. Quantitative judgements did not apply. All that mattered was to recognize the chance when it offered. Perhaps his father was at that moment clearing the way for him. 'Show me what to do and help me to do it,' he prayed.

Arthur Box-Bender had been to Mass before. After the last gospel, when the priest left the altar, he looked at his watch and picked up his bowler hat. Then when the priest appeared differently dressed and came within a few feet of him, he surreptitiously tucked his hat away again. The Absolution was sung, then priest and deacon walked round the catafalque, first sprinkling it with holy water, then censing it. The black cope brushed against Box-Bender's almost black suit. A drop of water landed on his left cheek. He did not like to wipe it off.

The pall was removed, the coffin borne down the aisle. Angela, uncle Peregrine and Guy fell in behind it and led the mourners out. Box-Bender modestly took a place behind the Lord Lieutenant. The nuns sang the Antiphon and then filed away from the gallery to their convent. The procession moved down the village street from the new church to the old, in silence broken only by the tread of the horse, the creaking of harness, and the turning of the wheels of the farm cart which bore the coffin; the factor walked at the old mare's head leading her.

It was a still day; the trees were dropping their leaves in ones and twos; they twisted and faltered in the descent as their crumpled brown shapes directed, but landed under the boughs on which they had once budded. Guy thought for a moment of Ludovic's note-book, of the 'feather in the vacuum' to which he had been compared and, by contrast, remembered boisterous November days when he and his mother had tried to catch leaves in the avenue; each one caught insured a happy day? week? month? which? in his wholly happy childhood. Only his father had remained to watch the transformation of that merry little boy into the lonely captain of Halberdiers who followed the coffin.

On the cobbled pavements the villagers whose work had kept them from church, turned out to see the cart roll past. Many who had come to the church broke away and went about their business. There was not room for many to stand in the little burying ground.

The nuns had lined the edges of the grave with moss and evergreen leaves and chrysanthemums, giving it a faint suggestion of Christmas decoration. The undertaker's men deftly lowered the coffin; holy water, incense, the few prayers, the silent Paternoster, the Benedictus; holy water again; the de profundis. Guy, Angela, and uncle Peregrine came forward, took the sprinkler in turn and added their aspersions. Then it was ended.

The group at the graveside turned away and, as they left the churchyard, broke into subdued conversation. Angela greeted those she had not met that morning. Uncle Peregrine made his choice of those who should come to the house for coffee. Guy encountered Lieutenant Padfield in the street.

'Nice of you to have come,' he said.

'It is a very significant occasion,' said the Lieutenant: 'Signifying what?' Guy wondered. The Lieutenant added, 'I'm coming back to the Hall. Reverend Mother asked me.'

When? How? Why? Guy wondered, but he said nothing except: 'You know the way?'

'Surely.'

The Lord Lieutenant had hung back, remaining in the public, Anglican graveyard, Box-Bender with him. Now he said: 'I won't bother your wife or your nephew. Just give them my sympathy, will you?' and, as Box-Bender saw him to his car, added: 'I had a great respect for your father-in-law. Didn't see much of him in the last ten years, of course. No one did. But he was greatly respected in the county.'

The funeral party walked back along the village street. Opposite the Catholic church and presbytery, the last building before the gates, was the 'Lesser House', a stucco façade and porch masking the much older structure. This was not in the convent's lease. It had fulfilled various functions in the past, often being used as a dower house. The factor lived there now. The blinds were in the windows, drawn down for the passing of the coffin. It was a quiet house; the street in front was virtually a cul-de-sac and at the back it was open to the park. It was here his father had suggested that Guy should end his days.

The convent school was prosperous and the grounds well kept even in that year when everywhere in the country box and yew were growing untrimmed and lawns were ploughed and planted with food-stuffs.

A gate tower guards the forecourt at Broome. Behind it lie two quadrangles, medieval in plan, Caroline in decoration, like a university college; as in most colleges there is a massive Gothic wing. Gervase and Hermione had added this, employing the same architect as had designed their church. At the main door stood the Reverend Mother and a circle of nuns. In the upper windows and in the turret where the Blessed Gervase Crouchback had been taken prisoner appeared the heads of girls, some angelic, some grotesque, like the corbels in the old church, all illicitly peeping down on the mourners.

The Great Hall had been given a plaster ceiling in the eighteenth century. Gervase and Hermione had removed it revealing the high timbers. In Guy's childhood the walls above the oak wainscot had been hung with weapons collected in many quarters and symmetrically arranged in great steely radiations of blades and barrels. These had been sold with the rest of the furniture. In their place hung a few large and shabby religious pictures of the kind which are bequeathed to convents, smooth German paintings of the nineteenth century portraying scenes of gentle piety alternating with lugubrious and extravagant martyrdoms derived at some distance from the southern baroque. Above the dais, where the panelling ran the full height of the room, a cinema screen held the place where family portraits had hung and in a corner were piles of tubular metal chairs and the posts of a badminton set. This hall was the school's place of recreation. Here the girls danced together in the winter evenings to the music of a gramophone and tender possessive friendships were contracted and repudiated; here in the summer was held the annual concert, and a costume play, chosen for its innocence of subject and for the multiplicity of its cast, was tediously enacted.

The nuns had spread a trestle table with as lavish a repast as the stringency of the times allowed. What was lacking in nourishment was compensated for by ingenuity of arrangement. Cakes compounded of dried egg and adulterated flour had been ornamented with nuts and preserved fruit that were part of the monthly bounty of their sister-house in America; the 'unsolicited gift' parcels which enriched so many bare tables at that time. Slices of spam had been cut into trefoils. The school prefects in their blue uniform dresses carried jugs of coffee already sweetened with saccharine. Box-Bender wondered if he might smoke and decided not.

With uncle Peregrine beside him to identify them, Guy made a round of the guests. Most asked what he was doing and he answered: 'pending posting'. Many reminded him of occurrences in his childhood he had long forgotten. Some expressed surprise that he was no longer in Kenya. One asked after his wife, then realized she had made a gaffe and entangled herself further by saying: 'How idiotic of me. I was thinking for the moment you were Angela's husband.'

'She's over there. He's over there.'

'Yes, of course, how utterly foolish of me. Of course I remember now. You're Ivo, aren't you?'

'A very natural confusion,' said Guy.

Presently he found himself with the solicitor.

'Perhaps we could have a few words in private?'

'Let us go outside.'

They stood together in the forecourt. The heads had disappeared from the windows now; the girls had been rounded up and corralled in their class-rooms.

'It always takes a little time to prove a will and settle up but I think your father left his affairs in good order. He chose to live very quietly but he was by no means badly off, you know. When he inherited, the estate was very large. He sold up at a bad time but he invested wisely and he never touched capital. He gave away most of the income. That is what I wanted to talk to you about. He made a large number of covenants, some to institutions, some to individuals. These of course terminate with his death. The invested money is left half to you and half to your sister for your lives and afterwards to her children and, of course, to your children if you have any. Death duties will have to be paid, but there will be a considerable residue. The total income which you will share has been in the last few years in the neighbourhood of seven thousand.'

'I had no idea it was so large.'

'No, he didn't spend seven hundred on himself. Now there is the question of the payments by covenant. Will you and your sister wish to continue them? There might be cases of real hardship if they were stopped. He was paying allowances to a number of individuals who, I believe, are entirely dependent on him.'

'I don't know about the institutions,' said Guy. 'I am sure my sister will agree with me in continuing the payments to individuals.'

'Just so. I shall have to see her about it.'

'How much is involved?'

'To individuals not more than two thousand; and, of course, many of the recipients are very old and unlikely to be a charge for many years more.

'There's another small point. He had some furniture at Matchet; nothing, I think, of any value. I don't know what you'll want to do with that. Some is at the hotel, some in store at the school. I should suggest selling it locally. There's quite a shortage of everything like that now. It was all well made, you will remember. It might get a fair price.'

The brass bedstead, the triangular wash-hand stand, the prie-dieu, the leather sofa, the object known to the trade as a 'club fender' of heavy brass upholstered on the top with turkey carpet, the mahogany desk, the book-case full of old favourites, a few chairs, the tobacco jar bearing the arms of New College, bought by Mr Crouchback when he was a freshman, the fine ivory crucifix, the framed photographs – all well made, as the lawyer said, and well kept – these were. what Mr Crouchback had chosen from his dressing-room and from the smoking-room at Broome to furnish the narrow quarters of his retreat. Angela had taken the family portraits and a few small, valuable pieces to Box-Bender's house in the Cotswolds. And then in the six days' sale silver and porcelain and tapestries, canopied beds, sets of chairs of all periods, cabinets, consoles; illuminated manuscripts, suits of armour, stuffed animals; no illustrious treasures, not the collection of an astute connoisseur; merely the accumulations and chance survivals of centuries of prosperous, unadventurous taste; all had come down into the front court where Guy now stood, and had been borne away and dispersed, leaving the whole house quite bare, except for the chapel; there the change of ownership passed unrecorded and the lamp still burned; not, as it happened, a thing of great antiquity; something Hermione had picked up in the Via Babuino. The phrase, often used of Broome, that its sanctuary lamp had never been put out, was figurative

All Guy's early memories of his father were in these spacious halls, as the central and controlling force of an elaborate régime which, for him, was typified by the sound of hooves on the cobbled forecourt and of the rake in the gravelled quadrangle; but in Guy's mind the house was primarily his mother's milieu; he remembered the carpet covered with newspaper and the flower petals drying for pot-pourri, his mother walking beside him by the lake under a sunshade, sitting beside him on winter afternoons helping him with his scrapbook. It was here that she had died leaving the busy house desolate to him and to his father. He had lost the solid image of his father as a man of possessions and authority (for even in his declining fortunes, up to the day of leaving Broome, Mr Crouchback had faithfully borne all his responsibilities, sitting on the bench and the county council, visiting prisons and hospitals and lunatic asylums, acting as president to numerous societies, as a governor of schools and charitable trusts, opening shows and bazaars and returning home after a full day to a home that usually abounded with guests) and saw him now only as the recluse of his later years in the smell of dog and tobacco in the small seaside hotel. It was to that image he had prayed that morning.

'No,' said Guy, 'I should like to keep everything at Matchet.'

Uncle Peregrine came down the steps.

'You should go and say goodbye to the Reverend Mother. Time to be moving off. The train leaves in twenty minutes. I wasn't able to reserve a coach for the return journey.'

On the way to the station Miss Vavasour came to Guy's side. 'I wonder,' she said, 'will you think it very impertinent to ask, but I should so much like to have a keepsake of your father; any little thing; do you think you could spare something?'

'Of course, Miss Vavasour. I ought to have thought of it myself. What sort of thing? My father had so few personal possessions, you know.'

'I was wondering, if no one else wants it, and I don't know who would, do you think I could have his old tobacco-jar?'

'Of course. But isn't there anything more personal? One of his books? A walking stick?'

'The tobacco-jar is what I should *like*, if it's not asking too much. It seems somehow specially personal. You must think me very foolish.'

'Certainly. Please take it by all means if that is what you would really like.'

'Oh, thank you. I can't tell you how grateful. I don't suppose I shall stay on much longer at Matchet. The Cuthberts have not been considerate. It won't be the same place without your father and the tobacco-jar will remind me – the smell you know.'

Box-Bender did not return to London. He had an allowance of parliamentary petrol. Angela had used it to come to Broome. He and she and the dog, Felix, drove back to their house in the Cotswolds.

Later that evening he said: 'Everyone had a great respect for your father.'

'Yes, that was rather the theme of the day, wasn't it?'

'Did you talk to the solicitor?'

'Yes.'

'So did I. Had you any idea your father was so well off? Of course it's your money, Angie, but it will come in very handy. There was something said about some pensions. You're not obliged to continue them you know.'

'So I gathered. But Guy and I will do so.'

'Mind you, one can't be sure they're all deserving cases. Worth looking into. After all your father was very credulous. Our expenses get heavier every year. When the girls come back from America, we shall have to meet all kinds of bills. It's a different matter with Guy. He hasn't anyone to support except himself. And he had his whack when he went to Kenya you know. He had no right to expect any more.'

'Guy and I will continue the pensions.'

'Just as you like, Angie. No business of mine. Just thought I'd mention it. Anyway, they'll all fall in one day.'

4

When Virginia Troy went to visit Dr Puttock for the second time, he received her cordially.

'Yes, Mrs Troy, I am happy to say that the report is positive.'

'You mean I *am* going to have a baby?'

'Without any doubt. These new tests are infallible.'

'But this is awful.'

'My dear Mrs Troy, I assure you that there is nothing whatever to worry about. You are thirty-three. Of course, it is generally advisable for a woman to enter her child-bearing period a little younger, but your general condition is excellent. I see no reason to anticipate any kind of trouble. Just carry on with your normal activities and come back to see me in three weeks so that I can see that everything is going along all right.'

'But it's all *wrong*. It's quite impossible for me to have a baby.'

'Impossible in what sense? I presume you had marital intercourse at the appropriate time.'

' "Marital?" ' said Virginia. 'Isn't that something to do with marriage?'

'Yes, yes, of course.'

'Well, I haven't seen my husband for four years.'

'Ah, I see; well. That's a legal rather than a medical problem, is it not? Or should I say social? One finds a certain amount of this kind of thing nowadays in all classes. Husbands abroad in the army or prisoners of war; that sort of thing. Conventions are not as strict as they used to be – there is not the same stigma attached to bastardy. I presume you know the child's father.'

'Oh, I know him all right. He's just gone to America.'

'Yes, I see that that is rather inconvenient, but I am sure you will find things turn out well. In spite of everything the maternity services run very smoothy. Some people even think that a disproportionate attention is given to the next generation.'

'Dr Puttock, you *must* do something about this.'

'*I*? I don't think I understand you,' said Dr Puttock icily. 'Now I am afraid I must ask you to make way for my other patients. We civilian doctors are run off our feet, you know. Give my kind regards to Lady Kilbannock.'

Virginia was remarkable for the composure with which she had hitherto accepted the vicissitudes of domesticity. Whatever the disturbances she had caused to others, her own place in her small but richly diverse world had been one of coolness, light, and peace. She had found that place for herself, calmly recoiling from a disorderly childhood and dismissing it from her thoughts. From the day of her marriage to Guy to the day of her desertion of Mr Troy and for a year after, she had achieved a *douceur de vivre* that was alien to her epoch; seeking nothing, accepting what came and enjoying it without compunction. Then, ever since her meeting with Trimmer in fog-bound Glasgow, chill shadows had fallen, deepening daily. 'It's all the fault of this damned war,' she reflected, as she went down the steps into Sloane Street. 'What good do they think they're doing?' she asked herself as she surveyed the passing uniforms and gasmasks. 'What's it all *for*?'

She went to her place of business in Ian Kilbannock's office and telephoned to Kerstie in 'Ciphers'.

'I've got to see you. How about luncheon?'

'I was going out with a chap.'

'You must chuck him, Kerstie. I'm in trouble.'

'Oh, Virginia, not again.'

'The first time. Surely you know what people mean when they say "in trouble"?'

'Not *that*, Virginia?'

'Just that.',

'Well, that is something, isn't it. All right, I'll chuck. Meet me in the club at one.'

The officer's club at HOO HQ was gloomier in aspect than the canteens at No. 6 Transit Camp. It had been designed for other purposes. The walls were covered with ceramic portraits of Victorian rationalists, whiskered, hooded and gowned. The wives and daughters of the staff served there under the wife of General Whale, who arranged the duties so that the young and pretty were out of sight in the kitchen and pantry. Mrs

Whale controlled, among much else, the tap of a coffee urn. Whenever one of these secluded beauties appeared by the bar, Mrs Whale was able to raise a cloud of steam which completely concealed her. Mrs Whale had resisted the entry of the female staff but had been overborne. She made things as disagreeable for them as she could, often reprimanding them: 'Now you can't sit here coffee-housing. You're keeping the men from the tables and *they* have work to do.'

She said precisely this when Virginia set about expounding her situation to Kerstie.

'Oh Mrs Whale, we've only just arrived.'

'You've had plenty of time to eat. Here's your bill.'

The nondescript colonel who was liberating Italy was in fact looking for a place. He took Virginia's warm chair gratefully.

'I should like to boil that bitch in her own stew,' said Virginia as they left.

They found a dark corner outside and there she described her visit to Dr Puttock. Eventually Kerstie said: 'Don't worry, darling, I'll go and talk to him myself. He dotes on me.'

'Go soon.'

'This evening on the way home. I'll tell you what he says.'

Virginia was already at Eaton Terrace when Kerstie returned. She was wearing the clothes she wore all day and was sitting as she had first sat down, doing nothing, waiting.

'Well,' she said, 'how did it go?'

'We'd better both have a drink.'

'Bad news?'

'It was all rather disturbing. Gin?'

'What did he say, Kerstie? Will he do it?'

'*He* won't. He was frightfully pompous. I've never known him like it before. Most welcoming at first until I told him what I'd come about. Talked about professional ethics; said I was asking him to commit a grave crime; asked me, would I go to my bank manager and suggest he embezzled money for me. I said, yes, if I thought there was any chance of his doing it. That softened him a little bit. I explained about you and how you were broke. Then he said: "She won't find it a cheap

76

operation." That rather gave him away. I said: "Come off it. You know there *are* doctors who do this kind of thing," and he said: "One has heard of such cases – in the police courts usually." And I said: "I bet you know one or two who haven't been caught. It goes on all the time. It just happens Virginia and I have never had to inquire before." Then I sucked up to him a lot and reminded him how he had always looked after me when I had babies. I suppose it wasn't strictly *à propos* but it seemed to soften him; so at last he said he did know the name of someone who might help, and as a family friend, not as a doctor, he might give me the name. Well, I mean to say, he's always been a doctor to me not a family friend. He's never been in the house except to charge a guinea a time; but I didn't bring that up. I said: "Well, come on. Write it down," and then, Virginia, he rather shook me. He said: "No. *You* write it down," and I put out a hand to take a piece of paper off his desk and he said: "Just a minute," and he took out a pair of scissors and cut the address off the top. "Now," he said, "you can write this name and address. I haven't heard of the man for some time. I don't know if he's still practising. If your friend wants an appointment, she had better take a hundred pounds with her in notes. That's the best I can do. And remember I'm not doing it. I have no knowledge of this matter. I have never seen your friend." Do you know, he had me so nervous I could hardly write.'

'But you got the name?'

Kerstie took the slip of paper from her bag and handed it to her.

'Brook Street?' said Virginia. 'I thought it would be someone in Paddington or Soho. No telephone number. Let's look him up.'

They found the name and respectable address but when they tried to ring him up they were told the number was 'unobtainable'.

'I'm going round there now,' said Virginia. 'The hundred pounds will have to wait. I must have a look at him. You wouldn't like to come too?'

'No.'

'I wish you would, Kerstie.'

'No. The whole thing's given me the creeps.'

So Virginia went alone. There was no taxi in Sloane Square. She took the tube to Bond Street and picked her way through the American soldiers to the once quiet and fashionable street. When she reached the place where the house should have stood, she found a bomb crater flanked on either side with rugged cliffs of brick and plaster. Usually at such places there was a notice stating the new address of the former occupants. Virginia searched with her electric torch and learned that a neighbouring photographer and a hat shop had removed elsewhere. There was no spoor of the abortionist's passage. Perhaps he lay with his instruments somewhere under the rubble.

She was near Claridge's Hotel and from old habits sought refuge there in her despair. Lieutenant Padfield was standing by the fireplace straight before her. She turned away, seeming not to see him, and wearily walked down the corridor to Davies Street; then thought: 'What the hell? *I* can't start cutting people,' turned again and smiled.

'Loot, I didn't recognize you. One's like a pit-pony coming in from the blackout. Will you buy a girl a drink?'

'Just what I was about to suggest. I have to go out in a minute – to Ruby at the Dorchester.'

'Is that where she lives now? I used to go to her parties in Belgrave Square.'

'You should go see her. People don't go to see her as much as they used. She's a very significant and lovely person. Her memory is fantastic. Yesterday she was telling me all about Lord Curzon and Elinor Glyn.'

'I won't keep you, but I feel I need a drink.'

'It seems they were both interested in the occult.'

'Yes, Loot, yes. Just give me a drink.'

'It's not a thing that has ever greatly interested me, the occult. I'm interested in live people mostly. I mean, I'm interested in Ruby remembering, more than in what she remembers. Now some days back I was at a Catholic Requiem in Somerset county. It was the live people there I found significant. There were a lot of them. It was Mr Gervase Crouchback's funeral at Broome.'

'I saw he had died,' said Virginia. 'It's years since we met. I was fond of him once.'

'A lovely person,' said the Lieutenant.

'Surely you never knew him, Loot?'

'Not personally, only by repute. He was reputed as very fine indeed. I was glad to learn that he was so well off.'

'Not Mr Crouchback, Loot; you've got that wrong. He was ruined long ago.'

'There were people like that in the States twelve years ago. Wiped out in the crash. But they got it all back again.'

'Mr Crouchback wasn't like that, I assure you.'

'From what I hear he wasn't ever "ruined". It was just that the way things were over here after the first war, real estate didn't produce any income. Not only it didn't pay – it was a regular loss. When Mr Crouchback sold up, he not only got a price for the land; he saved himself all he had been paying out every year to keep things going. He wouldn't let the place run down. Sooner than that he'd clear out altogether. That was how he reckoned it. There were some valuable things, too, he sold out of the house. So he ended up a very substantial person.'

'What a lot you know about everyone, Loot.'

'Well, yes. I've been told before now I'm funny that way.'

Virginia was not a woman who left things unsaid.

'I know all about you and my divorce.'

'Mr Troy is an old and valued client of my firm,' said the Lieutenant. 'There was nothing personal about it. Business before friendship.'

'You still look on me as a friend?'

'Surely.'

'Then go and find a taxi.'

That aptitude never failed the Lieutenant. As Virginia drove back to Eaton Terrace, men and women emerged into the dim headlights signalling vigorously to the cab, waving bank-notes. She had a brief sense of triumph that she was sitting secure in the darkness; then the full weight of her failure bowed her, literally, so that she was crouched with her head near her knees when they drew up at the house where she lodged. Kerstie was on the door-step.

'What luck. Keep the taxi,' and then: 'Everything all right?'

'No, nothing. I saw the Loot.'

'At the doctor's? I should have thought that's one place he wouldn't be.'

'At Claridge's. He came clean.'

'But how about the doctor?'

'Oh, he was no good. Blitzed.'

'Oh dear. I tell you what; I'll ask Mrs Bristow in the morning. She knows everything.' (Mrs Bristow was the charwoman.) 'Must go now. I'm going to poor old Ruby.'

'You'll find the Loot.'

'I'll give him socks.'

'He says we're friends. I expect I'll be in bed when you get back.'

'Good night.'

'Good night.'

Virginia went alone into the empty house. Ian Kilbannock was away for some nights conducting a party of journalists round an assault course in Scotland. The dining-room table was not laid. Virginia went down into the larder, found half a loaf of greyish bread, some margarine, a segment of imitation cheese and ate them at the kitchen table.

She was not a woman to repine. She accepted change, though she did not so express it to herself, as the evidence of life. A mile of darkness away, in her hotel sitting-room, Ruby repined. Her brow and the skin round her old eyes were taut with 'lifting'. She looked at the four unimportant people who sat round her little dinner-table and thought of the glittering guests in Belgrave Square; thirty years of them, night after night, the powerful, the famous, the promising, the beautiful: thirty years' work to establish and impose herself ending now with – what where their names? what did they do? – these people sitting with electric fires behind their chairs talking of what? 'Ruby, tell us about Boni de Castellane.' 'Tell us about the Marchesa Casati.' 'Tell us about Pavlova.' Virginia had never sought to impose herself. She had given parties, too; highly successful ones, all over Europe and in certain select parts of America. She could not remember the names of her guests;

many she had not known at the time. As she ate her greasy bread in the kitchen she did not contrast her present lot with her past. Now, as it had been for the past month, she was aghast at the future.

Next morning Kerstie came early to Virginia's room.

'Mrs Bristow's here,' she said. 'I can hear her banging about. I'll go down and tackle her. You keep out of it.'

Virginia did not take long preparing herself for these days. There was no longer the wide choice in her wardrobe or the expensive confusion on her dressing-table. She was ready dressed, sitting on her bed waiting, fiddling with her file at a broken fingernail, when Kerstie at length came back to her.

'Well, that was all right.'

'Mrs Bristow can save me?'

'I didn't let on it was you. I rather think she suspects Brenda and she's always had a soft spot for her. She was most sympathetic. Not at all like Dr Puttock. She knows just the man. Several of her circle have been to him and say he's entirely reliable. What's more he only charges twenty-five pounds. I'm afraid he's a foreigner.'

'A refugee?'

'Well, rather more foreign than that. In fact he's black.'

'Why should I mind?' asked Virginia.

'Some people might. Anyway, here's the name and address. Dr Akonanga, 14 Blight Street, W2. That's off the Edgware Road.'

'Different from Brook Street.'

'Yes and quarter the price. Mrs Bristow doesn't think he has a telephone. The thing to do is go to his surgery early. He's very popular in his district, Mrs Bristow says.'

An hour later Virginia was on the doorstep of number fourteen. No bombs had fallen in Blight Street. It was a place of lodging houses and mean tobacconists, that should have been alive with children. Now the Pied Piper of the state schools had led them all away to billets and 'homes' in the country, and only the elderly and the slatternly remained of its inhabitants. The word 'Surgery' was lettered on what had once been a shop window. A trousered woman, with her hair in a turban was smoking at the door.

'Do you know if Dr Akonanga is at home?'

'He's gone.'

'Oh dear.' Virginia suffered again all the despair of the previous evening. Her hopes had never been firm or high. It was Fate. For weeks now she had been haunted by the belief that in a world devoted to destruction and slaughter this one odious life was destined to survive.

'Been gone nearly a year. The government took him.'

'You mean he's in prison?'

'Not him. Work of national importance. He's a clever one, black as he may be. What it is, there's things them blacks know what them don't that's civilized. That's where they put him.' She pointed to a card on the jamb of the door which read: *DR AKONANGA, nature-therapeutist and deep psychologist, has temporarily discontinued his practice. Parcels and messages to* and there followed an address two doors from the bombed house where she had peered into the darkness the evening before.

'Brook Street? How odd.'

'Gone up in the world,' said the woman. 'What I say, it takes a war for the clever ones to be appreciated.'

Virginia found a cab in the Edgware Road and drove to the new address, once a large private house, now in military occupation. A sergeant sat in the hall.

'Can I see your pass, please?'

'I'm looking for Dr Akonanga.'

'Your pass, please.'

Virginia showed an identity card issued by HOO HQ.

'That's OK,' said the sergeant. 'You can't miss him. We always know when the doctor's at work. Hark.'

From high overhead at the top of the wide staircase came sounds which could only be the beat of a tom-tom. Virginia climbed towards it thinking of Trimmer who had endlessly, unendurably crooned 'Night and Day' to her. The beat of the drum seemed to be saying: 'You, you, you.' She reached the door behind which issued the jungle rhythm. It seemed otiose to add the feeble tap of her knuckles. She tried the handle and found herself locked out. There was a bell with the doctor's name above it. She pressed. The drumming stopped. A key turned. Virginia was greeted by a small, smiling, nattily dressed Negro, not in his first youth; there was grey in his sparse little tangle of beard; he was wrinkled and simian and what should have been the whites of his eyes were the colour of Trimmer's cigarette-stained fingers; from behind him there came a faint air blended of spices and putrefaction. His smile revealed many gold capped teeth.

'Good morning. Come in. How are you? You have the scorpions?'

'No,' said Virginia, 'no scorpions this morning.'

'Pray come in.'

She stepped into a room whose conventional furniture was augmented with a number of hand-drums, a bright statue of the Sacred Heart, a cock, decapitated but unplucked, secured with nails to the table top, its wings spread open like a butterfly's, a variety of human bones including a skull, a brass cobra of Benares ware, bowls of ashes, flasks from a chemical laboratory stoppered and holding murky liquids. A magnified photograph of Mr Winston Churchill glowered down upon the profusion of Dr Akonanga's war-stores, but Virginia did not observe them in detail. It was the fowl that caught her attention.

'You are not from HOO HQ?' asked Dr Akonanga.

'Yes, as a matter of fact I am. How did you guess?'

'I have been expecting scorpions for three days. Major Allbright assured me they were being flown from Egypt. I explained they are an essential ingredient for one of my most valuable preparations.'

'There's always a delay nowadays in getting what one wants, isn't there? I don't know Major Allbright I'm afraid. Mrs Bristow sent me to you.'

'Mrs Bristow? I am not sure I have the honour –'

'I've come as a private patient,' said Virginia. 'You've treated lots of her friends. Women like myself,' she explained with her high incorrigible candour, 'who want to get rid of babies.'

'Yes, yes. Perhaps a long time ago in what you would call

83

the "piping days" of peace. All that is changed. I am now in
the government service. General Whale would not like it if
resumed my private practice. Democracy is at stake.'

Virginia shifted her gaze from the headless fowl to the un
familiar assembly of equipment. She noticed a copy of *No
Orchids for Miss Blandish.*

'Dr Akonanga,' she asked, 'what can you think you are doing
that is more important than me?'

'I am giving Herr von Ribbentrop the most terrible dreams,
said Dr Akonanga with pride and gravity.

What dreams troubled Ribbentrop that night, Virginia could
not know. She dreamed she was extended on a table, pinioned
headless and covered with blood-streaked feathers, while a
voice within her, from the womb itself, kept repeating: 'You
you, you.'

5

LUDOVIC'S command was stationed in a large, requisitioned
villa in a still desolate area of Essex. The owners had been
ready to move out when they saw and heard, a few flat fields
away, the bulldozers move in to prepare the new aerodrome; a
modest enough construction, a single cross of runway, a dozen
huts, but enough to annihilate the silence they had sought
there. They left behind them most of their furniture, and Ludovic's quarters in what had been designed as the nurseries were
equipped with all he required. He had never shared the taste
of Sir Ralph and his friends for bric-à-brac. There was a certain likeness between his office and Mr Crouchback's sitting
room at Matchet, without the characteristic smell of pipe and
retriever. Ludovic did not smoke and he had never owned a
dog.

When he was appointed, he was told: 'It's no business of
yours who your "clients" are or where they are going. You
simply have to see they're comfortable during the ten days they
spend with you. Incidentally, you will be able to make yourself pretty comfortable too. I don't imagine the change will be

unwelcome' – looking at his file – 'after your experiences in the Middle East.'

For all his tutelage under Sir Ralph Brompton in the arts of peace Ludovic lacked Jumbo Trotter's zest for comfort and his ingenuity in pursuing it. He shared a batman with his staff-captain, Fremantle; his belt and boots always shone. He cherished an old trooper's fetish for leather. His establishment drew a special scale of rations, for it catered for 'clients' who were taking vigorous physical exercise and suffering, most of them, from nervous anxiety. Ludovic ate heavily but without discrimination. His life was the life of the mind and there was little to occupy it in his official duties. The staff-captain had charge of administration; three athletic officers performed the training and these brave young men went in fear of Ludovic. They had less information even than he about the identity of their pupils. They did not know even the initial letters of the departments they served, and they believed, rightly, that when they visited the market town, security police in plain clothes offered them drinks and tried to draw them into indiscretion on the subject of their employment. They reported at the end of each course on the prowess of their 'clients'. Ludovic transcribed and where necessary paraphrased their verdicts and forwarded them in a nest of envelopes to the sponsors.

One morning at the end of November he settled to this, which was almost his only task. Training reports lay on his desk. *PT OK*, he read, *but a nervous type. Got worse. Had to be pushed out for last jump. NBG.* – *His excellent physique is not matched by psychological stamina*, he wrote. Then he consulted Roget and under the heading of Prospective Affections found: 'Cowardice, pusillanimity, poltroonery, dastardness, abject fear, funk, dunghill-cock, coistril, nidget, Bob Acres, Jerry Sneak.' 'Nidget' was a new word. He moved to the dictionary and found: '*Nidget*; an idiot. A triangular horseshoe used in Kent and Sussex.' Not applicable. 'Dunghill-cock' was good, but perhaps too strong. Major Hound had been a dunghill-cock. He tried 'coistril' and found only: '*Coistrel*: a groom, knave, base fellow' and the quotation: 'the swarming rabble of our coistrell curates.'

His eyes followed the columns, like a prospector's panning

for gold. Everywhere in the dross of 'coition ... cojuror ... colander' nuggets gleamed. '*Coke-upon-Littleton:* cant name of a mixed drink ...' – He seldom frequented the bar in the ante-room. He could hardly call for Coke-upon-Littleton. Perhaps it could be used in rebuke. 'Fremantle, it seemed to me you had had one too many Cokes-upon-Littleton last night.' – 'Coke' he noted was pronounced 'cook'. '*Colaphize:* to buffet and knock ...'; and so browsed happily until recalled to his duties by the entrance of his staff-captain with an envelope marked 'secret'. He hastily completed the report: *Failed to eradicate faults in training. Not recommended for active operations*, and signed at the foot of the sheet.

'Thank you, Fremantle,' he said. 'You can take the confidential reports, seal them and give them to the despatch rider to take back. What did you think of our last batch?'

'Not up to much.'

'A rabble of coistrell curates?'

'Sir?'

'Never mind.'

Each batch of 'clients' left early in the morning to be succeeded by the next in the late afternoon two days later. The intervening period was one of ease for the staff when, if they were in funds, they could go to London. Only the chief instructor, who was a man of few pleasures, remained on duty that day. He did not like to be long parted from the gymnastic apparatus in which the station abounded, and was resting in the ante-room from a vigorous hour on the trapeze when the staff-captain found him. He refused a drink. The staff-captain mixed himself a pink gin at a bar, scrupulously entered it in the ledger, and said after a pause:

'Don't you think the old man is getting rather rum lately?'

'I don't see much of him.'

'Can't understand half he says these days.'

'He had a bad time escaping from Crete. Weeks in an open boat. Enough to make anyone rum.'

'He was babbling about curates just now.'

'Religious mania, perhaps,' said the chief instructor. 'He doesn't give me any trouble.'

Upstairs Ludovic opened the envelope, removed the roll of

the 'clients' arriving next day and scanned it cursorily. An all military batch he noted. He had only one slight cause of uneasiness. So much remained from his early training that he would not have liked to find an officer of the Household Cavalry under his command. This had not occurred yet, nor did it now. But there was a name of more evil omen. The list was alphabetically arranged and at its head stood: 'Crouchback, G. T/Y Capt. RCH.'

Even in the moment of horror his new vocabulary came pat. There was one fine word which exactly defined his condition: 'Colaphized'. It carried a subtle echo, unsupported by its etymology, of 'collapse'.

To be struck twice in a month after two years' respite; to be struck where he should have been most sheltered, in the ivory tower of *avant garde* letters, in the keep of his own seemingly impregnable fastness, was a disaster beyond human calculation. He had read enough of psychology to be familiar with the word 'trauma'; to know that to survive injury without apparent scar gave no certainty of abiding health. Things had happened to Ludovic in the summer of 1941, things had been done by him, which, the ancients believed, provoked a doom. Not only the ancients; most of mankind, independently, cut off from all communications with one another, had discovered and proclaimed this grim alliance between the powers of darkness and justice. Who was Ludovic, Ludovic questioned, to set his narrow, modern scepticism against the accumulated experience of the species?

He opened his dictionary and read: '*Doom:* irrevocable destiny (usually of adverse fate), final fate, destruction, ruin, death.' He turned to Roget and found '*Nemesis*: Eumenides; keep the wound green; *lex talionis*; ruthless; unforgiving, inexorable; implacable, remorseless.' His sacred scriptures offered no comfort that morning.

At the same time as Ludovic was contemplating the arcane operation of Nemesis in the lowlands of Essex, Kerstie was causing dismay in Eaton Terrace by revealing the effects of causality in the natural order.

Ian had returned from his tour of the Highlands. He had

dismissed his party of journalists on the platform at Edinburgh and delayed a night to visit his mother at the castellated dwelling on the Ayrshire coast which his grandfather, the first baron, had built as the family seat. The main building had been requisitioned and, though massive, was being eroded by soldiers. The Dowager Lady Kilbannock lived in the factor's house and there gratefully entertained Ian's sons in their school holidays. It was his first visit since the beginning of the war. He was still savouring the unaccustomed warmth of his welcome.

He had arrived in London that morning but had no intention of reporting back to his office until afternoon. Virginia was there to help his depleted secretariat deal with the telephone. He had bathed after his night journey, shaved, and breakfasted, lit a cigar from a box given him by his mother, and was prepared for an easy morning, when Kerstie had joined him. The cipher clerks worked irregular hours according to the press of business. She had been on night shift and returned home hoping for a bath. She was not pleased to find that Ian had used all the hot water. In her vexation she sprang the news of Virginia's predicament.

Ian's first words were: 'Good God. At her age. After all her experience;' and then: 'Well, she can't have it here.'

'She's in an odd mood,' said Kerstie. 'She seems to have lost all her spirit. The country must still be teeming with helpful doctors or for that matter midwives. I believe a lot of them make a bit on the side that way. She happens to have struck it unlucky twice. Now she's just given up trying. Talks about Fate.'

Ian drew deeply at his cigar, wondered why Scotland was still stocked with commodities that had long disappeared from the south, then turned gentler thoughts towards Virginia. He had momentarily seen himself as a figure of melodrama driving her from his door. Now he said:

'Has she thought of the Loot?'

'As a doctor?'

'No, no. As a husband. She should marry someone. That's what a lot of girls do, who funk an operation.'

'I don't think the Loot likes women.'

'He's always about with them. But he wouldn't really do. What she needs is a chap who's just off to Burma or Italy. Lots of chaps marry on embarkation leave. She needn't announce the happy event until a suitable time. When he comes home, if he does come home, he won't be likely to ask to see its birth certificate. He'll be proud as Punch to find a child to greet him. It happens all the time.' He smoked in silence before the gas fire, while Kerstie went up to change and wash in cold water. When she returned, wearing one of Virginia's 1939 suits, he was still thinking of Virginia.

'How about Guy Crouchback?' he asked.

'How about him?'

'I mean as a husband. He's off to Italy quite soon, I believe.'

'What a disgusting idea. I like Guy.'

'Oh, so do I. Old friends. But he's been keen on Virginia. She told me he made a pass at her when she first came back to London. They were saying in Bellamy's that he's been left a lot of money lately. Come to think of it, he was once married to Virginia in the remote ages. You'd better put the idea into her head. Let it lie there and fructify. She'll do the rest. But she must look sharp.'

'Ian, you absolutely nauseate me.'

'Well perhaps I'd better have a word with her at the office as her boss. Got to see to the welfare of one's command.'

'There are times I really detest you.'

'Yes, so does Virginia. Well, who else do you suggest for her? I dare say one of the Americans would be the best bet. The trouble is that, from the litter of contraceptives they leave everywhere, it looks as though they lacked strong philoprogenitive instincts.'

'You couldn't get Trimmer recalled?'

'And undo the work of months? Not on your life. Besides Virginia hates him more than anyone. She wouldn't marry him, if he came to her in his kilt escorted by bagpipes. He fell in love with her, remember? That was what sickened her. He used to sing "Night and Day" about her, to *me*. "Like the beat, beat, beat of the tom-tom, when the jungle shadows fall." It was excruciating.'

Kerstie sat close to Ian by the fireplace in the cloud of rich smoke. It was not affection that drew her but the warmth of the feeble blue flames.

'Why don't you go to Bellamy's,' she asked, 'and talk to your beastly friends there?'

'Don't want to run into anyone from HOO HQ. Officially I'm still in Scotland.'

'Well, I'm going to sleep. I don't want to talk any more.'

'Just as you like. Cheer up,' he added, 'if she can't qualify for a ward for officers' wives, I believe there are special state maternity homes now for unmarried factory-girls. Indeed, I know there are. Trimmer visited one during his Industrial Tour and was a great success there.'

'Can you imagine Virginia going to one of them?'

'Better than her staying here. Far better.'

Kerstie did not sleep long but when she came downstairs at noon, she found that the lure of Bellamy's had proved stronger than Ian's caution and that the house was empty save for Mrs Bristow who was crowning her morning's labour with a cup of tea and a performance on the wireless of 'Music while you Work'.

'Just off, ducks,' she said using a form of address that had become prevalent during the blitz. 'I've got a friend says she can give me another doctor as might help your friend.'

'Thank you, Mrs Bristow.'

'Only he lives in Canvey Island. Still you can't find things where you want them now, can you ducks? Not with the war.'

'No, alas.'

'Well, I'll bring the name tomorrow. So long.'

Kerstie did not think Canvey Island a promising resort and was confirmed in this opinion when, a few minutes later, Virginia telephoned from her office.

'Canvey Island? Where's that?'

'Somewhere near Southend I think.'

'That's out.'

'It's Mrs Bristow's last hope.'

'*Canvey Island.* Anyway, that's not what I rang up about. Tell me, does Ian know about me?'

'I think he does.'

'You told him?'

'Well, yes.'

'Oh, I don't mind but, listen, he's just done something very odd. He's asked me to lunch with him. Can you explain that?'

'No, indeed not.'

'It's not as though he didn't see all too much of me every day at home and in the office. He says he wants to talk to me privately. Do you think it's about my trouble.'

'I suppose it might be.'

'Well, I'll tell you all about it when I come back.'

Kerstie considered the matter. She was a woman with moral standards which her husband did not share. Finally she tried to telephone to Guy but a strange voice answered from the shade of the megalosaurus saying that Captain Crouchback had been posted to another department and was inaccessible.

An aeroplane rising half a mile distant, and thunderously skimming the chimneys of the house, an obsolete bomber such as was adapted for parachute training, roused Ludovic from the near-stupor into which he had fallen. He rose from his deep chair and at his desk entered on the first page of a new notebook a *pensée*: *The penalty of sloth is longevity.* Then he went to the window and gazed blankly through the plate glass.

He had chosen these rooms because they were secluded from the scaffolds and platforms where the training exercises took place in front of the house. He faced, across half an acre of lawn, what the previous owners had called their 'arboretum'. Ludovic thought of it merely as 'the trees'. Some were deciduous and had now been stripped bare by the east wind that blew from the sea, leaving the holm oaks, yews, and conifers in carefully contrived patterns, glaucous, golden, and of a green so deep as to be almost black at that sunless noon; they afforded no pleasure to Ludovic.

Where, he asked himself, could he hide during the next ten days? It did not occur to him to go on leave. He had had all the leave that was due to him and his early training had left him with a superstitious regard for orders. Jumbo Trotter would have devised a dozen perfectly regular means of absenting himself. He would, if all else failed, have posted himself to a senior officers' 'refresher' course. Ludovic had never sought to master the byways of military movement. He stared at the arboretum and remembered the saw: 'The place to hide a leaf is in a tree.'

He went downstairs and across the hall to the ante-room. Captain Fremantle was still there with the chief instructor.

'Sit down. Sit down,' he said, for he had never experienced, and had not sought to introduce under his command, the easy manners of the Officers' House at Windsor or at the Halberdiers' Depot. 'Here is the nominal roll of tomorrow's batch.' He handed it over and then he lingered. 'Fremantle,' he said, 'does my name appear anywhere?'

'Appear, sir?'

'I mean are the men under instruction aware of my name?'

'Well, sir, you usually meet them and speak to them the first night, don't you? You begin: "I am the commandant. My name is Ludovic. I want you all to feel free to come to me with any difficulties."'

This had indeed been the custom which Ludovic had inherited from his more genial predecessor in office, and very unnerving his baleful stare, as he spoke these formalities of welcome, had proved to more than one apprehensive 'client'. None had ever come to him with any difficulty.

'Do I? Is that what I say?'

'Well, something like that usually, sir.'

'Ah, but if I *don't* meet them, could they find out who I am? Is there a list of the establishment posted anywhere? Does my name appear on standing orders? Or daily orders?'

'I think it does, sir. I'll have to check on that.'

'I want all orders in future to be signed by you "Staff captain for Commandant". And have any notices that need it, retyped with my name omitted. Is that clear?'

'Yes, sir.'

'And I shan't be coming into the mess. I shall take all my meals in my office for the next week or so.'

'Very good, sir.'

Captain Fremantle regarded him with puzzled concern.

'You may thinks this rather strange, Fremantle. It's a question of security. They are tightening it up. As you know, this station is on the secret list. There have been some leaks lately. I received orders this morning that I was to go, as it were, "under-ground". You may think it all rather extravagant. I do myself. But those are our orders. I shall start the new régime today. Tell the mess corporal to serve my lunch upstairs.'

'Very good, sir.'

He left them and walked out of the french windows towards the trees.

'Well,' said the chief instructor, 'what d'you make of that?'

'He didn't get any orders this morning. I went through the mail. There was only one "secret" envelope—the nominal roll we always get.'

'Persecution mania,' said the chief instructor. 'It can't be anything else.'

Ludovic walked alone among the trees. What had been paths were ankle deep in dead leaves and cones and pine needles. His glossy boots grew dull. Presently he turned back and, avoiding the french windows, entered by a side door and the back stairs. On his table lay a great plate of roast meat – a week's ration for a civilian – a heap of potatoes and cold thick gravy, and beside it a pudding of sorts. He gazed at these things, wondering what to do. The bell did not work nor, had it done so, were the mess orderlies trained to answer it. He could not bear to sit beside this distasteful plethora waiting to see what would become of it. He took to the woods once more. Now and then an aeroplane came in to land or climbed roaring above him. Dusk began to fall. He was conscious of damp. When at last he returned to his room, the food was gone. He sat in his deep chair while the gathering dusk turned to darkness.

There was a knock at the door. He did not answer. Captain Fremantle looked in and the light from the passage revealed Ludovic sitting there, empty-handed, staring.

'Oh,' said Captain Fremantle, 'I'm sorry, sir. I was told you had gone out. Are you all right, sir?'

'Quite all right, thank you. Why should you fear otherwise? I like sometimes to sit and think. Perhaps if I smoked a pipe, it would seem more normal. Do you think I should buy a pipe?'

'Well, that's rather a matter of taste, isn't it, sir?'

'Yes, and to me it would be highly disagreeable. But I will buy a pipe, if it would make you easier in your mind about me.'

Captain Fremantle withdrew. As he shut the door he heard Ludovic switch on the light. He returned to the ante-room.

'The old man's stark crazy,' he reported.

It was part of the very light veil of secrecy which enveloped Ludovic's villa that its location was not divulged to the 'clients'. It was known officially as No. 4 Special Training Centre. Those committed to it were ordered to report at five in the afternoon to the Movement Control office in a London terminus, where they were mustered by a wingless Air Force officer and thence conveyed into Essex by motor bus. They did not see this airman again until the day of departure. His contribution to the war effort was to travel with them in the dark and see that none deserted or fell into conversation with subversive agents.

Foreign refugees who composed many of the training courses were obfuscated by this stratagem and when caught and tortured by the Gestapo could only give the unsatisfactory answer that they were taken in the dark to an unknown destination, but Englishmen had little difficulty in identifying their route.

When Guy arrived at the rendezvous he found a group of officers which grew to twelve in number. None was higher than captain in rank; all were older than the lean young athletes of the Parachute Regiment. Guy was the oldest of them by some five or six years. They came from many different regiments and like him had been chosen ostensibly for their knowledge of foreign languages and their appetite, if not for adventure, at least for diversity in the military routine. The last to report was a Halberdier, and Guy recognized his one-time subaltern, Frank de Souza.

'Uncle! What on earth are you doing here? Are you on the staff of this Dotheboys Hall they're taking us to?'

'Certainly not. I'm coming on the course with you.'

'Well, that's the most cheering thing I've heard about it yet.

It can't be as arduous as they make out if they take old sweats like you.'

They sat together at the back of the bus and throughout the hour's drive talked of the recent history of the Halberdiers. Colonel Tickeridge was now brigadier; Ritchie-Hook a major-general. 'He can't bear it and he's not much use at it either. He's never to be found at his own headquarters. Always biffing about in front.' Erskine now commanded the 2nd Battalion; de Souza had had D Company until a few weeks ago; then he had put in for a posting, claiming a hitherto unrevealed proficiency in Serbo-Croat. 'I suppose they might call it "battle weariness",' he said. 'Anyway, I wanted a change. Four years is too long in the same outfit for a man who's naturally a civilian. Besides it wasn't the same. There aren't many of the original battalion left. Not many casualties really. We had a suicide in the company. I never knew what about. A militia-man – perfectly cheerful all day and shot himself in his tent one evening. He left a letter to the CSM saying he hoped he would not cause any trouble. A few men got badly hit and sent home. Only one officer, Sarum-Smith, killed, but chaps got shunted about, first one, then another of the temporary officers were sent off on courses and never came back; half the senior NCO's were superannuated; the new young gentlemen were a dreary lot; until one suddenly realized the whole thing had changed. And then in Italy there were Americans all over the place clamouring for dough-nuts and Coca-Cola and ice-cream. So I decided to put my knowledge of Jugo-Slavia to use.'

'What do you know about it, Frank?'

'I once spent a month in Dalmatia, a most agreeable place, and I mugged up a bit of the language from a tourists' phrase book – enough to satisfy the examiners.'

Guy related his own drab history culminating in his meeting with the Electronic Selector in HOO HQ.

'Did you come across old Ralph Brompton there?'

'Do *you* know him, Frank?'

'Oh, rather. In fact it was he who told me about this Partisan Liaison Mission.'

'When you were in Italy?'

'Yes; he wrote. We're old friends.'

'How very odd. I thought all his friends were pansies.'

'Not at all. Nothing of the sort, I assure you. In fact,' de Souza added with an air of mystification, 'I shouldn't be surprised if half this bus load weren't friends of Ralph Brompton's one way or another.'

As he said this an unmilitary-looking man, in a beret and greatcoat, turned round in the seat in front of them and scowled at de Souza, who said in a voice of parody: 'Hullo, Gilpin. Did you see any good shows in towns?'

Gilpin grunted and turned back, and then de Souza in fact began to talk about the theatre.

The welcome at their destination was cordial and efficiently organized. Orderlies were standing by to take their baggage up to their rooms. 'I've put you two Halberdiers together,' said Captain Fremantle. 'Here's the ante-room. I shall be saying a few words after dinner. Meanwhile I expect you can all do with a drink. Dinner will be in half an hour.'

Guy went up. De Souza remained below. As Guy returned he paused on the stairs, hearing his own name mentioned. De Souza and Gilpin were in conversation in what they took to be privacy; Gilpin was plainly rebuking de Souza, who with uncharacteristic humility was attempting to exculpate himself.

'Crouchback's all right.'

'That's as may be. You had no call to bring up Brompton's name. You've got to watch out who you talk to. You can't trust anyone.'

'Oh, I've known old Crouchback since 1939. We joined the Halberdiers on the same day.'

'Yes, and Franco plays a nice game of golf I've been told. What's the name "Halberdiers" got to do with it? I reckon you've been picking up a little too much free and easy, Eighth Army esprit de bloody corps.'

The two moved to the ante-room, and Guy, puzzled, followed them after a minute. Seeing de Souza without his 'British warm' Guy noticed that he wore the ribbon of the MC.

That evening Captain Fremantle addressed them:

'I am the staff captain. My name is Fremantle. The commandant wishes you to feel free to come to me with any difficulties ...' He read the standing orders, explained the arrangements of messing and security.

The chief instructor followed him giving them the programme of the course; five days' instruction and physical training; then the qualifying five jumps from an aeroplane at times to be determined by the conditions of the weather. He gave them some encouraging figures about the rarity of fatalities. 'Every now and then you get a "Roman candle". Then you've had it. We've had a few cases of men fouling their ropes and making a bad landing. On the whole it's a lot safer than steeple-chasing.'

Guy had never ridden in a steeple-chase and, looking about him, he reflected that no one in the audience, nor the speaker either, seemed likely to have done so.

They went to bed early. De Souza said: 'All army courses are like prep schools – all that welcoming of the new boys. But we seem to have struck one of the better-class establishments. Dinner wasn't at all bad. The programme sounds reasonable. I think we are going to be happy here.'

'Frank, who's Gilpin?'

'Gilpin? Chap in the Education Corps. I think he's a school teacher in civil life. A bit earnest.'

'What's he doing here?'

'The same as the rest of us, I expect. He wants a change.'

'How do you come to know him?'

'I know all sorts, uncle.'

'One of Sir Ralph's set?'

'Oh, I shouldn't suppose so. Would you?'

For two days the squad 'limbered up'. The PT instructor showed a solicitude for Guy's age which he did not at all resent.

'Take it easy. Don't do too much at first, sir. Anyone can see you've been at an office desk. Stop the moment you feel you've had enough. We take them all sizes and shapes here. Why last month we had a man so heavy he had to use two parachutes.'

On the third day they jumped off a six foot height and rolled on the grass when they landed. On the fourth day they jumped from ten foot and in the afternoon were sent up a scaffolding higher than the house from which in parachute harness they jumped at the end of a cable which, sprung and weighted, set them gently on their feet at the end of the drop. Here they were sharply scrutinized by the chief instructor for symptoms of hesitation in taking the plunge.

'You'll be all right, Crouchback,' he said. 'Rather slow off the mark, Gilpin.'

During these days Guy experienced a mild stiffness and was massaged by a sergeant specially retained for this service. There was no night-flying from the adjoining aerodrome. Guy slept excellently and enjoyed a sense of physical well-being. It did not irk him as it irked others of the squad, that they were confined to the grounds.

Early on de Souza showed curiosity about the head of their little school. 'The commandant, does he exist? Has anyone seen him? It's like one of those ancient oriental states where the viziers bring messages from an invisible priest-king.'

Later he said: 'I've seen food going up the back stairs. He's shut up somewhere on the top storey.'

'Perhaps he's a drunk.'

'More than likely. I came home in a ship where the OC Troops was a raging dipsomaniac, locked in his cabin for the entire voyage.'

Later he reported: 'It can't be drink. I've seen the plates coming down empty. Chap with the horrors can't eat. At least our OC Troops didn't.'

'I expect it's the warder's dinner.'

'That's what it is. He's either drunk or insane and he has to have a man sitting with him night and day to see he doesn't commit suicide.'

Later he said to a group in the ante-room: 'There's nothing wrong with the commandant. He's being held prisoner. There's been a palace plot and his staff are selling the rations on the black market. Or do you think the whole place has been taken over by the Gestapo? Where could parachutists most safely land? At a parachute training base. They shot everyone except the commandant. They have to keep him to sign the bumf. Meanwhile they get particulars of all our agents. There's that instructor who's always fooling about with a camera. Says he's making "action studies" to correct faulty positions in jumping. Of course what he's really doing is making records of us all. They'll be microfilmed and sent out via Portugal. Then the Gestapo will have a complete portrait gallery and they can pick us up as soon as we show our faces. We ought to organize a rescue party.' Gilpin snorted with contempt at this fantasy and left the room. 'An earnest fellow,' said de Souza, with, Guy thought he could detect, an infinitesimal *nuance* of bravado, 'just as I told you. What's more he's windy about tomorrow's jump.'

'So am I.'

'So am I,' said others of the group.

'I don't believe you are, Guy,' said de Souza.

'Oh, yes,' said Guy untruthfully, 'I'm windy as hell.'

Part of the apparatus erected on the front lawn was the fuselage of an aeroplane. It was fitted with metal seats along the sides; an aperture had been cut in the floor; it was a replica of the machine from which they would jump and on the final afternoon of training they were drilled there by the 'despatching officer'.

He gave the warning order: 'Coming into target area,' removed the cover from the manhole. 'First pair ready.'

Two of the squad sat opposite one another with legs dangling. 'Number one. Jump.' His arm came down.

The first man precipitated himself on the grass and number three took his place. 'Number two jump.' And so on, again and again throughout the afternoon until they moved briskly and thoughtlessly. 'You don't have to think of anything. Just watch my hand. The parachute has a slip rope and opens automatically. Once you're out all you have to think about is keeping your legs together and rolling lightly when you land.'

But there was an air of apprehension in the ante-room that evening. De Souza worked his joke about the 'mystery man' in command for all it was worth.

'I saw a "face at the window",' he reported. 'A huge, horrible, pallid face. It stared straight down at me and then disappeared. Obviously seized by the guards. It was the face of a man totally abandoned to despair. I dare say they keep him under drugs.'

Gilpin said: 'What's this about "Roman Candles"?'

'When the parachute doesn't open and you fall plump straight.'

'How does that happen?'

'Faulty packing, I believe.'

'And the packing is left to a lot of girls. You'd only need one fascist agent on the assembly line and she could kill hundreds of men – thousands probably. There would be no way of catching her and her "Roman candles". Why are they called "Roman candles", anyway, if it isn't a fascist trick? I'm as ready as the next man to take a reasonable risk. I don't like the idea of trusting my life to some girl in a packing station – so-called refugees perhaps – Polish and Ukrainian agents as likely as not.'

'You *are* windy, aren't you, Gilpin?'

'I'm calculating the risk, that's all.'

One of the younger 'clients' said: 'If these buggers think they're going to get me to jump out of an aeroplane sober, they'd better think again.'

De Souza said: 'Of course, it's perfectly possible that the commandant is the head of the organization. They won't let him appear because he can't speak English – only Ukrainian. But he comes out at night and repacks the parachutes so that they won't open. It takes hours, of course, so he has to sleep all day.'

But the joke was wearing thin.

'For Christ's sake,' said Gilpin in admonition, and they all fell silent. De Souza saw he had lost the sympathy of his audience.

'Uncle,' he said that night, 'I believe you and I are the only ones who aren't windy and I'm not so sure about myself.'

When all the lights were out, Ludovic emerged from his retreat and stumbled to the edge of the dark trees, breathed for a few minutes the scent of sodden leaves, which carried no fond memories for him, and then returned to his room to write: *Those who take too keen an interest in the outside world, may one day find themselves locked outside their own gates.*

It was not an entirely original *pensée*. He had come on it and vaguely remembered it, in an undergraduate magazine that Sir Ralph had received and left among his litter. It seemed to him apt.

Next morning was almost windless; there was a pale suggestion of sunshine; jolly jumping weather.

'If it stays like this,' said the chief instructor as though offering a special, unexpected treat, 'we may be able to get in a night drop at the end of the course.'

He went early to the dropping-ground, a barren heath some miles distant, to see that it was suitably marked and to set up the loud-speaker apparatus through which he admonished his pupils as they fell towards him. The squad drove to the aerodrome, where their arrival seemed unexpected.

'It's always like this,' said the despatching officer. 'They've nothing else to do except lay on a flight for us, but at the last minute there's always difficulties.'

The dozen soldiers sat in the Nissen hut loud with jazz where a flying officer regarded them incuriously over the *Daily Mirror*. Presently he strolled out.

'Isn't there any way of turning off that music?' asked Guy. A knob was found. There was a brief respite of silence, then a blue-grey arm appeared from behind a door, manipulated the machine, and the music was resumed in even greater volume.

After half an hour the despatching officer returned. He was accompanied by the young man who had studied the *Daily Mirror*.

'I've ironed that out,' he said. 'All set?'

The flying officer wore some additions to his costume. 'The crate's really in for overhaul,' he said, 'but I dare say we can make it.'

They all trooped across the runway and climbed into the shabby old aeroplane. They put on their parachute harness and the despatching officer examined it cursorily. The rip-cords were clipped to a steel bar above the trap. There was very little light in the fuselage. Guy sat next to Gilpin, who was the man before him, No. 7 to his No. 8 in the order they had rehearsed.

'I wish they'd get on with it,' he said, but further conversation was obviated by the roar of the engines. Gilpin looked queasy

It was one of the objects of the exercise to accustom the squad to flying conditions. They were not taken direct to the dropping-area but in a long circle, wheeling over the sea and then coming inshore again. Very little could be seen from the portholes. The harness was more uncomfortable than it had seemed on the ground. They sat bowed and cramped, in twilight, noise, and the smell of petrol. At length the despatching officer and his sergeant opened the man-hole. 'Coming into the target area,' he warned. 'First pair ready.'

De Souza was No. 1. He slipped out cleanly at the fall of the hand and No. 3 took his place.

'Wait for it,' said the despatching officer. There was an interval of a minute between each drop as the machine banked and returned to its target. Soon Gilpin and Guy sat face to face. The landscape below turned vertiginously. 'Don't look down. Watch my hand,' said the despatching officer. Gilpin did not raise his eyes to the signal. The despatching officer gave the command: 'No. 7. Jump.'

But Gilpin sat rigid, feet dangling over the abyss, hands gripping the edge, gazing down. The despatching officer said nothing until the machine had completed its steep little circle then to Guy: 'You next. No. 8. Jump.'

Guy jumped. For a second, as the rush of air hit him, he lost consciousness. Then he came to himself, his senses purged of the noise and smell and throb of the machine. The hazy November sun enveloped him in golden light. His solitude was absolute.

He experienced rapture, something as near as his earthbound soul could reach to a foretaste of paradise, *locum refrigerii lucis et pacis*. The aeroplane seemed as far distant as will, at the moment of death, the spinning earth. As though he had cast the constraining bonds of flesh and muscle and nerve, he found himself floating free; the harness that had so irked him in the narrow, dusky, resounding carriage now almost imperceptibly supported him. He was a free spirit in an element as fresh as on the day of its creation.

All too soon the moment of ecstasy ceased. He was no

suspended motionless; he was falling fast. An amplified voice from below exhorted him: 'You're swinging No. 7. Steady yourself with the ropes. Keep your legs together.' At one moment he had the whole wide sky as his province; at the next the ground sprang to meet him as though he were being thrown by a horse. As his boots touched, he rolled as he had been taught. He felt a heavy blow on the knee as though he had landed on a stone. He lay in the sedge, dazed and breathless; then, as he had been taught, disengaged his harness. He attempted to stand, suffered a sharp pain in his knee and toppled once more to the ground. One of the instructors approached: 'That was all right. No. 7. Oh, it's you, Crouchback. Anything wrong?'

'I think I've hurt my knee,' said Guy.

It was the same knee he had twisted on guest night at the Halberdier barracks.

'Well, sit quiet till the jump's over. Then we'll attend to you.'

Again and again the aeroplane swooped overhead filling the sky with parachutes. Finally Gilpin landed quite near him, his qualms subdued. The sturdy, unmilitary figure joined him, infused with an unfamiliar jauntiness.

'Well, that wasn't so bad, was it?' he said.

'Highly enjoyable, up to a point,' said Guy.

'I missed my cue the first time,' said Gilpin. 'Don't know how it happened. I was like that square-bashing. Never got the trick of "instinctive, unquestioning obedience to orders", I suppose.'

Guy wanted to ask whether he had been 'assisted' through the man-hole. He refrained and, since Gilpin was the last of the squad, there was never anyone to know except the readers of his confidential report.

'I expect we shall do another jump this afternoon,' said Gilpin. 'I feel quite ready for one now.'

'I'm damned if I do,' said Guy.

That evening Captain Fremantle reported to Ludovic: 'One casualty, sir. Crouchback.'

'Crouchback?' said Ludovic vaguely as though the name was new to him. 'Crouchback?'

'One of the Halberdiers, sir. We thought he was a bit old for the job.'

'Yes,' said Ludovic. 'One of those accidents with, how do you describe them – "Roman candles"?'

'Oh, no. Nothing as bad at that. Just a sprain, I think.' Ludovic dissembled his chagrin at this news. 'We've sent him over to the RAF hospital for an X-ray. They'll probably keep him there for a bit. Will you be going over to see him?'

'No, I can't manage that, I'm afraid. I have a lot of work on hand. Telephone and find the result of the X-ray. Perhaps later you or one of the instructors might visit him and see that he is comfortable.'

Captain Fremantle knew exactly how much work Ludovic had on hand. The former commandant had always made a point of visiting injured 'clients'; even, on rare occasions, attending their funerals.

'Very good, sir,' said Captain Fremantle.

'Oh, and, by the way, you might tell the mess-corporal shall be dining down tonight.'

There was a mood of exuberance, almost of exultation, in the ante-room that evening. The eleven surviving members of the squad had made their second jump in weather of undisturbed tranquillity. They had overcome all their terrors of the air and were confident of finishing the course with honour. Some sprawled at their ease in the armchairs and sofas; some stood close together laughing loud and long. Even Gilpin was not entirely aloof from the general conviviality. He said: 'I don't mind admitting now I didn't quite like the look of it the first time,' and accepted a glass of bottled beer from the despatching officer who had that morning ignominiously bundled him into space and stepped firmly on his fingers as he clutched the edge of the man-hole in vain resistance to the force of the slip-stream.

Into this jolly company Ludovic entered like the angel of death. No one had believed the literal detail of de Souza's fantasies but their repetition and enlargement had created an aura of mystery and dread about the commandant who lurked overhead and was seen and heard by none, which Ludovic's appearance did nothing to dispel.

He overtopped the largest man in the room by some inches. There was at that time a well-marked contrast in appearance between the happy soldiers destined for the battlefield and those who endangered their digestions and sanity at office telephones. Standing before and above those lean and flushed young men, Ludovic's soft bulk and pallor suggested not so much the desk as the tomb. Complete silence fell. 'Present me,' Ludovic said, 'to these gentlemen.'

Captain Fremantle led him round. He laid a clammy hand in each warm, dry palm and repeated each name as Captain Fremantle uttered it '... de Souza ... Gilpin ...' as though he were reciting the titles of a shelf of books he had no intention of reading.

'Can I get you a drink, sir?' de Souza boldly asked.

'No, no,' said Ludovic from the depths of his invisible sarcophagus. 'I too have my rules of training to observe.' Then he surveyed the hushed circle 'One of you have been incapacitated, I learn. You are now an eleven without a spare man, without A. N. Other. What is the news of Captain A. N. Other, Fremantle?'

'Crouchback, sir? Nothing new since I saw you. The X-ray is tomorrow.'

'Keep me informed. I am anxious about Captain A. N. Other. Pray continue with your festivities, gentlemen. They sounded hilarious from upstairs. Continue. My presence is entirely informal.'

But the young officers emptied their glasses and laid them aside.

Gilpin's eyes were on the level of Ludovic's breast.

'You are wondering,' Ludovic said sternly and suddenly, 'how I acquired the Military Medal.'

'No, I wasn't,' said Gilpin. 'I was just wondering what it was.'

'It is the award for valour given to "Other Ranks". I won it in flight – not in such a flight as you have enjoyed today. I won it by running away from the enemy.'

Had there been any suggestion of mirth in Ludovic's manner,

his hearers would have been ready enough to laugh. As things were, they stood abashed. Ludovic took a large steel watch from the pocket below his ribbons. 'It is time for dinner,' he said. 'Lead on, Fremantle.'

Hitherto at this station it had been the habit to drop into the mess at any time up to half an hour of dinner being announced and to sit anywhere. Tonight Ludovic took the head of the table. The chief instructor took the foot and there was some competition to sit as near him as possible. At length two unhappy men found themselves obliged to take their places on either side of Ludovic.

'Do you say Grace in your mess?' Ludovic asked one of them.

'Only on guest nights, sir.'

'And this is not a guest night. It is the antonym. We are commemorating the absence of Captain A. N. Other. Do you know a Grace, Fremantle? Does no one know a Grace? Well, we will eat graceless.'

The dinner that night was particularly good. The oppression of Ludovic's presence could not keep the hungry young men from their food. A murmur of conversation spread from the foot of the table but did not quite reach the head where Ludovic ate copiously and with a peculiar precision and intent care in the handling of knife and fork – 'like a dentist', de Souza described it later – in his own simply constructed solitude, as remote and impenetrable as Guy's brief excursion in the skies. When he had finished he rose and without a word softly and heavily left the room. But his going did not appreciably raise the general spirits. Everyone discovered he was weary, and after the nine o'clock news went up to bed. De Souza was sorry Guy was not with him to discuss the evening's gruesome apparition. He had already dubbed the commandant 'Major Dracula' and his mind was teeming with necrophilic details which Gilpin, he knew, would condemn as bourgeois. Downstairs the staff lingered. They had been a cosy little band. The awe in which they held Ludovic had not seriously threatened their comfort. Now, it came to each of them, a dislocation impended, perhaps of absurdity, perhaps of enormity; something, at any rate, profoundly inimical to their easy routine.

'I'm not altogether sure of the form,' said the chief instructor. 'What does one do if one's commanding officer goes mad? I mean who reports it to whom?'

'He may get better.'

'He was a damn sight worse tonight.'

'Do you think the clients noticed?'

'I don't see how they could help it. After all, this batch aren't refugees.'

'He's not actually *done* anything yet.'

'But what will he do when he does?'

Next day was fine and the routine was repeated but that evening there was little exhilaration. Even the youngest and fittest were complaining of bruises and strains, and all found that familiarity did not entirely expunge the natural reluctance, inherent in man, to fling himself into space. Ludovic appeared at luncheon and dinner, without éclat now. At dinner he introduced one topic only, and then to Captain Fremantle, saying: 'I think I shall get a dog.'

'Yes sir. Jolly things to have about.'

'I don't want a jolly dog.'

'Oh, no, I see, sir, something for protection.'

'*Not* for protection.' He paused and surveyed the stricken staff-captain, the curious and silent diners. 'I require something for *love*.'

No one spoke. A savoury, rather enterprising for the date, was brought to him. He ate it in a single, ample mouthful. Then he said: 'Captain Claire had a Pekinese.' After a pause he added: 'You would not know Captain Claire. He came out of Crete, too – *without a medal*.' Another pause, a matter of seconds by their watches; of hours in the minds of his hearers. 'I require a loving Pekinese.'

Then as though impatient of a discussion on which his mind was already decided, he rose from the table as suddenly as he had done the night before, stalked out giving an impression that even then there was awaiting him on the further side of the oak door the animal of his choice, which he would gather to himself and bear away into the haunted shades that were his true habitat.

He shut the door behind him but through the heavy oak

panels his voice could be heard singing a song, not of his own youth; one which a father or uncle must have sung reminiscently to the extraordinary little boy that was to become Ludovic:

> 'Father won't buy me a bow – wow – wow – wow.
> Father won't buy me a bow – wow – wow.
> I've got a little cat and I'm very fond of that
> But what I want's a bow – wow – wow – wow.'

'It might be a good thing,' the chief instructor later said to Captain Fremantle, 'to sound one of the more responsible of the clients and see what they make of the old man.'

Next day the wind was blowing hard from the east. All the morning the squad sat about waiting on weather reports until at noon the chief instructor announced that the exercise was cancelled. Captain Fremantle, who during the past thirty-six hours had become increasingly nervous in the contemplation of Ludovic's evident decline, welcomed the respite as an opportunity to carry out the chief instructor's plan.

He chose de Souza.

'Someone ought to go and call at the hospital. Care to come and see your fellow Halberdier? We might lunch out. There's quite a decent black-market road-house not far away.'

They went into the wind without a soldier-driver. As soon as they were clear of the villa Captain Fremantle said: 'Of course I know it's not strictly the thing to discuss a senior officer but you seem to me a sensible sort of fellow and I wanted to ask you unofficially and in confidence whether any of you chaps have noticed anything odd about the commandant.'

'Major Dracula?'

'Major Ludovic. Why do you call him that?'

'It's just the name he's got with our squad. I don't think anyone ever told us his real name. He is certainly singular. Has he not always been like this?'

'No. It's been coming on, especially the last few days. He was never exactly bonhomous; kept himself to himself; but there was nothing you could actually put your finger on.'

'And now there is?'

'Well, you saw him the last two nights.'

'Yes, but you see I didn't know him before. I had a theory but from what you tell me it seems I was wrong.'

'What did you think?'

'I thought he was dead.'

'I don't quite get you.'

'In Haiti they call them "Zombies". Men who are dug up and put to work and then buried again. I thought perhaps he had been killed in Crete or wherever it was. But clearly I was wrong.'

Captain Fremantle began to wonder if he had been wise in his choice of confidant.

'I wouldn't have mentioned the matter if I'd thought you would make a joke of it,' he said crossly.

'It was merely a hypothesis,' de Souza conceded airily; 'and of course it was based on the brief period I have had him under observation. I dare say the real explanation is quite prosaic. He's just going off his rocker.'

'You mean a case for the psychiatrist?'

'Oh, that's not what I mean at all. *They* never do any good. I should get him a Pekinese and keep him hidden as much as you can. In my experience the more responsible posts in the army are largely filled by certifiable lunatics. They don't cause any more trouble than the sane ones.'

'If you're going to treat it all as a joke ...' Captain Fremantle began.

'It will certainly be a joke to Guy Crouchback,' said de Souza. 'I expect he's in need of one. Air Force jokes are deeply depressing.'

They reached the hospital, a temporary and unsightly structure. A flag of the RAF flapped furiously overhead. Crouched against the wind they mounted the concrete ramp and entered.

A long-haired youth in Air Force uniform sat at a table by the door with a cup of tea before him and a cigarette adhering to his lower lip.

'We have come to see Captain Crouchback.'

'D'you know where to find him?'

'No. Perhaps you can tell us.'

'I don't know, I'm sure. Did you say "captain"? We don't take army blokes here.'

'He came yesterday for an X-ray.'

'You can try Radiology.'

'Where's that?'

'It'll tell you on the board,' said the airman.

'I suppose it would be no good putting that man on a charge for insolence?' said Captain Fremantle.

'Not the smallest,' said de Souza. 'It isn't an offence in the Air Force.'

'Surely you're wrong there?'

'Not wrong; merely facetious.'

It was not a busy hospital and this was its least busy hour. The patients had been fed, and left, it was supposed, to sleep; the staff were feeding themselves. No one was in the room marked 'Radiology'. The two soldiers wandered down empty corridors whose floors were coated with some dark, slightly sticky substance designed to muffle their footsteps.

'There must be someone on duty somewhere.'

Seeing a door labelled 'No visitors', de Souza opened it and entered. He found an inflamed and apparently delirious man who broke into complaint that his bed was overrun with poisonous insects.

'DT's, I suppose,' said de Souza. 'Perhaps if we ring his bell someone will think he has taken a turn for the worse and come with sedatives.'

He rang and at length an orderly appeared.

'We're looking for an army officer named Crouchback.'

'This isn't him. This one's on the danger list. You'd better come out,' and when they were once more in the corridor he added: 'Never saw anything like it before. Some joker in Alex gave him a parcel "by hand of officer only" to take to London. It was full of scorpions and they escaped.'

'What risks you boys in blue do run for us! But how do we find Captain Crouchback?'

'You might ask at the registrar's.'

They found an office and an officer.

'Crouchback? No, never heard of him.'

'You keep a list of the inmates?'

'Of course we do. What d'you think?'

'No Crouchback on it? He came yesterday.'

'I wasn't on yesterday.'

'Could we see the officer who was?'

'He's off today.'

'It sounds like a plain case of abduction,' said de Souza.

'Look here, I don't know who the devil you two are or how you got in or what you think you're doing.'

'Security check up. Just routine,' said de Souza. 'We shall make our report to the proper quarter.'

When they left the building the wind blew so fiercely that speech was impossible until they reached the shelter of the car. Then Captain Fremantle said : 'I say, you know, you shouldn't have spoken to that chap like that. It might get us into trouble.'

'Not *us*. You perhaps. My identity, you must remember is a carefully guarded secret. Now for the black market.'

The road-house offered shelter from the gale but none of the luxuries of Ruben's. Indeed, it differed from neighbouring hotels only in enjoying a larger share of the rations sold by Captain Fremantle's own quartermaster-sergeant. They were able to eat, however, with more zest than under Ludovic's sinister regard.

'Pity we didn't get to see Crouchback,' said Captain Fremantle at length. 'They must have moved him.'

'These oubliettes open and close constantly in army life. You don't think he was kidnapped on the commandant's orders? He harped rather, did he not, on the absence of Captain A. N. Other? You might almost call it "gloating".' Stirred by the heavy North African wine de Souza's imagination rolled into action as though at a 'story conference' of jaded script-writers. 'In assuming insanity we have been accepting altogether too simple an explanation of your commander's behaviour. We are in deep political waters, Fremantle. I was surprised to meet old Uncle Crouchback at the bus station; a man clearly far too old for fooling about with parachutes. I should have been suspicious but I was thinking of the simple, zealous officer I knew in 1939. Four years of total war can change a man. They have changed me. I left an unimportant but conspicuous part of my left ear in Crete. Uncle Crouchback was sent here with a purpose. Perhaps to watch Major Ludovic; perhaps to be watched by him. One or other is a fascist agent; perhaps both. Uncle Crouchback has been working at HOO HQ – a notorious nest of conspiracy. Perhaps sealed orders were sent to your Ludovic, giving no explanation; curtly remarking "the above-mentioned officer is expendable". Someone was remarking the other evening that it would not be difficult to arrange for a "Roman Candle". Crouchback's number in the squad was already known. No doubt Ludovic and his accomplices had arranged a trap of the kind.'

Captain Fremantle's simple mind, warmed, too, by the purple ferruginous vintage, was caught by the idea.

'As a matter of fact,' he said, 'that was the first thing the commandant asked when I reported Crouchback's accident. "A Roman Candle?" he asked as though it was the most natural thing in the world.'

'It would have seemed natural. The commandant was not to know the hour of the assassination. It might have been on the first afternoon; it might have been yesterday. But Crouchback's little accident saved him – for the time being. Now they have caught up with him. I don't think you or I will ever see my old comrade-in-arms again.'

They discussed and elaborated the possibilities of plot, counterplot, and betrayal. Captain Fremantle was a simple man. Before the war he had served in a lowly capacity in an insurance company. His post for the last three years had given him an occasional glimpse into arcane matters. Too many strange persons had briefly passed through his narrow field of vision for him to be totally unaware of the existence of an intricate world of deception and peril that lay beyond his experience. Roughly speaking he was ready to believe anything he was told. De Souza confused him only by suggesting so much.

Later, as they drove back, de Souza developed a new plot.

'Are we being too contemporary?' he asked. 'We are thinking in terms of the thirties. Both uncle Crouchback and your Major Dracula came to manhood in the twenties. Perhaps we should look for a love motive. Your commandant is plainly as queer as a coot and Uncle Crouchback's sex-life has always been something of a mystery. He never made his mark as a *coureur* when I served with him. This may well be a simple old-fashioned case of blackmail or, better still, of amorous jealousy.'

'Why "better still"?'

Captain Fremantle was far out of his depth.

'Altogether less sordid.'

'But how do you know the commandant has any connexion with Crouchback's disappearance?'

'It is our working hypothesis.'

'I simply don't know whether to take you seriously or not.'

'No, you don't, do you? But you must admit you have enjoyed our little outing. It's given you something to think about.'

'I suppose it has, in a way.'

It was a baffled and bemused staff-captain who returned in the early afternoon to his headquarters. He had been deputed to make tactful inquiries of the most responsible-seeming of the officers under instruction as to whether he and his fellow officers had noticed any little oddities in the behaviour of his commandant. He had found himself investigating a mystery, perhaps a murder, whose motives lay in the heights of international politics or the depths of unnatural vice. Captain Fremantle was not at his ease in such matters.

The house, when they reached it, seemed empty. It was certainly silent save for the howling of the wind in the chimneys. One RASC private was on duty at the garage. Everyone else, confined to quarters without employment, had gone to bed, except Major Ludovic who, Captain Fremantle was informed, had left by car while they were still in the aerodrome, taking a driver with him and remarking in the phrase universally used by commanding officers to explain their absence from their posts, that he was 'called to a conference'.

'I think perhaps I'll go and lie down too,' said de Souza. 'Thank you for the outing.'

The staff captain looked at his tidy office where no new papers had arrived since morning. Then he, too, took his puzzled head to his pillow. The African wine gently asserted its drowsy powers. He slept until the batman came in to put up the blackout screen in his window.

'Sorry, sir,' said the man as he discovered the tousled figure; 'didn't know you was here.'

Captain Fremantle slowly came to himself.

'Time I showed a leg,' he said. Then: 'Is the commandant back?'

'Yessir,' said the man grinning.

'What's the joke, Ardingly?' There was a confidence and cordiality between these two to which Ludovic, who shared Ardingly's services, was a stranger. 'The major, sir. He's going on funny.'

'Funny?'

Phantasmagoric memories came into Captain Fremantle's quickening mind. 'Going on funny?'

'Yessir. He's been and got a little dog.'

'And he is going on funny with it?'

'Well, not a bit like the major, sir.'

'Perhaps I'd better go and see.'

'Perhaps you'd say "acting soft",' Ardingly conceded.

Captain Fremantle had lain down to rest with the minimum of preparation. He had removed his boots, anklets, and tunic. Now he arose and put on service dress and followed the corridor into Major Ludovic's part of the house. Pausing outside the door he heard from inside a clucking noise, as though a countrywoman were feeding poultry. He knocked and entered.

The floor of Ludovic's room was covered with saucers containing milk, gravy, spam, biscuits, Woolton sausage, and other items of diet, some rationed, some on points, some free to the full purse. Here and there the food had been rudely spilt; none of it seemed to have appealed to the appetite of the Pekinese puppy which crouched under Ludovic's bed in a nest of shredded paper. It was a pretty animal with eyes as prominent as Ludovic's own. Ludovic was on all fours making the noises which had been audible outside; he was, at first sight, all khaki trouser-seat, like Jumbo Trotter at the billiard-table; a figure from antiquated farce, 'caught bending', inviting the boot. He raised to Fremantle a face that was radiant with simple glee; there was no trace of embarrassment or of resentment at the intrusion. He wished to share with all the overflowing delight of his heart.

114

'Cor,' he said, 'just take a dekko at the little perisher. Wouldn't fancy anything I give him. Had me worried. Thought he was sick. Thought I ought to call in the M O. Then I turned me back for a jiffy and blessed if he hasn't polished off the last number of *Survival*. How d'you call that for an appetite?' Then falling into a fruity and, to Captain Fremantle, blood-curdling tone of infatuation, he addressed himself to the puppy: 'What'll kind staff-captain-man say if you won't eat his nice grub, eh? What'll kind editor-man say if you eat his clever paper?'

Guy meanwhile lay in bed less than a mile from Ludovic and his pet. There were, as de Souza had remarked, oubliettes which from time to time opened and engulfed members of His Majesty's forces. Thus it had happened to Guy. He was clothed in flannel pyjamas not his own; his leg was encased in plaster and it seemed to him that he had lost all rights of property over that limb. He was left alone in a hut so full of music that the wind swept over it unheard. It was the Emergency Ward of the aerodrome. Here he had been delivered in an ambulance from the R A F hospital, where a young medical officer had informed him that he required no treatment. 'Just lie up, old boy. We'll have another look at you in a few weeks and then take the plaster off. You'll be quite comfortable.'

Guy was not at all comfortable. There were no fellow patients in the ward. Its sole attendant was a youth who, sitting on Guy's bed, announced, as soon as the stretcher-party had left: 'I'm a C O.'

'Commanding Officer?' Guy asked without surprise.

Anything seemed possible among these inhabitants.

'Conscientious Objector.'

He explained his objections at length above the turmoil of jazz. They were neither political nor ethical but occult, being in someway based on the dimensions of the Great Pyramid.

'I could have lent you a book about it, but it got pinched.'

There was no malice in this youth nor was there the power to please. Guy asked for something to read. 'There was a welfare bloke came with some books once. I reckon someone must have flogged them. They weren't the sort of books anyone could read anyway. They don't take in any papers in the RAF. Any news they want they hear on the blower.'

'Can't you stop this infernal noise?'

'What noise was that?'

'The wireless.'

'Oh no. I couldn't do that. It's laid on special. Piped all through the camp. It isn't wireless anyway. Some of it's records. You'll soon find you get so you don't notice it.'

'Where are my clothes?'

The conscientious objector looked vaguely round the hut. 'Don't seem to be here, do they? Perhaps they got left behind. You'll have to see Admin about that.'

'Who's Admin?'

'He's a bloke comes round once a week.'

'Listen,' said Guy, 'I've got to get out of here. Will you telephone to the parachute school and ask Captain Fremantle to come here?'

'Can't hardly do that.'

'Why on earth not?'

'Only Admin's allowed to telephone. What's the number of this school?'

'I don't know.'

'Well, there you are.'

'Can I see Admin?'

'You'll see him when he comes round.'

For an excruciating day Guy lay staring at the corrugated iron roof while the sounds of jazz wailed and throbbed around him. Very frequently the attendant brought him cups of tea and plates of inedible matter. During the watches of the second night he formed the resolution to escape.

The wind had dropped in the night. His fellows, he reflected, would now be starting for their fifth jump. With pain and enormous effort he hobbled across the ward supporting himself by the ends of the empty beds. In a corner stood the almost hairless broom with which the attendant was supposed to dust the floor. Using this as a crutch, Guy stumbled into the open. He recognized the buildings; the distance across the asphalt yard to the officers' mess would have been negligible to a whole man. For the first time since his unhappy landing Guy felt the full pain of his injury. Sweating in the chill November morning he accomplished the fifty difficult paces. It was not an excursion which would have passed without notice at the Halberdier barracks. Here it was no one's business either to stop him or to help him.

At length he subsided in an armchair.

One or two pilots gaped but they accepted the arrival of this pyjama'd cripple with the same indifference as they had shown him when he had arrived in uniform with his batch of parachutists. He shouted to one of them above the noise of the music: 'I want to write a letter.'

'Go ahead. It won't disturb me.'

'Is there such a thing as a piece of paper and a pen?'

'Don't see any, do you?'

'What do you fellows do when you want to write a letter?'

'My old man taught me: "Never put anything in writing," he used to say.'

The pilots gaped. One went out; another came in.

Guy sat and waited; not in vain. After an hour the party of parachutists arrived, led on this occasion by Captain Fremantle.

The staff captain had slept (twice) on the problem of Guy's disappearance. He now gave no notional assent to any of de Souza's 'hypotheses', but an aura of mystery remained, and he was quite unprepared for the apparition of Guy in flannel pyjamas waving a broom. He came cautiously towards him.

'Thank God you've come,' said Guy with a warmth to which Captain Fremantle was little accustomed.

'Yes. I have to see the AO about a few things.'

'You've got to get me out of here.'

Captain Fremantle had more than three years' experience of the army and, as the facts of Guy's predicament were frantically explained, the staff-solution came pat: 'Not my pigeon. The SMO will have to discharge you.'

'There's no medical officer here. Only some kind of orderly.'

'He won't do. Must be signed for by the SMO.'

The eleven 'clients' were morose. Their former exhilaration had subsided with their fears. This last jump was merely a disagreeable duty. De Souza saw Guy and approached him.

'So you are safe and well, uncle,' he said.

Guy had served as the source of invention to beguile a wet day. That joke was over. De Souza now wished to finish his course early and get back to London and a waiting girl.

'I'm being driven insane, Frank.'

'Yes,' said de Souza, 'yes, I suppose you are.'

'The staff-captain says he can't do anything about me.'

'No. No. I don't suppose he can. Well, I'm glad to have seen you all right. It looks as if they wanted us to take off.'

'Frank, do you remember Jumbo Trotter in barracks?'

'No. Can't say I do.'

'He might be able to help me. Will you telephone to him as soon as you get back? Just tell him what's happened to me and where I am. I can give you his number.'

'But *shall* I get back. That is the question uppermost in my mind at the moment. We put our lives in jeopardy every time we go up in that aeroplane – or rather every time we leave it. Perhaps you'll find me in the next bed to you insensible. Perhaps I shall be dead. I am told you dig your own grave – those are the very words of the junior instructor – if the parachute doesn't open – burrow into the earth five feet deep and all they have to do is shovel the sides down on one. I keep reminding Gilpin of that possibility. In that rich earth a richer dust concealed. In my case a corner that shall be for ever Anglo-Sephardi.'

'Frank, will you telephone to Jumbo for me?'

'If I survive, uncle, I will.'

Guy stumbled back to his bed.

'Wasn't it a bit cold out there?' asked the conscientious objector.

'Bitterly.'

'I was wondering who'd got my brush.'

Guy lay on the bed, exhausted by his efforts. His plastered leg ached more than it had done at any time since his injury Presently the conscientious objector came in with tea.

'Got some books out of the Squadron Leader's office,' he said, giving him two tattered pictorial journals which, from their remote origin in juvenile humour, were still dubbed 'comics'; but for their price they would have been more appropriately named 'penny-dreadfuls' for the incidents portrayed were uniformly horrific.

An aeroplane came in to land.

'Was that the parachute flight?' Guy asked.

'Couldn't say, I'm sure.'

'Be a good fellow. Go and find out. Ask if anyone was hurt.'

'They wouldn't tell me a thing like that. Don't suppose they'd know, anyway. They just drop them out and come back. Ground staff collect the bodies.'

Guy studied the Squadron Leader's 'comic'.

Wherever he went de Souza left his spoor of unreasonable anxiety.

Few things were better calculated to arouse Jumbo's sympathies than the news that a Halberdier had fallen into the hands of the Air Force. Those who knew him only slightly would not have recognized him as a man of swift action. In Guy's case his normal gentle pace became a stampede. Not Jumbo alone with his car, driver, and batman, but the Transit Camp Medical Officer in his car with his orderly, and an ambulance and its crew all sped out of London into Essex. The right credentials were produced, the right manumissions completed; Guy's clothes were collected from the hospital, his remaining baggage from the Training Centre, Guy himself from the emergency ward, and he was back in London in his quiet room before de Souza, Gilpin, and their fellows had been marshalled into the bus for their return to the 'dispersal centre'.

Next morning Captain Fremantle reported to his commandant with the customary sheaf of confidential reports. He found Ludovic at a desk clear of all papers. The Pekinese puppy was in sole occupation of that oaken surface on which had been indited so many of Ludovic's *pensées*; he gave intermittent attention to the efforts being made to divert him with a ping-pong ball, a piece of string, and an india-rubber.

'What are you going to call him, sir?' Captain Fremantle asked in the obsequious tones which usually provoked a rebuff. This afternoon he was received more kindly.

'I'm giving it a lot of thought. Captain Claire called his dog Freda. That name is precluded by the difference of sex. I knew a dog called Trooper once – but he was a much bigger animal of quite different character.'

'Something Chinese, perhaps?'

'I shouldn't like that at all,' said Ludovic severely. 'It would remind me of Lady Cripps's Fund.' He looked with distaste at the documents offered him. 'Work,' he said. 'Routine. All right, leave them here.' He tenderly bore the puppy to its basket. 'Stay there,' he said. 'Daddy's got to earn you your din-din.'

Captain Fremantle saluted and withdrew. Ludovic found the necessary forms and began his work of editing.

'*De Souza O.K.*' he read, and baldly translated: *The above named officer has satisfactorily completed his course and is highly recommended for employment in the field.*

Of Gilpin he wrote: *Initial reluctance was overcome but with evident effort. It is recommended that further consideration should be given to the stability of this officer's character before he is passed as suitable.*

With deliberation he left Guy to the last. The chief instructor had written: *NBG. Too old. Spirit willing – flesh weak.* Ludovic paused, seeking the appropriate, the inevitable words for the sentence he was determined to pronounce. As a child he had been well grounded in Scripture and was familiar with the tale of Uriah the Hittite in its resonant Jacobean diction, but though tempted, he eschewed all archaisms in composing this *pensée. A slight accident,* he wrote, *in no way attributable to this officer's infirmity or negligence, prevented his completing the full course. However he showed such outstanding aptitude that he is recommended for immediate employment in action without further training.*

He folded the papers, marked them *Most Secret,* put them in a nest of envelopes and summoned his staff-captain.

'There,' he said to the puppy, 'Daddy's finished his horrid work. Did you think you'd been forgotten? Was you jealous of the nasty soldier-men?'

When Captain Fremantle reported, he found Ludovic with the puppy on his heart, buttoned into his tunic, only its bright white head appearing.

'I've decided what to call him,' Ludovic said. 'You may think it rather a conventional name but it has poignant associations for me. His name is Fido.'

6

THE Transit Camp, despite all Jumbo's manifest will to give Guy a position of privilege there – he had come during the last year to regard him almost as a contemporary; no longer as an adventurous temporary officer but as a seasoned Halberdier cruelly but unjustly relegated like himself to an unheroic role – was not an ideal place for the bedridden. It had served well as a place to leave in the early morning for HOO HQ and as a place to return to late from Bellamy's. It was not the place to spend day and night – particularly such nights as Guy now suffered, made almost sleepless by the throb and dead weight of his plastered knee. For two days the relief from music and from the attentions of the conscientious objector was solace enough. Then a restless melancholy began to afflict him. Jumbo noticed it.

'You ought to see more fellows,' he said. 'It's awkward here in some ways. Can't have a lot of women coming in and out. Oughtn't really to have civilians at all. Isn't there anyone who'd take you in? Nothing easier than to draw lodging allowances.'

Guy thought: Arthur Box-Bender? He would not be welcome. Kerstie Kilbannock? Virginia was living there.

'No,' he said. 'I don't believe there is.'

'Pity. How would it be if I sent a message to your club? Your porter might send some fellows round. How's the knee today by the way?'

Guy was not seriously injured – something had been cracked, something else twisted out of place; he was in slightly worse condition than he had been after the Halberdier guest night; no more than that – but he was hampered and in pain. His calf and ankle were swollen by the constriction of the plaster.

'I believe I shall be a lot more comfortable without this thing on it.'

'Who put it on?'

'One of the Air Force doctors.'

'Soon get that off,' said Jumbo. 'I'll send my man up at once.'

Obediently the RAMC major attached to the camp – one of the lighter posts of that busy service – came to Guy's room with a pair of shears and laboriously removed the encumbrance.

'I suppose it's all right doing this,' he said. 'They ought to have sent me the X-ray pictures, but of course they haven't. Does it seem more comfortable like that?'

'Much.'

'Well, that's the important thing. I dare say a spot of heat might help. I'll send along a chap with a lamp.'

This reincarnation of Florence Nightingale did not appear. The swelling of calf and ankle slightly subsided; the knee grew huge. Instead of a continuous ache Guy suffered from frequent agonizing spasms when he moved in the bed. They were on the whole preferable.

The immediate result of Jumbo's appeal to Bellamy's was a visit from Lieutenant Padfield. He came in the morning, when most men and women in London were ostensibly busy, bearing the new number of *Survival* and a Staffordshire figure of Mr Gladstone; also a fine bunch of chrysanthemums, but these were not for Guy.

'I'm on my way to the Dorchester,' he explained. 'Ruby had rather a misfortune last night. One of our generals over here is a great admirer of *Peter Pan*. Ruby asked him to dinner to meet Sir James Barrie. She kindly asked me too. I was surprised to learn Barrie was still alive. Well, of course, he isn't. We waited an hour for him and when at last she rang for dinner they said room-service was off and that there was a red warning anyway. "That's what it is," she said. "He's gone down to a shelter. Ridiculous at his age." So we got no dinner and the general was upset and so was Ruby.'

'You do lead a complicated life, Loot.'

'The same sort of thing is happening all the time in New York, they tell me. All the social secretaries are in Washington. So I thought, a few flowers . . .'

'You might take her Mr Gladstone too, Loot. It was a very kind thought but, you know, I've nowhere to put him.'

'Do you think Ruby would really like it? Most of her things are French.'

'Her husband was in Asquith's cabinet.'

'Yes, of course he was. I'd forgotten. Yes, that would make a difference. Well I must be going.' The Lieutenant dallied at the door uncertainly regarding the earthenware figure. 'The Glenobans sent you many messages of condolence.'

'I don't know them.'

'And so did your Uncle Peregrine – such an interesting man ... You know I don't really think this would go well in Ruby's room.'

'Give it to the Glenobans.'

'Are they Liberals?'

'I dare say. Lots of Scotch are.'

'I might change it for a highlander. There was one in the same shop.'

'I'm sure the Glenobans would prefer Mr Gladstone.'

'Yes.'

At length the Lieutenant departed on his work of mercy, leaving Guy to *Survival*.

This was the issue on which little Fido had gorged. It had gone to press long before Everard Spruce received Ludovic's manuscript. Guy turned the pages without interest. It compared unfavourably in his opinion with the Squadron Leader's 'comic' particularly in the matter of draughtsmanship. Everard Spruce, in the days when he courted the marxists, dissembled a discreditable, personal preference for Fragonard above Léger by denying all interest in graphic art, affirming stoutly and correctly that the Workers were solidly behind him in his indifference. 'Look at Russia,' he would say. But the Ministry of Information in the early days of *Survival*, before the Russian alliance, had pointed out that since Hitler had proclaimed a taste for 'figurative' painting, defence of the cosmopolitan *avant garde* had become a patriotic duty in England. Spruce submitted without demur and *Survival* accordingly displayed frequent 'art supplements', chosen by Coney and Frankie.

There was one such in the current issue, ten shiny pages of squiggles. Guy turned from them to an essay by the pacific expatriate Parsnip, tracing the affinity of Kafka to Klee. Guy had not heard of either of these famous names.

His next caller was his uncle, Peregrine.

Uncle Peregrine, like the Lieutenant, had ample leisure. He brought no gift, supposing his attendance was treat enough. He sat holding his umbrella and soft, shabby hat and looked at his nephew reproachfully.

'You should take more care of yourself,' he said, 'now that you are the head of the family.'

He was five years younger than Guy's father but he looked rather older; an imperfect and ill-kept cast from the same mould.

When the Lieutenant spoke of Peregrine Crouchback as 'interesting' he was making a unique judgement. A man of many interests certainly, well read, widely travelled, minutely informed in many recondite subjects, a discerning collector of bibelots; a man handsomely apparelled and adorned when he did duty at the papal court; a man nevertheless assiduously avoided even by those who shared his interests. He exemplified the indefinable numbness which Guy recognized intermittently in himself; the saturnine strain which in Ivo had swollen to madness, terror of which haunted Box-Bender when he studied his son's letters from prison-camp.

In 1915 Uncle Peregrine contracted a complicated form of dysentery on his first day in the Dardanelles and was obliged to spend the rest of the war as ADC to a colonial governor who repeatedly but vainly cabled for his recall. In the nineteen twenties he had hung about the diplomatic service as honorary attaché. Once Ralph Brompton, as first secretary, had been posted to the same embassy, and had sought to make him the chancery butt; unsuccessfully; his apathetic self-esteem was impervious to ridicule; no spark could be struck from that inert element. For the last decade, after the decline in the value of the pound, Uncle Peregrine had made his home in London, in an old-fashioned flat near Westminster Cathedral, at whose great functions he sometimes assisted in various liveries. Perhaps he was a legitimate object of interest to an inquiring foreigner like the Lieutenant. He could have occurred nowhere else but in England and in no period but his own.

Uncle Peregrine quite enjoyed the war. He was naturally frugal and welcomed the excuse to forgo wine and food, to wear his old clothes and to change his linen weekly. He was quite without fear for his own safety when the bombs were falling. He rejoiced to see so many of his gloomier predictions of foreign policy fulfilled. For a time he busied himself with the despatch of parcels to distressed civilians in enemy hands. Lately he had found more congenial work. There was a 'salvage drive' in progress in the course of which public-spirited citizens were exhorted to empty their shelves so that their books could be pulped to produce official forms and *Survival*. Many rare and beautiful volumes perished before it occurred to the ministry that they could more profitably be sold. A committee was then authorized to survey two centuries of English literature laid out, backs uppermost, in what had once been a school gymnasium; male and female, the old buffers poked among the bindings, making their choice of what should be saved, priced, and put into the market. They met two or three times a week for their business, in which, as in all matters, Uncle Peregrine was scrupulously honest; but he exercised the prerogative of pre-emption enjoyed by the stall-holders of charitable bazaars. He invariably asked a colleague to decide the price of anything he coveted; if it fell within his means, he paid and bore it off. Not more than twenty items had been added to his little library in this way, but every one was a bibliophile's treasure. The prices were those which the old amateurs remembered to have prevailed in the lean last years of peace.

'A young American protégé of mine told me you were here,' he continued. 'You may remember meeting him with me. It doesn't seem much of a place,' he added critically surveying Guy's room. 'I don't think I ever heard of it before.'

He inquired into the condition of Guy's knee and into the treatment he was receiving. Who was his medical man? 'Major Blenkinsop? Don't think I've ever heard of him. Are you sure he understands the knee? Highly specialized things, knees.' He spoke of an injury he himself sustained many years before on a tennis-lawn at Bordighera. 'Fellow I had then didn't understand knees. It's never been quite the same since.'

He picked up *Survival*, glanced at the illustrations, remarked without hostility: 'Ah, *modern*', and then passed on to public affairs. 'Shocking news from the eastern front. The Bolshevists are advancing again. Germans don't seem able to stop them. I'd sooner see the Japanese in Europe – at least they have a king and some sort of religion. If one can believe the papers we are actually helping the Bolshevists. It's a mad world, my masters.'

Finally he said: 'I came with an invitation. Why don't you move into my flat until you are fit? There's plenty of room, I've still got Mrs Corner; she does what she can with the rations. The lift works – which is more than a lot of people can claim. There's a Dutch Dominican – not that I approve of Dominicans in the general way – giving a really interesting series of Advent conferences at the Cathedral. You can see he doesn't like the way the war's going. You'd be better off than you are here. I'm at home most evenings,' he added as though that constituted an inestimable attraction.

It was the measure of Guy's melancholy that he did not at once reject the offer; that in fact he accepted it.

Jumbo arranged for an ambulance to take him to his new address. The lift, as promised, bore him up to the large, dark, heavily furnished flat and Mrs Corner, the housekeeper, received him as an honourably wounded soldier.

Not very far away Colonel Grace-Groundling-Marchpole was studying a list submitted to him for approval.

'Crouchback?' he said. 'Haven't we a file on him?'

'Yes. The Box-Bender case.'

'I remember. *And* the Scottish nationalists.'

'And the priest in Alexandria. There's been nothing much on him since.'

'No. He may have lost contact with his headquarters. It's just as well we didn't pull him in at the time. If we let him go to Italy he may lead us into the neo-fascist network.'

'It won't be so easy keeping track of him there. The Eighth Army is not security conscious.'

'No. It's a moot point. On the whole, perhaps, the noes have it.'

He wrote: *This officer cannot be recommended for secret work in Italy*, and turned to the name of de Souza.

'Communist party member of good standing,' he said. 'Quite sound at the moment.'

The room in which Guy was to spend six weeks and make a momentous decision, had seldom been occupied during Uncle Peregrine's tenancy. Its window opened on a brick wall. It was furnished with pieces from the dispersal of Broome. Guy lay in a large old bed ornamented with brass knobs. Here Major Blenkinsop paid him a cursory visit.

'Still pretty puffy, eh? Well, the only thing is to keep it up.'

Through Jumbo's good offices Guy was able to lay in some gin and whisky. The circle of his acquaintants had widened in the last four years. During his first days at the flat he received several visitors, Ian Kilbannock among them. After twenty minutes of desultory gossip he said: 'You remember Ivor Clair?'

'Yes, indeed.'

'He's joined the Chindits in Burma. Surprising, don't you think?'

Guy thought of his first view of Ivor in the Borghese Gardens. 'Not altogether.'

'The whispering campaign took some time to reach the Far East. Or perhaps he got bored with viceregal circles.'

'Ivor doesn't believe in sacrifice. Who does nowadays? But he had the will to win.'

'I can't think of anything more sacrificial than plodding about in the jungle with those desperadoes. I don't know what he thinks he's going to win there.'

'There was a time I was very fond of Ivor.'

'Oh, I'm *fond* of him. Everyone is and everyone has forgotten his little *faux pas* in Crete. That's what makes it so rum his charging off to be a hero *now*.'

When Ian left, Guy brooded about the antithesis between the acceptance of sacrifice and the will to win. It seemed to have personal relevance, as yet undefined, to his own condition.

He re-read the letter from his father which he carried always in his pocket book. *'The Mystical Body doesn't strike attitudes or stand on its dignity. It accepts suffering and injustice ... Quantitative judgements don't apply.'*

There was a congress at Teheran at the time entirely occupied with quantitative judgements.

7

AT the end of the first week of that December, History records, Mr Winston Churchill introduced Mr Roosevelt to the Sphinx. Fortified by the assurances of their military advisers that the Germans would surrender that winter, the two puissant old gentlemen circumambulated the colossus and silently watched the shadows of evening obliterate its famous features. Some hours later that same sun set in London not in the harsh colours of the desert but fading into the rain where no lamps shone on the wet paving. At that hour, with something of the bland, vain speculation which had been expressed on the faces of the leaders of the Free World, Uncle Peregrine stood at his front-door and regarded the woman who had rung his bell.

'I've come to see Guy Crouchback,' she said.

There was no light on the landing. The light in the hall was a mere glimmer. Uncle Peregrine found the blackout congenial and observed the regulations with exaggerated rigour.

'Does he expect you?'

'No. I've only just heard he was here. You don't remember me, do you? Virginia.'

'Virginia?'

'Virginia Crouchback, when you knew me.'

'Oh,' he said. 'You are, are you?' Uncle Peregrine was never really disconcerted but sometimes, when a new and strange fact was brought to his notice, he took a little time to assimilate it. 'It is a terrible evening. I hope you did not get wet coming here.'

'I took a cab.'

'Good. You must forgive my failure to recognize you. It's

rather dark and I never knew you very well, did I? Are you sure Guy will want to see you?'

'Pretty sure.'

Uncle Peregrine shut the front-door and said: 'I was at your wedding. Did we meet after that?'

'Once or twice.'

'You went to Africa. Then someone said you had gone to America. And now you want to see Guy?'

'Yes, please.'

'Come in here. I'll tell him.' He led Virginia into the drawing-room. 'You'll find plenty to interest you here,' he added as though presaging a long wait. 'That is, if you're interested in things.'

He shut the door behind him. He also shut Guy's before he announced in a low tone: 'There's a young woman here who says she's your wife.'

'Virginia?'

'So she claims.'

'Good. Send her in.'

'You *wish* to see her?'

'Very much.'

'If there's any trouble, ring. Mrs Corner is out, but I shall hear you.'

'What sort of trouble, Uncle Peregrine?'

'*Any* sort of trouble. You know what women are.'

'Do *you*, Uncle Peregrine?'

He considered this for a moment and then conceded: 'Well, no. Perhaps I don't.'

Then he went out, led Virginia back and left husband and wife together.

Virginia had taken trouble with her appearance. Kerstie was away, attending St Nicholas' Day festivities at her son's prep school, and Virginia had borrowed some of the clothes she had lately sold her. She bore no visible signs of her pregnancy, or, in Guy's eyes, of the many changes which had occurred in her since their last meeting. She came straight to his bed, kissed him, and said: 'Darling. What a long time it's been.'

'February 14th, 1940,' said Guy.

'As long as that? How can you remember?'

'It was a big day in my life, a bad day, a climacteric ... I've heard news of you. You work in Ian's office and live with him and Kerstie.'

'Did you hear something else, rather disgusting?'

'I heard rumours.'

'About Trimmer?'

'That was Ian's story.'

'It was all quite true.' Virginia shuddered. 'The things that happen to one! Anyway, that's all over. I've had a dreary war so far. I almost wish I'd stayed in America. It all seemed such fun at first, but it didn't last.'

'I found that,' said Guy. 'Not perhaps in quite the same way. The last two years have been as dull as peace.'

'You might have come and seen me.'

'I made rather an ass of myself at our last meeting, if you remember.'

'Oh, *that*,' said Virginia. 'If you only knew the asses I've seen people make of themselves. *That's* all forgotten.'

'Not by me.'

'Ass,' said Virginia.

She drew a chair up, lit a cigarette and asked fondly about his injuries. 'So brave,' she said. 'You know you really are brave. *Parachuting.* I'm scared even sitting in an aeroplane, let alone jumping out.' Then she said: 'I was awfully sorry to see your father's death.'

'Yes. I had always expected him to live much longer – until the last few months.'

'I wish I'd seen him again. But I dare say he wouldn't have wanted it.'

'He never came to London,' said Guy.

Virginia for the first time looked round the sombre room. 'Why are you here?' she asked. 'Ian and Kerstie say you're rich now.'

'Not *now*. The lawyers are still busy. But it looks as if I may be a bit better off eventually.'

'I'm dead broke,' said Virginia.

'That isn't at all like you.'

'Oh, you'll find I've changed in a lot of ways. What can I do to amuse you? We used to play piquet.'

'I haven't for years. I don't suppose there are any cards in the house.'

'I'll bring some tomorrow, shall I?'

'If you're coming tomorrow.'

'Oh, yes, I'll come. If you'd like me to, that's to say.'

Before Guy could answer the door opened and Uncle Peregrine entered.

'I just came to see you were all right,' he said.

What did he suspect? Assassination? Seduction? He stood studying the pair of them as the statesmen had studied the Sphinx, not really expecting an utterance, but dimly conscious of the existence of problems beyond his scope. Also, and more simply, he wanted to have another look at Virginia. He was unaccustomed to such visitors and she in particular had lurid associations for him. Well travelled, well read, well informed, he was a stranger in the world. He had understood few of the jokes which in bygone days Ralph Brompton used to devise at his expense. Virginia was a Scarlet Woman; the fatal woman who had brought about the fall of the house of Crouchback; and, what was more, to Uncle Peregrine she fully looked the part. Not for him to read the faint, indelible signature of failure, degradation, and despair that was written plain for sharper eyes than his. In the minutes which had passed since he had shown her in to Guy, he had not attempted to resume his reading. He had stood by his gas-fire considering what he had seen during his brief passage. He had returned to confirm his impression.

'I'm afraid I haven't any cocktails,' he said.

'Good gracious no. I should think not.'

'Guy often has some gin, I believe.'

'All gone,' said Guy, 'until Jumbo's next visit.'

Uncle Peregrine was fascinated. He could not bring himself to leave. It was Virginia who made the move.

'I must be off,' she said, though in fact she had nowhere at all to go. 'But I'll come back now I know what you need. Cards and gin. You won't mind having to pay for them, will you?'

Uncle Peregrine led her to the door; he followed her into the lift; he stood with her on the benighted steps and gazed with her into the rain.

'Will you be all right?' he asked. 'You might find a cab at Victoria.'

'I'm only going to Eaton Terrace. I'll walk.'

'It's a long way. Shall I see you home?'

'Don't be an ass,' said Virginia, stepping down into the rain. 'See you tomorrow.'

It was, as Uncle Peregrine observed, a long way. Virginia strode out bravely, flickering her torch at the crossings. Even on that inclement evening every doorway held an embraced couple. The house, when she reached it, was quite empty. She hung up her coat to dry. She washed her underclothes. She went to the cupboard where she knew Ian kept a box of sleeping pills. Kerstie never needed such things. Virginia took two and lay unconscious while the sirens gave warning of a distant, inconsiderable 'nuisance raid'.

At Carlisle Place Uncle Peregrine returned to Guy's room. 'I suppose it's quite usual nowadays,' he said, 'divorced people meeting on friendly terms?'

'It has been so for a long time, I believe, in the United States.'

'Yes. And, of course, she has lived there a lot, hasn't she? That would explain it. What's her name?'

'Troy, I think. It was when I last saw her.'

'Mrs Troy?'

'Yes.'

'Funny name. Are you sure you don't mean Troyte? There are people near us at home called Troyte.'

'No. Like Helen of Troy.'

'Ah,' said Uncle Peregrine. 'Yes. Exactly. Like Helen of Troy. A very striking woman. What did she mean about paying for the gin and the cards. Is she not well off?'

'Not at all, at the moment.'

'What a pity,' said Uncle Peregrine. 'You would never guess, would you?'

When Virginia came next evening she greeted Uncle Peregrine as 'Peregrine'; he bridled and followed her into Guy's room. He watched her unpack her basket, laying gin, angostura bitters, and playing-cards on the table by the bed. He insisted on paying for her purchases, seeming to derive particular pleasure from the transaction. He went to his pantry and brought glasses. He did not drink gin himself, nor did he play piquet, but he hung about the scene fascinated. When at length he left them alone, Virginia said: 'What an old pet. Why did you never let me meet him before?'

She came daily, staying sometimes for half an hour, sometimes for two hours, insinuating herself easily into Guy's uneventful routine so that her visits became something for him to anticipate with pleasure. She was like any busy wife visiting any bed-ridden husband. It was seldom that they saw one another alone. Uncle Peregrine played the part of duenna with an irksome assumption of archness. On Sunday Virginia came in the morning, and while Uncle Peregrine was at the cathedral, she asked Guy: 'Have you thought what you're going to do after the war?'

'No. It's hardly the time to make plans.'

'People are saying the Germans will collapse before the spring.'

'I don't believe it. And even if they do, that's only the beginning of other troubles.'

'Oh, Guy, I wish you were more cheerful. There's fun ahead, always. If I didn't think that, I couldn't keep going. How rich are you going to be?'

'My father left something like two hundred thousand pounds.'

'Goodness.'

'Half goes to Angela and a third to the government. Then for the next few years we have to find a number of pensions. I get the rent for Broome, that's another three hundred.'

'What does all that mean in income?'

'I suppose about two thousand eventually.'

'Not beyond the dreams of avarice.'

'No.'

'But better than a slap with a wet fish. And you had a pittance before. How about Uncle Peregrine? He must have a bit. Is that left to you.'

'I've no idea. I should have thought to Angela's children.'

'That could be changed,' said Virginia.

That day there was a pheasant for luncheon. Mrs Corner,

133

who had come to accept Virginia's presence without comment, laid the dining-room table for two and Guy ate awkwardly on his tray while Virginia and Uncle Peregrine made a lengthy meal apart.

On the tenth day Uncle Peregrine did not return until after seven o'clock. Virginia was then on the point of leaving when he entered the room, a glint of roguish purpose in his eye.

'I haven't seen you,' he said.

'No. I've missed you.'

'I wonder whether by any possible, happy chance you are free this evening. I feel I should like to go out somewhere.'

'Free as the air,' said Virginia. 'How lovely.'

'Where would you like to go? I'm not much up in restaurants, I am afraid. There is a fish place near here, opposite Victoria Station, where I sometimes go.'

'There's always Ruben's,' said Virginia.

'I don't think I know it.'

'It will cost you a fortune,' said Guy from his bed.

'*Really*,' said Uncle Peregrine appalled at this breach of good manners. 'I should *hardly* have thought that a matter to discuss in front of my guest.'

'Of course it is,' said Virginia. 'Guy's quite right. I was only trying to think of somewhere cosy.'

'The place I speak of is certainly quiet. It has always struck me as discreet.'

'*Discreet?* Gracious. I don't think I've ever in my life been anywhere "discreet". How heavenly.'

'And since the sordid subject has been raised,' added Uncle Peregrine, looking reproachfully at his nephew, 'let me assure you it is *not* particularly cheap.'

'Come on. I can't wait,' said Virginia.

Guy watched the departure of this oddly-matched couple with amusement in which there was an element of annoyance. If Virginia was doing nothing that evening, he felt, her proper place was by his side.

They walked to the restaurant through the damp dark. Virginia took his arm. When, as happened at crossings and turnings, he tried with old-fashioned etiquette to change sides and put himself in danger of passing vehicles, she firmly retained er hold. At no great distance they found the fish shop and climbed the stairs at its side to the restaurant overhead. New to Virginia, well-known to the unostentatious and discriminating, the long room with its few tables receded in a glow of Edwardian, rose-shaded lights. Peregrine Crouchback shed his old coat and hat and handed his umbrella to an ancient porter and then said with an effort: 'I expect you want, that's to say, I mean, wash your hands, tidy up, ladies' cloakroom, somewhere I believe up those stairs.'

'No thanks,' said Virginia, and then added, as they were being shown to a table: 'Peregrine, have you ever taken a girl out to dinner before?'

'Yes, of course.'

'Who? When?'

'It was some time ago,' said Uncle Peregrine vaguely.

They ordered oysters and turbot. Virginia said she would like to drink stout. Then she began: 'Why have you never married.'

'I was a younger son. Younger sons didn't marry in my day.'

'Oh, rot. I know hundreds who have.'

'It was thought rather *outré* among landed people, unless of course they found heiresses. There was no establishment for them. They had a small settlement which they were expected to leave back to the family – to their nephews, other younger sons. There had to be younger sons of course in case the head of the family died young. They came in quite useful in the last war. Perhaps we are rather an old-fashioned family in some ways.'

'Didn't you ever want to marry?'

'Not really.'

Uncle Peregrine was not at all put out by these direct personal questions. He was essentially imperturbable. No one, so far as he could remember, had ever shown so much interest in him. He found the experience enjoyable, even when Virginia pressed further.

'Lots of affairs?'

'Good heavens, no.'

'I'm sure you aren't a pansy.'

'Pansy?'

'You're not homosexual?'

Even this did not disconcert Uncle Peregrine. It was a subject he had rarely heard mentioned by a man; never by a woman. But there was something about Virginia's frankness which struck him as childlike and endearing.

'Good gracious, no. Besides the "o" is short. It comes from the Greek not the Latin.'

'I knew you weren't. I can always tell. I was just teasing.'

'No one has ever teased me about *that* before. But I knew a fellow once in the diplomatic service who had that reputation. There can't have been anything in it. He ended up as an ambassador. They would hardly have appointed a fellow like *that*. He was rather a vain, dressy fellow. I dare say that was what made people talk.'

'Peregrine, have you never been to bed with a woman?'

'Yes,' said Uncle Peregrine smugly, 'twice. It is not a thing I normally talk about.'

'Do tell.'

'Once when I was twenty and once when I was forty-five. I didn't particularly enjoy it.'

'Tell me about them.'

'It was the same woman.'

Virginia's spontaneous laughter had seldom been heard in recent years; it had once been one of her chief charms. She sat back in her chair and gave full, free tongue; clear, unrestrained, entirely joyous, with a shadow of ridicule, her mirth rang through the quiet little restaurant. Sympathetic and envious faces were turned towards her. She stretched across the table cloth and caught his hand, held it convulsively, unable to speak, laughed until she was breathless and mute, still gripping his bony fingers. And Uncle Peregrine smirked. He had never before struck success. He had in his time been at parties where others had laughed in this way. He had never had any share in it. He did not now know quite what it was that had won this prize, but he was highly gratified.

'Oh Peregrine,' said Virginia at last with radiant sincerity. 'I love you.'

He was not afraid to spoil his triumph with expatiation.

'I know most men go in for love affairs,' he said. 'Some of

hem can't help it. They can't get on at all without women, but
here are plenty of others – I dare say you haven't come across
hem much – who don't really care about that sort of thing,
but they don't know any reason why they shouldn't, so they
spend half their lives going after women they don't really want.
I can tell you something you probably don't know. There are
men who have been great womanizers in their time and when
they get to my age and don't want it any more and in fact can't
do it, instead of being glad of a rest, what do they do but take
all kinds of medicines to make them *want* to go on? I've heard
fellows in my club talking about it.'

'Bellamy's?'

'Yes. I don't go there much except to read the papers.
Awfully rowdy place it's become. I was put up as a young man
and go on paying the subscription, I don't know why. I don't
know many fellows there. Well, the other day I heard two of
them who must have been about my age, talking of which
doctor was best to make them *want* women. All manner of
expensive treatments. You can't explain that, can you?'

'I knew a man called Augustus who did just that.'

'Did you? And he told you about it? Extraordinary.'

'Why is it different from going for a walk to get up an
appetite for luncheon?'

'Because it's Wrong,' said Uncle Peregrine.

'You mean "wrong" according to your religion?'

'Why, how else could anything be wrong?' asked Uncle
Peregrine with the perfect simplicity and continued his disserta-
tion on the problems of sex: 'There's another thing. You only
have to look at the ghastly fellows who are a success with
women to realize that there isn't much point in it.'

But Virginia was not attending. She began to make a little
pagoda of the empty oyster-shells on her plate. Without raising
her eyes, she said: '*I'm* rather thinking of becoming a
Catholic.'

It has been said of Uncle Peregrine that he was never disconcerted. Exception must be made of the abrupt access of
displeasure which now struck him. It is one of the established
delights of celibacy to discourse frankly, even grossly, of the
vagaries of lust to an attractive woman; it was one which Uncle

Peregrine had never before experienced and he was enjoying it stupendously. Now she had rudely let drop the guillotine.

'Oh,' he said. 'Why?'

'Don't you think it would be a good thing?'

'It depends on your reasons.'

'Isn't it always a good thing?'

The waiter reproachfully re-arranged the oyster-shells on Virginia's plate before removing it.

'Well, isn't it?' she pressed. 'Come on. Tell. Why are you so shocked suddenly? I've heard an awful lot one way and another about the Catholic Church being the church of sinners.'

'Not from me,' said Uncle Peregrine.

The waiter brought them their turbot.

'Of course, if you'd sooner not discuss it . . .'

'I'm not really competent to,' said the Privy Chamberlain, the Knight of Devotion and Grace of the Sovereign Order of St John of Jerusalem. 'Personally I find it very difficult to regard converts as Catholics.'

'Oh, don't be so stuck up and snubbing. What about Lady Plessington? She is a pillar, surely?'

'I have never felt quite at ease with Eloise Plessington where religion is concerned. Anyway, she was received into the Church when she married.'

'Exactly.'

'And you, my dear, were not.'

'Do you think it might have made a difference – with Guy and me, I mean – if I had been?'

Uncle Peregrine hesitated between his acceptance in theory of the operation of divine grace and his distant but quite detailed observation of the men and women he had known, and relapsed to his former 'I'm really not competent to say.'

A silence fell on the pair; Uncle Peregrine deploring the turn the conversation had taken, Virginia considering how she could give further impetus in that direction. They ate their turbot and were brought coffee before their plates were removed. Diners were not encouraged to linger over their tables in those days. At length Virginia said: 'You see I rather hoped for your support in a plan of mine. I've got a bit tired of knocking about. I thought of going back to my husband.'

'To Troy?'

'No, no. To Guy. After all he is my real husband, isn't he? thought becoming a Catholic might help. No amount of vorces count in your Church, do they? I suppose we shall ave to go to some registry office to make it legal, but e're already married in the eyes of God – he's told me).'

'Lately?'

'Not very lately.'

'Do you think he wants you back?'

'I bet I could soon make him.'

'Well,' said Uncle Peregrine, 'that alters everything.' He oked at her with eyes of woe. 'It was *Guy* you've been ming to see all these last days?'

'Of course. What did you think? ... Oh, Peregrine, did you ink I had designs on *you*?'

'The thought had crossed my mind.'

'You thought perhaps I might provide your third –' She sed a word, then unprintable, which despite its timeless bscenity did not make Uncle Peregrine wince. He even found attractive on her lips. She was full of good humour and mis- hief now, on the verge of another access of laughter.

'That was rather the idea.'

'But surely that would have been Wrong?'

'Very Wrong indeed. I did not seriously entertain it. But it curred often, even when I was sorting the books. You could ave moved into the room Guy is now in. I don't think Mrs orner would have seen anything objectionable. After all, ou are my niece.'

Virginia's laughter came again, most endearing of her harms.

'Darling Peregrine. And you wouldn't have needed any of ose expensive treatments your chums in Bellamy's recom- end?'

'In your case,' said Uncle Peregrine with his cavalier grace, am practically sure not.'

'It's perfectly sweet of you. You don't think I'm laughing *at* ou, do you?'

'No, I don't believe you are.'

139

'Any time you want to try, dear Peregrine, you're quite welcome.'

The pleasure died in Peregrine Crouchback's sad old face

'That wouldn't be quite the same thing. Put like that I find the suggestion embarrassing.'

'Oh dear, have I made a floater?'

'Yes. It was all a fancy really. You make it sound so practical. I found I looked forward to seeing you about the flat. don't you know? It wasn't much more than that.'

'And I want a husband,' said Virginia. 'You wouldn't consider that?'

'No, no. Of course that would be quite impossible.'

'Your religion again.'

'Well, yes.'

'Then it will have to be Guy. Don't you see now why I want to become a Catholic? He can't very well say no, can he?'

'Oh, yes, he can.'

'But knowing Guy you don't think he will, do you?'

'I really know Guy very little,' said Uncle Peregrine rather peevishly.

'But you'll help me? When the point comes up, you'll tell him it's his duty?'

'He's not at all likely to consult me.'

'But if he does? And when it comes to squaring Angela?'

'No, my dear,' said Uncle Peregrine, 'I'll be damned if I do.'

The evening had not gone as either of them had planned. Uncle Peregrine saw Virginia to her door. She kissed him, for the first time, on their parting. He raised his hat in the darkness, paid off the taxi and walked despondently home, where he found Guy awake, reading.

'Have a good time?' he asked.

'It is always good, so far as anything is nowadays, at that restaurant. It cost more than two pounds,' he added, his memory still sore from the imputation of parsimony.

'I mean, did you enjoy yourself?'

'Yes and no. More no than yes perhaps.'

'I thought Virginia seemed in cracking form.'

'Yes and no. More yes than no. She laughed a lot.'

'That sounds all right.'

'Yes and no. Guy, I have to warn you. That girl has *Designs*.'

'On you, Uncle Peregrine?'

'On you.'

'Are you sure?'

'She told me.'

'Do you think you should repeat it?'

'In the circumstances, yes.'

'Not yes and no?'

'Just yes.'

Sir Ralph Brompton had been schooled in the old diplomatic service to evade irksome duties and to achieve power by insinuating himself into places where, strictly, he had no business. In the looser organization of total war he was able to trip from office to office and committee to committee. The chiefs of HOO considered they should be represented wherever the conduct of affairs was determined. Busy themselves in the highest circles, they willingly delegated to Sir Ralph the authority to listen and speak for them and to report to them, in the slightly lower but not much less mischievous world of their immediate inferiors.

Liberation was Sir Ralph's special care. Wherever those lower than the Cabinet and the Chiefs of Staff adumbrated the dismemberment of Christendom, there Sir Ralph might be found.

On a morning shortly before Christmas in an office quite independent of HOO Sir Ralph dropped in for an informal chat on the subject of liaison with Balkan terrorists. The man whom he was visiting had been rather suddenly gazetted brigadier. His functions were as ill-defined as Sir Ralph's; they were dubbed 'co-ordination'. There had been times in Sir Ralph's professional career when he had been aware that certain of his colleagues and, later, of his staff were engaged in secret work. Strange men not of the service had presented credentials and made use of the diplomatic bag and the cipher room. Sir Ralph had fastidiously averted his attention from their activities. Now, recalled from retirement, he found a naughty relish in what he had formerly shunned. These two had risen to their positions by very different routes; their paths had never crossed.

Sir Ralph sported light herring-bone tweed, such as in peacetime he would not have worn at that season in London; brilliant black brogue shoes shone on his narrow feet. His long legs were crossed and he smoked a Turkish cigarette. The brigadier had bought his uniform ready-made. The buttons were dull. He wore a cloth belt. No ribbons decorated his plump breast. His false teeth held a pipe insecurely. An impersonal association, but a close one, united them. Their political sympathies were identical.

'It is a great thing getting control of Balkan Liberation shifted here from Cairo.'

'Yes, almost the whole Middle East set-up was hopelessly compromised with royalist refugees. We shall be able to use the few reliable men. The others will be found more suitable employment.'

'Iceland?'

'Iceland will be perfectly suitable.'

Lists were produced of the proposed liaison missions.

'De Souza got a very good report from the parachute school.'

'Yes. You don't think he'll be wasted in the field? He could be very useful to us here.'

'He can be very useful in the field. Gilpin failed. We can use him here until we open a headquarters in Italy.'

'Once our fellows get to Italy they'll be harder to keep under our own hand. They'll come under command of the army for a good many things. We've been accepted on the top level but we still have to establish confidence lower down. What we need is a good backing of conventional regimental soldiers in the subordinate posts. I see Captain Crouchback's name here, crossed off. I know him. I should have thought he was just what we need – middle-aged, Catholic, no political activities, a Halberdier, good record, excellent report from the parachute school.'

'Bad security risk, apparently.'

'Why?'

'They never give reasons. He is simply noted as unsuitable for employment in North Italy.'

'Entanglements with women?' suggested the brigadier.

'I should doubt it.'

There was a pause while Sir Ralph considered the fatuity of the security forces. Then he said: 'Only in North Italy?'

'That is what the report says.'

'In fact there would be no objection to his going to the Balkans?'

'Not according to this report.'

'I think he and de Souza might make a satisfactory team.'

For very many years Peregrine Crouchback's Christmases had been dismal occasions for himself and others. Bachelors, unless dedicated to some religious function or deluded by vice, are said to be unknown among the lower races and classes. Peregrine Crouchback was a bachelor by nature and the feast of the Nativity was to him the least congenial in the calendar. As a child, as the mere recipient of gifts and the consumer of rich, rather tasteless foods, he had conformed and rejoiced. But he had matured, so far as his peculiar condition could be called maturity, young. In his early manhood, as his niece and nephews became the centre of celebration at Broome, he sought refuge abroad. After the First World War, Arthur Box-Bender was added to the bereaved family; Ivo died but Box-Bender's children filled the nurseries at mid-winter. Finally Broome was emptied and Christmas ceased to be a family gathering. Uncle Peregrine did not repine. But between the wars, in a year whose quite recent date could have been establishd from the visitors' book but now seemed of immemorial antiquity, it had become habitual, almost traditional, for Uncle Peregrine to spend Christmas with some distant cousins of his mother, older than himself, name Scrope-Weld, who inhabited an agricultural island among the industrial areas of Staffordshire. The house was large, the hospitality, when he first went there, lavish, and one unloved, middle-aged bachelor less or more – 'Old Crouchers' even then to them, his seniors – did not depress the spirits of the 1920s. A forlorn relation was part of the furniture of Christmas in most English homes.

Mr and Mrs Scrope-Weld died, their son and his wife took their places; there were fewer servants, fewer guests, but always Uncle Peregrine at Christmas. In 1939 the greater part of the house was taken for a children's home; Scrope-Weld

143

went abroad with his regiment; his wife remained with three children, four rooms, and a nanny. Still Peregrine Crouchback was invited and he accepted. 'It is just the sort of thing one must not give up,' said Mrs Scrope-Weld. 'One must not make the war an excuse for unkindness.'

So it was in 1940, 1941, and 1942. The children grew sharper.

'Mummy do we have to have Uncle Perry here to spoil Christmas every year until he dies.'

'Yes, dear. He was a great friend and a sort of relation of your grandmother's. He'd be very hurt if he was not asked.'

'He seemed awfully hurt all the time he was here.'

'Christmas is often a sad time for old people. He's very fond of you all.'

'I bet he isn't fond of me.'

'Or me.'

'Or me.'

'Will he leave us any money?'

'Francis, that's an absolutely disgusting question. Of course he won't.'

'Well, I wish he'd hurry up and die anyway.'

And as Peregrine Crouchback left on the day after Boxing Day he reflected: 'Well, that's over for another year. They'd be awfully hurt if I didn't come.'

So it was in 1943. Loth to leave London he took the crowded train on Christmas Eve. Once he used to bring a Strasburg pie with him. Now the shops were empty. His only gift was a large, highly coloured Victorian album which he had extracted from 'salvage'.

That night, as always, they attended Mass. On Christmas Day they all made a formal visit to the library, now the common-room of the paid 'helpers', commended the sprigs of holly that they had disposed along the book-shelves and picture-frames and drank sherry with them before retiring to eat a middle-day dinner of turkey, an almost nefarious bird at that date, long cosseted with rationed food-stuffs. 'I feel so guilty eating it alone,' said Mrs Scrope-Weld, 'but it would go nowhere with the helpers and we couldn't possibly have reared another.' The children gorged. Peregrine and nanny nibbled. That evening there was a Christmas tree for the 'evacuees' in the staircase hall. On Boxing Day, as always, he went to Mass, walking alone through the chill morning, under the dripping avenue to the chapel on the edge of the park. Mrs Scrope-Weld had to milk and then do most of the work in cooking breakfast. One of the 'helpers' was there before him. They walked back together and she said: 'Perhaps this will be the last Christmas here.'

'Do you hope for that?'

'Well, of course, everyone hopes for peace. But I don't know where I shall be or what I shall be doing when it comes. I've got sort of used to the war.'

Later he went for a long, damp walk with his hostess. She said: 'You're really the only link with Christmas as it used to be. It is sweet of you coming so faithfully. I know it isn't a bit comfortable. Do you think things will ever be normal again?'

'Oh, no,' said Peregrine Crouchback. 'Never again.'

Meanwhile Guy and Virginia were together in London. Virginia said: 'Thank God HOO doesn't make a thing about Christmas.'

'In the Halberdiers we had to go to the sergeants' mess and they tried to make us drunk. In some regiments, I believe, the officers wait on the men at dinner.'

'I've seen photographs of it. Peregrine's away?'

'He always goes to the same people. Did he give you a present?'

'No. I wondered whether he would. I don't think he knew what would be suitable. He seemed less loving after our fish dinner.'

'He told me you had Designs.'

'On him?'

'On me.'

'Yes,' said Virginia. 'I have. Peregrine had designs on me.'

'Seriously?'

'Not really. The thing about you Crouchbacks is that you're effete.'

'Do you know what that means? It means you've just given birth.'

'Well, it's the wrong word then. You're just like Peregrine correcting my pronunciation of homosexual.'

'Why on earth were you talking to him about homosexuals? You don't think he's one, do you?'

'No, but I think all you Crouchbacks are over-bred and under-sexed.'

'Not at all the same thing. Think of Toulouse-Lautrec.'

'Oh, damn, Guy. You're evading my Designs.'

It was all as light as the heaviest drawing-room comedy and each had a dread at heart.

'You're dying out as a family,' she continued. 'Even Angela's boy, they tell me, wants to be a monk. Why do you Crouch-backs do so little —ing?' – and again she used without offence that then unprintable word.

'I don't know about the others. With me I think, perhaps, it's because I associate it with love. And I don't love any more.'

'Not me?'

'Oh, no, Virginia, not you. You must have realized that.'

'It is not so easy to realize when lots of people have been so keen, not so long ago. What about you, Guy, that evening in Claridges?'

'That wasn't love,' said Guy. 'Believe it or not it was the Halberdiers.'

'Yes. I think I know what you mean.'

She was sitting beside his bed, facing him. Between them lay the wicker table-tray on which they had been playing piquet. Now she ran a hand, light, caressing, exploring, up under the bed-clothes. Guy turned away and the pain of the sudden, instinctive movement made him grimace.

'No,' said Virginia. 'Not keen.'

'I'm sorry.'

'It's not a nice thing for a girl to have a face made at her like that.'

'It was only my knee. I've said I'm sorry,' and indeed he was, that he should so humiliate one whom he had loved.

But Virginia was not easily humiliated. Behind her last, locust years lay deep reserves of success. Almost all women in England at that time believed that peace would restore normality. Mrs Scrope-Weld in Staffordshire meant by 'normality' having her husband at home and the house to themselves; also certain, to her, rudimentary comforts to which she had always been used; nothing sumptuous; a full larder and cellar; a lady's maid (but one who did her bedroom and darned and sewed for the whole family), a butler, a footman (but one who chopped and carried fire-logs), a reliable, mediocre cook training a kitchen-maid to succeed her in simple skills, self-effacing house-maids to dust and tidy; one man in the stable, two in the garden; things she would never know again. So to Virginia normality meant power and pleasure; pleasure chiefly and not only her own. Her power of attraction, her power of pleasing was to her still part of the natural order which had been capriciously interrupted. War, the massing and moving of millions of men, some of whom were sometimes endangered, most of whom were idle and lonely, the devastation, hunger, and waste, crumbling buildings, foundering ships, the torture and murder of prisoners; all these were a malevolent suspension of 'normality'; the condition in which Virginia's power of pleasing enabled her to cash cheques, wear new clothes, lave her face with its accustomed unguent, travel with speed and privacy and attention wherever she liked, when she liked, and choose her man and enjoy him at her leisure. The interruption had been prolonged beyond all reason. The balance would soon come right, meanwhile –

'What did Peregrine say about my Designs?'

'He didn't specify.'

'What do you think he meant? What do *you* think of *me*?'

'I think you are unhappy and uncomfortable and you've no one you're specially interested in at the moment and that for the first time in your life you are frightened of the future.'

'And none of that applies to you?'

'The difference between us is that I only think of the past.'

Virginia seized on the, to her, essential point. 'But there's no one *you're* specially interested in at the moment, is there?'

'No.'

'And you've absolutely loved having me round the place the last few weeks, haven't you? Admit. We get along like an old Darby and Joan, don't we?'

'Yes, I've enjoyed your visits.'

'And I'm still your wife. Nothing can alter that?'

'Nothing.'

'I don't exactly say you've a duty to me,' Virginia conceded with her high, fine candour.

'No, Virginia, you hardly could, could you?'

'You thought I had duties to you once – that evening in Claridge's. Remember?'

'I've explained that. It was being on leave from camp, wearing a new uniform, starting a new life. It was the war.'

'Well, isn't it the war that's brought me here today, bringing you, as I thought, a lovely Christmas present?'

'You didn't think anything of the kind.'

Virginia began to sing a song of their youth about 'a little broken doll'. Suddenly both of them laughed. Guy said: 'It's no good, Ginny. I am sorry you are hard up. As you know, I'm a little better off than I was. I am willing to help you until you find someone more convenient.'

'Guy, what a beastly, bitter way to talk. Not like you at all. You would never have spoken like that in the old days.'

'Not bitter – limited. That's all I've got for you.'

Then Virginia said: 'I need more. There's something I've got to tell you and please believe that I was going to tell you even if this conversation had gone quite differently. You must remember me well enough to know I was never one for dirty tricks, was I?'

Then she informed him, without any extenuation or plea for compassion, curtly almost, that she was with child by Trimmer.

Ian and Kerstie Kilbannock returned to London from Scotland on the night of Childermas. He went straight to his office, she home, where Mrs Bristow was smoking a cigarette and listening to the wireless.

'Everything all right?'

'Mrs Troy's gone.'

'Where?'

'She didn't say. Gone for good, I wouldn't be surprised. She packed up everything yesterday morning and gave me a pound. You'd have thought either it would be something more or just friendly thanks after all this time. I nearly told her tipping's gone out these days. What I mean we all help one another as the wireless says. A fiver would have been more like if she wanted to show appreciation. I helped her down with the bags too. Well, she's lived a lot abroad, hasn't she? Oh, and she left you this.'

This was a letter:

Darling

I am sorry not to be here to say good-bye but I am sure you will be quite pleased to have me out of the house at last. What an angel you have been. I can never thank you or Ian enough. Let's meet very soon and I'll tell you all about everything. I've left a little token for Ian – a silly sort of present but you know how impossible it is to find anything nowadays.

All love
Virginia

'Did she leave anything else, Mrs Bristow?'

'Just two books. They're upstairs on the drawing-room table.'

Upstairs Kerstie found Pyne's *Horace*. Kerstie was no bibliophile but she had haunted the sale rooms and recognized objects of some value. Like Mrs Bristow's tip, she considered, it might have been something less or more. The elegant volumes were in fact Virginia's only disposable property, an inappropriate and belated Christmas present from Uncle Peregrine.

Kerstie returned to the kitchen.

'Mrs Troy left no address?'

'She's not gone far. I didn't catch what she said to the taxi driver but it wasn't a railway station.'

The mystery was soon solved. Ian telephoned. 'Good news,' he said. 'We've got rid of Virginia.'

'I know.'

'For good. She's been a sensible woman. I knew she had it in her. She's done just what I said she should – found a husband.'

'Anyone we know?'

'Yes, the obvious man. Guy.'

'Oh, no.'

'I assure you. She's in the office now. She's just handed in official notification that she is giving up war-work to be a housewife.'

'Ian, she can't do this to Guy.'

'They're going round to the registrar as soon as he can hobble.'

'He must be insane.'

'I've always thought he was. It's in the family, you know. There was that brother of his.'

There were depths of Scotch propriety in Kerstie, hard granite very near the surface. Life in London, life with Ian, had not entirely atrophied her susceptibility to moral outrage. It happened to her rarely but when shocked she suffered no superficial shiver but a deep seismic upheaval. For some minutes after Ian had rung off she sat still and grim and glaring. Then she made for Carlisle Place.

'Oh, good morning, my lady,' said Mrs Corner, very different in her address from Mrs Bristow, 'you've come to see Captain Guy, of course. You've heard his news?'

'Yes.'

'No surprise to me, I can assure you, my lady. I saw it coming. All's well that ends well. It's only natural really, isn't it, whatever the rights and wrongs were before, they are man and wife. She's moved in here in the room down the passage and she's giving up her work so she'll be free to take care of him.'

Throughout this speech Kerstie moved towards Guy's door. 'He will be pleased to see you,' Mrs Corner said opening it; 'he doesn't often get visitors in the morning.'

'Hallo, Kerstie,' said Guy. 'Nice of you to come. I expect you've heard of my change of life.'

She did not sit down. She waited until Mrs Corner had left them.

'Guy,' she said, 'I've only got a minute. I'm due at my office. I had to stop and see you. I've known you a long time if never very well. It just happens you're one of Ian's friends I really like. You may think it's no business of mine but I've got to tell you'; and then she delivered her message.

'But, dear Kerstie, do you suppose I didn't know?'

'Virginia told you?'

'Of course.'

'And you're marrying her in spite of – ?'

'Because of.'

'You poor bloody fool,' said Kerstie, anger and pity and something near love in her voice, 'you're being *chivalrous* – about *Virginia*. Can't you understand men aren't chivalrous any more and I don't believe they ever were. Do you really see Virginia as a damsel in distress?'

'She's in distress.'

'She's tough.'

'Perhaps when they *are* hurt, the tough suffer more than the tender.'

'Oh, come off it, Guy. You're forty years old. Can't you see how ridiculous you will look playing the knight errant? Ian thinks you are insane, literally. Can you tell me any sane reason for doing this thing?'

Guy regarded Kerstie from his bed. The question she asked was not new to him. He had posed it and answered it some days ago. 'Knights errant,' he said, 'used to go out looking for noble deeds. I don't think I've ever in my life done a single, positively unselfish action. I certainly haven't gone out of my way to find opportunities. Here was something most unwelcome, put into my hands; something which I believe the Americans describe as "beyond the call of duty"; not the normal behaviour of an officer and a gentleman; something they'll laugh about in Bellamy's.

'Of course Virginia is tough. She would have survived somehow. I shan't be changing her by what I'm doing. I know all that. But you see there's another –' he was going to say 'soul'; then realized that this word would mean little to Kerstie for all her granite propriety – 'there's another life to consider. What sort of life do you think her child would have, born unwanted in 1944?'

'It's no business of yours.'

'It was made my business by being offered.'

'My dear Guy, the world is full of unwanted children. Half the population of Europe are homeless – refugees and prisoners. What is one child more or less in all that misery?'

'I can't do anything about all those others. This is just one case where I can help. And only I, really. I was Virginia's last resort. So I couldn't do anything else. Don't you *see*?'

'Of course I don't. Ian is quite right. You're insane.'

And Kerstie left more angry than she had come.

It was no good trying to explain, Guy thought. Had someone said: 'All differences are theological differences'? He turned once more to his father's letter: *Quantitative judgements don't apply. If only one soul was saved, that is full compensation for any amount of 'loss of face'.*

BOOK THREE

The Death Wish

1

THE Dakota flew out over the sea, then swung inland. The listless passengers, British and American, all men, of all services and all of lowly rank, stirred and buckled themselves to the metal benches. The journey by way of Gibraltar and North Africa had been tedious and protracted by unexplained delays. It was now late afternoon and they had had nothing to eat since dawn. This was a different machine from the one in which Guy had embarked in England. None of those who had travelled with him that first sleepless night had continued to Bari. Crouching and peering through the little porthole, he caught a glimpse of orchards of almond; it was late February and the trees were already in full flower. Soon he was on the ground beside his kit-bag and valise, reporting to a transport officer.

His move-order instructed him to report forthwith to the Headquarters of the British Mission to the Anti-Fascist Forces of National Liberation (Adriatic).

He was expected. A jeep was waiting to take him to the sombre building in the new town where this organization was installed. Nothing reminded him of the Italy he knew and loved; the land of school holidays; the land where later he had sought refuge from his failure.

The sentry was less than welcoming.

'That's a Home Forces pass, sir. No use here.'

Guy still retained his HOO HQ pass and exhibited it.

'Don't know anything about that, sir.'

'I have orders to report to a Brigadier Cape.'

'He's not here today. You'll have to wait and see the security officer. Ron,' he said to a colleague, 'tell Captain Gilpin there's an officer reporting to the Brigadier.'

For some minutes Guy stood in the dark hall. This building was a pre-fascist structure designed in traditional style round a sunless *cortile*. A broad flight of shallow stone steps led up into the darkness, for the glass roof had been shattered and replaced by tarred paper. 'The light ought to come on any time now,' said the sentry. 'But you can't rely on it.'

Presently Gilpin appeared in the gloom.

'Yes?' he said. 'What can we do for you?'

'Don't you remember me at the parachute school with de Souza?'

'De Souza's in the field. What exactly is it you want?'

Guy showed him his move-order.

'First I've seen of this.'

'You don't imagine it's a forgery, do you?'

'A copy ought to have come to me. I don't *imagine* anything. It is simply that we have to take precautions.' In the twilight of the hall he turned the order over and studied its back. He read it again. Then he tried a new attack. 'You seem to have taken your time getting here.'

'Yes, there were delays. Are you in command here?'

'I'm not the senior officer if that's what you mean. There's a major upstairs – a Halberdier like yourself.' – He spoke the name of the Corps in a manner which seemed deliberately to dissociate himself from the traditions of the army; with a sneer almost. – 'I don't know what he does. He's posted as GSO 2 (Co-ordination). I suppose in a way you might say he was "in command" when the Brig. is away.'

'Perhaps I could see him?'

'Is that your gear?'

'Yes.'

'You'll have to leave it down here.'

'Do you suppose I wanted to carry it up?'

'Keep an eye on it, corporal,' said Gilpin, not, it seemed from any solicitude for its preservation; rather for fear of what it might contain of a subversive, perhaps, explosive, nature. 'You did quite right to hold this officer for examination,' he added. 'You can send him up to GSO 2 (Co-ordination)' – and without another word to Guy he turned and left him.

The second sentry led Guy to a door on the mezzanine. Four and a half years' of the vicissitudes of war had accustomed Guy to a large variety of reception. It had also accustomed im to meet from time to time the officer whose name he had ever learned, who now greeted him with unwonted warmth.

'Well,' he said, 'well, we do run across one another, don't we? I expect you're more surprised than I am. I saw your name on a bit of bumf. We've been expecting you for weeks.'

'Gilpin wasn't.'

'We try to keep as much bumf as we can from Gilpin. It isn't always easy.'

At that moment, as though symbolically, the bulb hanging from the ceiling glowed, flickered, and shone brilliantly.

'Still a major, I see,' said Guy.

'Yes, dammit. I was lieutenant-colonel for nearly a year. Then there was a reorganization at brigade. There didn't seem a job for me there any more. So I drifted into this outfit.'

The electric bulb, as though symbolically, flickered, glowed, and went out. 'They haven't really got the plant working yet,' said the major superfluously. 'It comes and goes.' And their conversation was carried on in intermittent periods of vision and obscurity as though in a storm of summer lightning.

'D'you know what you're going to do here?'

'No.'

'I didn't when I was posted. I don't now. It's a nice enough outfit. You'll like Cape. He's not long out of hospital – got hit at Salerno. No more active soldiering for him. He'll explain the set-up when you see him tomorrow. He and Joe Cattermole had to go to a conference at Caserta. Joe's a queer fellow, some sort of professor in civil life; frightfully musical. But he works like the devil. Takes everything off *my* shoulders – and Cape's. Gilpin is a pest as you saw. Joe's the only man who can stand him. Joe likes everyone – even the Jugs. Awfully good-natured fellow, Joe; always ready to stand in and take extra duty.'

They spoke of the Halberdiers, of the achievements and frustrations of Ritchie-Hook, of the losses and reinforcements, recruiting, regrouping, reorganization, and cross-posting that was changing the face of the Corps. The light waxed, waned, flickered, expired as the familiar household names of Guy's innocence resounded between them. Then the anonymous major turned his attention to Guy's affairs and booked him a

155

room at the officer's hotel. When the light next went out, the sun had set and they were left in total darkness. An orderly came in bearing a pressure-lamp.

'Time to pack it up,' said the major. 'I'll see you settled in Then we can go out to dinner.'

'I'll just sign you in,' said the major at the entrance of the club. Guy looked over his shoulder but the signature was as illegible as ever; indeed Guy himself, entered in his writing shared a vicarious anonymity. 'If you're going to be in Bar any time, you'd better join.'

'I see it's called the "Senior Officers' Club".'

'That doesn't mean anything. It's for fellows who are used to a decent mess. The hotel is full of Queen Alexandra's nurses in the evenings. Women are a difficulty here,' he continued as they made their way into the ante-room – this new, rather outlandish building had been made for a seminary of Uniate Abyssinians, who had been moved to Rome at the fall of the Italian Ethiopian Empire; the chief rooms were domed in acknowledgement of their native tukals and fanes. 'The locals are strictly out of bounds. No great temptation, either, from what I've seen. Thoroughly unsavoury, and, anyway, they only want Americans. They pay anything and don't mind what they're getting. There are a few secretaries and ciphereens but they're all booked. If you're lucky you get fixed up with a nurse. They get two evenings a week. Cape's got one – a bit long in the tooth but very friendly. It's easier for fellows who've been in hospital. Joe was in hospital when he came out of Jugland but he doesn't seem to have taken advantage. I have to rely on WAAFs mostly; they come through sometimes on the way to Foggia. They talk a lot of rot about Italy.'

'The WAAFs do?'

'No, no. I mean people who've never been here. *Romantic* – my God. That's where the club comes in. It *is* like a mess at home, isn't it? English rations, of course.'

'No restaurants open?'

'Strictly out of bounds. There's nothing for the wops to eat in this town except what they can scrounge off the RASC dump.'

'No wine?'

'There's a sort of local red vino if you like it.'

'Fish, surely?'

'That's kept for the wops. Good thing, too, by the smell of it.'

The exhilaration which Guy had experienced at finding himself abroad after two years of war-time England flickered and died like the bulb at Headquarters.

'Shops?' Guy asked: 'I've always heard that there are some fine things to be found in Apulia.'

'Nothing, old boy, nothing.'

A civilian waiter bought them their pink gins. Guy asked him in Italian for olives. He answered in English almost scornfully: 'No olives for senior officers,' and brought American pea-nuts.

Under the blue-washed cupola where the dusky, bearded clerics had lately pursued their studies, Guy surveyed the heterogeneous uniforms and badges and saw his own recent past, his probable future. This was Southsands again; it was the transit camp, the Station Hotel in Glasgow; it was that lowest circle where he had once penetrated, the unemployed officers' pool.

'I say,' said Guy's host, 'cheer up. What's wrong? Homesick?'

'Homesick for Italy,' said Guy.

'That's a good one,' said the major, puzzled, but appreciative that a joke had been made.

They went into what had been the refectory. Had Guy been homesick for war-time London, he would have found solace here, for Lieutenant Padfield was dining with a party of three Britons. Since Christmas the Lieutenant had not been seen about London.

'Good evening, Loot. What are you up to?'

'I'll join you later, may I?'

'You know that Yank?' asked the major.

'Yes.'

'What does he do?'

'That no one knows.'

'He's been hanging round Joe Cattermole lately. I don't

157

know who's brought him here tonight. We try to be matey with the Yanks in office hours but we don't much encourage them off duty. They've got plenty of places of their own.'

'The Loot's a great mixer.'

'What d'you call him?'

'Loot. It's American for Lieutenant, you know.'

'Is it? I didn't. How absurd.'

Dinner, as Guy had been forewarned, included no succulent, redolent Italian dishes but he gratefully drank the 'vino', poor as it was; wine in any form had been scarcer and more costly than ever in the last two months in London. The major drank nothing with his food. He told Guy in detail of his last WAAF and of the WAAF before her. The differences were negligible. Presently the Lieutenant came across to them bearing a cigar-case. 'I can't wear them myself,' he said. 'I think these are all right. Not from the PX. Our minister in Algiers gave me a box.'

'A woman's only a woman but a good cigar is a smoke,' said the major.

'Which reminds me,' said the Lieutenant, 'that I have never written to congratulate you and Virginia. I read about you in *The Times* when I was staying with the Stitches in Algiers. It's *very* good news.'

'Thank you.'

The Halberdier major having accepted, bitten, and lit the cigar he was offered, felt obliged to say: 'Bring up a pew. We haven't met, but I've seen you with Joe Cattermole.'

'Yes, he's the most useful fellow here in my job.'

'Would it be insecure to ask what that is?'

'Not at all. Opera. We're trying to get the opera going, you know.'

'I didn't.'

'It's the most certain way to the Italian heart. There's not much difficulty about orchestras. The singers seem all to have gone off with the Germans.' He spoke of the various opera houses of occupied Italy; some had been gutted by bombs, others had escaped with a little damage. Bari was unscathed. 'But I must rejoin my hosts,' he said, rising.

The major hesitated on the brink of so private a topic; then

unged: 'Did I gather from what that fellow said that you've
st got married?'

'Yes.'

'Rotten luck being posted abroad at once. I say, I'm afraid
was talking out of turn a bit, giving you advice about the
cal market.'

'I don't think my wife would mind.'

'Wouldn't she? Mine would – and I've been married eleven
ars.' He paused, brooding over that long stretch of inter-
ittent rapture, and added: 'At least, I think she would.' He
used again. 'It's a long time since I saw her. I dare say,' he
ncluded with the resigned, cosmic melancholy that Guy had
ways associated with him, 'that she wouldn't really care a
t.'

They returned to the ante-room. The major's spirits had
nk at the thought of the possibility of his wife's indifference
his adventures with the WAAFs. He called for whisky.
en he said: 'I say, do you believe that fellow's really going
und getting up operas? What does he mean about "the way
the Italian heart"? We've just beaten the bastards, haven't
e? What have they got to sing about? I don't believe even the
anks would be so wet as to lay on entertainments for them.
you ask me, it's cover for something else. Once you leave
gimental soldiering, you run up against a lot of rum things
ou didn't know went on. This town's full of them.'

In London at that moment there was being enacted a scene
f traditional domesticity. Virginia was making her *layette*. It
as a survival of the schoolroom, incongruous to much in
er adult life, that she sewed neatly and happily. It was thus
e had spent many evenings in Kenya working a quilt that
as never finished. Uncle Peregrine was reading aloud from
rollope's *Can You Forgive Her?* Presently she said: 'I've
nished my lessons, you know.'

'Lessons?'

'Instructions. Canon Weld says he's ready to receive me any
me now.'

'I suppose he knows best,' said Uncle Peregrine dubiously.

'It's all so easy,' said Virginia. 'I can't think what those novelists make such a fuss over – about people "losing their faith". The whole thing is clear as daylight to me. I wonder why no one ever told me before. I mean it's all quite obvious really, isn't it, when you come to think of it?'

'It is to me,' said Uncle Peregrine.

'I want you to be my godfather, please. And that doesn't mean a present – at least not anything expensive.' She plied her needle assiduously showing her pretty hands. 'It's really you who have brought me into the Church, you know.'

'I? Good heavens, how?'

'Just by being such a dear,' said Virginia. 'You do like having me here, don't you?'

'Yes, of course, my dear.'

'I've been thinking,' said Virginia. 'I should like to have the baby here.'

'Here? In this flat?'

'Yes. Do you mind?'

'Won't it be rather inconvenient for you?'

'Not for me. I think it will be cosy.'

'*Cosy*,' said Peregrine aghast. '*Cosy*.'

'You can be godfather to the baby too. Only, if you don't mind, if he's a boy I shouldn't think I'll call him Peregrine. I think Guy would like him to be called Gervase, don't you?'

And Ludovic was writing. Since the middle of December he had without remission written 3,000 words a day; more than a hundred thousand words. His manner of composition was quite changed. Fowler and Roget lay unopened. He felt no need now to find the right word. All words were right. They poured from his pen in disordered confusion. He never paused; he never revised. He barely applied his mind to his task. He was possessed, the mere amanuensis of some power, not himself, making for – what? He did not question. He just wrote. His book grew as little Trimmer grew in Virginia's womb without her conscious collaboration.

It was the aim of every Barinese to obtain employment under the occupying forces. Whole families in all their ramifications had insinuated themselves into the service of the officers' hotel. Six senile patriarchs supported themselves on long mops from dawn to dusk gently polishing the linoleum floor of the vestibule. They all stopped work as Guy passed between them next morning and then advanced crablike to expunge his foot-prints.

He walked to the office he had visited the evening before. The morning sunlight transformed the building. There had once been a fountain in the *cortile*, Guy now observed; perhaps it would one day play again. A stone triton stood there gaping last poor descendant of grand forebears, amid spiky vegetation. The sentry was engaged in conversation with a despatch-rider and let Guy pass without question. He met Gilpin on the stairs.

'How did you get in?'

'I'm attached here, don't you remember?'

'But you haven't got a pass. How long will it take those men to learn that an officer's uniform means nothing? They had no business to let you through without a pass.'

'Where do I get one?'

'From me.'

'Well, perhaps it might save trouble if you gave me one.'

'Have you got three photographs of yourself?'

'Of course not.'

'Then I can't make out a pass.'

At this moment a voice from above said: 'What's going on, Gilpin?'

'An officer without a pass, sir.'

'Who?'

'Captain Crouchback.'

'Well give him a pass and send him up.'

This was Brigadier Cape. The voice became a man on the landing; a lame, lean man, wearing the badges of a regiment of lancers. When Guy presented himself, he said: 'Keen fellow, Gilpin. Takes his duties very seriously. Sorry I wasn't here yesterday. I can't see you at the moment. I've got some Jugs coming in with a complaint. The best thing you can do is to get Cattermole to put you in the picture. Then we'll find where you fit in.'

Major Cattermole had the next room to Brigadier Cape. He

was of the same age as Guy, tall, stooping, emaciated, totally unsoldierly, a Zurbarán ascetic with a joyous smile.

'Balliol 1921–1924,' he said.

'Yes. Were we up together?'

'You wouldn't remember me. I led a very quiet life. I remember seeing you about with the bloods.'

'I was never a blood.'

'You seemed one to me. You were a friend of Sligger's. He was always very nice to me but I was never in his set. I wasn't in any set. I wasted my time as an undergraduate, working. I had to.'

'I think you used to speak at the Union?'

'I tried. I wasn't any good. So you're going across to Jugoslavia?'

'Am I?'

'That seems to be why you're here. How I envy you. I came out in the new year and the doctors won't let me go back. I was there for the Sixth Offensive but I crocked up. They had to carry me for the last two weeks. I was only an encumbrance. The partisans never leave their wounded. They know what the enemy would do to them. We had men of seventy and girls of fifteen in our column. A few hour's halt and then "pokrit" – "forward". I don't know what my academic colleagues would have made of it. We ate all our donkeys in the first week. At the end we were eating roots and bark. But we got clean through and an aeroplane picked me up with the rest of the wounded. Didn't you have a pretty hard crossing from Crete?'

'Yes, how did you know?'

'It was all in the dossier they sent us. Well, I don't have to tell you what real exhaustion means. Did you get hallucinations?'

'Yes.'

'So did I. You've made a better recovery than I. They say I'll never be fit to go into the field again. I'm stuck in an office, briefing other men. Let's get to work.'

He unrolled a wall-map. 'The position is fluid,' he said, a curious official insincerity masking his easier, early manner. 'This is as up to date as we can make it.'

And for twenty minutes he delivered what was plainly a set

exposition. Here were the 'liberated areas'; this was the route of one brigade, that of another; here was the headquarters of a division, there of a corps. A huge, intricately involved campaign of encirclements and counter-attacks took shape in Cattermole's precise, donnish phrases.

'I had no idea it was on this scale,' said Guy.

'No one has. No one will, as long as there's a royalist government in exile squatting in London. The partisans are pinning down three times as many troops as the whole Italian campaign. Beside's von Weich's Army Group there are five or six divisions of Cetnics and Ustachi – perhaps those names are unfamiliar. They are the Serb and Croat Quislings. Bulgarians, too. There must be half a million enemy over there.'

'There seem to be plenty of partisans,' Guy observed, pointing to the multitude of high formations scored on the map.

'Yes,' said Major Cattermole, 'yes. Of course not all the regiments are quite up to strength. It's no good putting more men in the field than we can equip. And we're short of almost everything – artillery, transport, aeroplanes, tanks. We had to arm ourselves with what we could capture. Until quite lately those men in Cairo were sending arms to Mihajlovic to be used against our own people. We're doing a little better now. There's a trickle of supplies, but it isn't easy to arrange drops for forces on the move. And the Russians have at last sent in a mission – headed by a general. You can have no idea, until you've seen them, what that will mean to the partisans. It's something I have to explain to all our liaison officers. The Jugoslavs accept us as allies but they look on the Russians as leaders. It is part of their history – well, I expect you know as well as I do about Pan-Slavism. You'll find it still as strong as it was in the time of the Czars. Once, during the Sixth Offensive, we were being dive-bombed at a river crossing and one of my stretcher bearers – a boy from Zagreb University – said quite simply: "Every bomb that falls here is one less on Russia." We are foreigners to them. They accept what we send them. They have no reason to feel particularly grateful. It is they who are fighting and dying. Some of our less sophisticated men get confused and think it is a matter of politics. I'm sure you won't make that mistake but I deliver this little lecture to everyone. There are no politics in war-time; just love of country and love of race – and the partisans know we belong to a different country and a different race. That's how misunderstandings sometimes arise.'

At this moment Brigadier Cape put his head in at the door and said: 'Joe, can you come in for a minute?'

'Study the map,' said Major Cattermole to Guy. 'Learn it. I'll be back soon.'

Guy was well instructed in military map-reading. He did as he was told, wondering where in that complicated terrain his own future lay.

Next door Cape sat at his table staring resentfully at a gold hunter watch, handsomely engraved on the back with a crown and inscription. 'You know all about this, of course, Joe?'

'Yes, I told Major Cernic to report it to you.'

'He was in a great state about it.'

'Can you blame him?'

'But what am I supposed to do?'

'Report it to London.'

'It's the hell of a thing to have happened just when the Jugs were beginning to trust us.'

'They'll never trust us as long as they know there's an emigré government in London. Properly handled this might be the opportunity for repudiating them.'

'There's no doubt it's genuine, I suppose?'

'None whatever.'

'Not a political move?'

'Not on our part. It's exactly what it purports to be – a presentation watch inscribed in London to Mihajlovic as Minister of War. A Serb brought it out, who was ostensibly coming to the partisans. Fortunately he got drunk at Algiers and showed it to a young American I know, who was passing through. He tipped me off, so the partisans arrested the agent as soon as he arrived.'

'He was going to have gone across? You know the odd thing about it is that it shows there must be a means of communication between Tito's chaps and Mihajlovic's.'

'Only through the enemy.'

'Damn,' said Cape, 'damn. I'd just as soon the fellow got his watch as have all this rumpus. What happened to the Serb?'

'He was dealt with.'

'This isn't soldiering as I was taught it,' said Cape.

Major Cattermole returned to Guy. 'Sorry to leave you. Just a routine matter. I'd pretty well finished my tutorial and the Brigadier is free to see you. He'll tell you where you are going and when.

'You are in for a unique experience, whatever it is. The partisans are a revelation – literally.'

When Major Cattermole spoke of the enemy he did so with the impersonal, professional hostility with which a surgeon might regard a malignant, operable growth; when he spoke of his comrades in arms it was something keener than loyalty, equally impersonal, a counterfeit almost of mystical love as portrayed by the sensual artists of the high baroque.

'Officers and men,' he proclaimed exultantly, 'share the same rations and quarters. And the women too. You may be surprised to find girls serving in the ranks beside their male comrades. Lying together, sometimes, for warmth, under the same blanket, but in absolute celibacy. Patriotic passion has entirely extruded sex. The girl partisans are something you will never have seen before. In fact, one of the medical officers told me that many of them had ceased to menstruate. Some were barely more than schoolchildren when they ran away to the mountains leaving their bourgeois families to collaborate with the enemy. I have seen spectacles of courage of which I should have been sceptical in the best authenticated classical text. Even when we have anaesthetics the girls often refuse to take them. I have seen them endure excruciating operations without flinching, sometimes breaking into song as the surgeon probed, in order to prove their manhood. Well, you will see for yourself. It is a transforming experience.'

Seven years previously J. Cattermole of All Souls had published *An Examination of Certain Redundances in Empirical Concepts*; a work popularly known as 'Cattermole's Redundances' and often described as 'seminal'. Since then he had been transformed.

Brigadier Cape's head appeared again at the door.

'Come on, Crouchback.' And Guy followed him next door.

'Glad to see you. You're the third Halberdier to join our out-fit. I'd gladly take all I can get. I think you know Frank de Souza. He's on the other side at the moment. I know you've spent the evening with our G2. You haven't got a parachute badge up.'

'I didn't qualify, sir.'

'Oh, I thought you did. Something wrong somewhere. Any-way, we've got two or three places now where we can land. Do you speak good Serbo-Croat?'

'Not a word. When I had my interview I was only asked about my Italian.'

'Well, oddly enough that isn't a disadvantage. We've had one or two chaps who spoke the language. Some seem to have joined up with the partisans. The others have been sent back with complaints of "incorrect" behaviour. The Jugs prefer to provide their interpreters – then they know just what our chaps are saying and who to. Suspicious lot of bastards. I suppose they have good reason to be. You've heard Joe Cattermole's piece about them. He's an enthusiast. Now I'll give you the other side of the picture. But remember Joe Cattermole's a first-class chap. He doesn't tell anyone, but he did absolutely splendidly over there. The Jugs love him and they don't love many of us. And Joe loves the Jugs, which is something more unusual still. But you have to take what he says with a grain of salt. I expect he told you about the partisans pinning down half a million men. The situation, as I see it, is rather different. The Germans are interested in only two things. Their com-munications with Greece and the defence of their flank against an allied landing in the Adriatic. Our information is that they will be pulling out of Greece this summer. Their road home has to be kept clear. There's nothing else they want in Jugo-slavia. When the Italians packed up, the Balkans were a total loss to them. No question now of cutting round to the Suez Canal. But they are afraid of a large-scale Anglo-American advance up to Vienna. The Americans very naturally prefer to land on the Côte d'Azur. But as long as there's any danger of an Adriatic landing the Germans have to keep a lot of men in Jugoslavia, and the Jugs, when they take time off from fighting one another, are quite a nuisance to them. The job of this mission is to keep the nuisance going with the few bits and pieces we are allowed.

'When the partisans talk about their "Offensives", you know, they are German offensives, not Jug. Whenever the Jugs get too much of a nuisance, the Germans make a sweep and clear them off, but they have never yet got the whole lot in the bag. And it looks more and more likely that they never will.

'Now, remember, we are soldiers not politicians. Our job is simply to do all we can to hurt the enemy. Neither you nor I are going to make his home in Jugoslavia after the war. How they choose to govern themselves is entirely their business. Keep clear of politics. That's the first rule of this mission.

'I shall be seeing you again before you move. I can't tell you at the moment where you'll be going or when. You won't find Bari a bad place to hang about in. Report to GSO2 every day. Enjoy yourself.'

Few foreigners visited Bari from the time of the Crusades until the fall of Mussolini. Few tourists, even the most assiduous, explored the Apulian coast. Bari contains much that should have attracted them; the old town full of Norman building, the bones of St Nicholas enshrined in silver; the new town spacious and commodious. But for centuries it lay neglected by all save native businessmen. Guy had never before set foot there.

Lately the place had achieved the unique, unsought distinction of being the only place in the Second World War to suffer from gas. In the first days of its occupation a ship full of 'mustard' blew up in the harbour, scattering its venom about the docks. Many of the inhabitants complained of sore throats, sore eyes, and blisters. They were told it was an unfamiliar, mild, epidemic disease of short duration. The people of Apulia are inured to such afflictions.

Now, early in 1944, the city had recovered the cosmopolitan, martial stir it enjoyed in the Middle Ages. Allied soldiers on short leave, some wearing ironically enough, the woven badge of the crusader's sword, teemed in its streets; wounded filled its hospitals; the staffs of numberless services took over the new, battered office-buildings which had risen as monuments to the

Corporative State. Small naval craft adorned the shabby harbour. Bari could not rival the importance of Naples, that prodigious, improvised factory of war. Its agile and ingenious criminal class consisted chiefly of small boys. Few cars flew the pennons of high authority. Few officers over the rank of brigadier inhabited the outlying villas. Foggia drew the *magistras* of the Air Force. Nothing very august flourished in Bari, but there were dingy buildings occupied by Balkan and Zionist emissaries; by a melancholic English officer who performed a part not then known as 'disc-jockey', providing the troops with the tunes it was thought they wished to hear; by a euphoric Scotch officer surrounded by books with which he hoped to inculcate a respect for English culture among those who could read that language; by the editors of little papers, more directly propagandist and printed in a variety of languages; by the agents of competing intelligence systems; by a group of Russians whose task was to relabel tins of American rations in bold Cyrillic characters, proclaiming them the produce of the USSR, before they were dropped from American aeroplanes over beleaguered gangs of Communists; by Italians, even, who were being coached in the arts of local democratic government. The allies had lately much impeded their advance by the destruction of Monte Cassino, but the price of this sacrilege was being paid by the infantry of the front line. It did not trouble the peace-loving and unambitious officers who were glad to settle in Bari.

They constituted a little world of officers – some young and seedy, some old and spruce – sequestered from the responsibilities and vexations of command. Such men of other rank as were sometimes seen in the arcaded streets were drivers, orderlies, policemen, clerks, servants, and sentries.

In this limbo Guy fretted for more than a week while February blossomed into March. He had left Italy four and a half years ago. He had then taken leave of the crusader whom the people called 'il santo inglese'. He had laid his hand on the sword that had never struck the infidel. He wore the medal which had hung round the neck of his brother, Gervase, when the sniper had picked him off on his way up to the line in Flanders. In his heart he felt stirring the despair in which his brother, Ivo, had starved himself to death. Half an hour's scramble on the beach near Dakar; an ignominious rout in Crete. That had been his war.

Every day he reported to headquarters. 'No news yet,' they said. 'Communications have not been satisfactory for the last few days. The Air Force aren't playing until they know what's going on over there.'

'Enjoy yourself,' Brigadier Cape had said. That would not have been the order of Ritchie-Hook. There was no biffing in Bari.

Guy wandered as a tourist about the streets of the old town. He sat in the club and the hotel. He met old acquaintances and made new ones. Leisure, bonhomie, and futility had him in thrall.

After a brief absence Lieutenant Padfield reappeared in the company of a large and celebrated English composer whom UNRRA had mysteriously imported. On the Sunday they drove Guy out on the road south to visit the beehive dwellings where the descendants of Athenian colonists still lived their independent lives. Near by was a small, ancient town where an Italian family had set up an illicit restaurant. They did not deal in paper currency but accepted petrol, cigarettes, and medical supplies in exchange for dishes of fresh fish cooked with olive oil and white truffles and garlic.

The Lieutenant left his car in the piazza before the locked church. There were other service vehicles there, and when they reached the house on the water-front they found it full of English and Americans; among them Brigadier Cape and his homely hospital nurse.

'I haven't seen you,' said the Brigadier, 'and you haven't seen me,' but the nurse knew all about the musician, and after luncheon insisted on being introduced. They all walked together along the quay. Guy and the Brigadier a pace behind the other three. This place had been left untouched by the advancing and retreating armies. The inhabitants were taking their siestas. To seaward the calm Adriatic lapped against the old stones; in the harbour the boats lay motionless. Guy remarked, tritely enough, that the war seemed far away.

The Brigadier was in ruminative mood. He had eaten largely;

other pleasures lay ahead. 'War,' he said. 'When I was at Sandhurst no one talked about war. We learned about it, of course – a school subject like Latin or geography; something to write exam papers about. No bearing on life. I went into the army because I liked horses, and I've spent four years in and out of a stinking, noisy tank. Now I've got a couple of gongs and a game leg and all I want is quiet. Not *peace*, mind. There's nothing wrong with war except the fighting. I don't mind betting that after five years of peace we shall all look back on Bari as the best days of our life.'

Suddenly the musician turned and said: 'Crouchback has the death wish.'

'Have you?' asked the Brigadier with a show of disapproval.

'Have I?' said Guy.

'I recognized it the moment we met,' said the musician. 'I should not mention it now except that Padfield was so liberal with the wine.'

'Death wish?' said the Brigadier. 'I don't like the sound of that. Time we were off, Betty.'

He took the nurse's arm and limped back towards the piazza. Guy saluted as Halberdiers did. The Lieutenant tipped his cap in a gesture that was part benediction, part a wave of farewell. The musician bowed to the nurse.

Then he turned towards the open sea and performed a little parody of himself conducting an orchestra, saying: 'The death wish. The death wish. On a day like this.'

Two days later, when Guy reported, the Brigadier asked: 'How's the death wish today? There's an aeroplane to take you into Croatia tonight. Joe will give you the details.'

Guy had made no preparations for this journey except to prepare himself. He walked to the old town where he found a dilapidated romanesque church where a priest was hearing confessions. Guy waited, took his turn and at length said: 'Father, I wish to die.'

'Yes. How many times?'

'Almost all the time.'

The obscure figure behind the grill leant nearer. 'What was it you wished to do?'

'To die.'

'Yes. You have attempted suicide?'

'No.'

'Of what, then, are you accusing yourself? To wish to die is quite usual today. It may even be a very good disposition. You do not accuse yourself of despair?'

'No, father; presumption. I am not fit to die.'

'There is no sin there. This is a mere scruple. Make an act of contrition for all the unrepented sins of your past life.'

After the Absolution he said: 'Are you a foreigner?'

'Yes.'

'Can you spare a few cigarettes?'

In Westminster Cathedral at almost the same time Virginia made her first confession. She told everything; fully, accurately, without extenuation or elaboration. The recital of half a life-time's mischief took less than five minutes 'Thank God for your good and humble confession,' the priest said. She was shriven. The same words were said to her as were said to Guy. The same grace was offered. Little Trimmer stirred as she knelt at the side-altar and pronounced the required penance; then she returned to her needle-work.

That evening she said to Uncle Peregrine, as she had said before: 'Why do people make such a *fuss*? It's all so easy. But it is rather satisfactory to feel that I shall never again have anything serious to confess as long as I live.'

Uncle Peregrine made no comment. He did not credit himself with any peculiar gift of discernment of spirits. Most things which most people did or said puzzled him, if he gave them any thought. He preferred to leave such problems in higher hands.

2

SUMMER came swiftly and sweetly over the wooded hills and rich valleys of Northern Croatia. Bridges were down and the rails up on the little single-track railway-line that had once led from Begoy to Zagreb. The trunk road to the Balkans ran east. There the German lorries streamed night and day without interruption and the German garrisons squatted waiting the order to retire. Here, in an island of 'liberated territory' twenty miles by ten, the peasants worked their fields as they had always done, subject only to the requisitions of the partisans; the priests said Mass in their churches subject only to the partisan security police who lounged at the back and listened for political implications in their sermons. In one Mohammedan village the mosque had been burned by Ustachi in the first days of Croatian independence. In Begoy itself the same gang, Hungarian trained, had blown up the Orthodox church and desecrated the cemetery. But there had been little fighting. As the Italians withdrew the Ustachi followed and the partisans crept in from the hills and imposed their rule. More of their fellows joined them, slipping in small, ragged bodies through the German lines; there were shortages of food but no famine. There was a tithe levied but no looting. Partisans obeyed orders and it was vital to them to keep the good-will of the peasants.

The bourgeois had all left Begoy with the retreating garrison. The shops in the little high street were empty or used as billets. The avenues of lime had been roughly felled for firewood. But there were still visible the hall-marks of the Habsburg Empire. There were thermal springs, and at the end of the preceding century the town had been laid out modestly as a spa. Hot water still ran in the bath house. Two old gardeners still kept some order in the ornamental grounds. The graded paths, each with a 'view-point', the ruins of a seat and of a kiosk, where once invalids had taken their prescribed exercise, still ran through boskage between the partisan bivouacs. The circle of villas in the outskirts of the town abandoned precipitately by their owners had been allotted by the partisans to various official purposes. In the largest of these the Russian mission lurked invisibly.

Two miles from the town lay the tract of flat grazing land which was used as an airfield. Four English airmen had charge of it. They occupied one side of the quadrangle of timbered buildings which comprised a neighbouring farm-house. The military mission lived opposite, separated by a dung heap. Both bodies were tirelessly cared for by three Montenegran war-widows; they were guarded by partisan sentries and attended by an 'interpreter' named Bakic, who had been a political exile in New York in the thirties and picked up some English there. Both missions had their wireless-sets with which to communicate with their several headquarters. A sergeant signaller and an orderly comprised Guy's staff.

The officer whom Guy succeeded had fallen into a melancholy and was recalled for medical attention; he had left by the aeroplane that brought Guy. They had had ten minutes' conversation in the light of the flare-path while a party of girls unloaded the stores.

'The comrades are a bloody-minded lot of bastards,' he had said. 'Don't keep any copies of signals in clear. Bakic reads everything. And don't say anything in front of him you don't want repeated.'

The Squadron Leader remarked that this officer had been 'an infernal nuisance lately. Suffering from persecution mania if you ask me. Wrong sort of chap to send to a place like this.'

Joe Cattermole had fully instructed Guy in his duties. They were not exacting. At this season aeroplanes were coming in to land at Begoy almost every week, bringing, besides supplies, cargoes of unidentified Slavs in uniform, who disappeared on landing and joined their comrades of the higher command. They took back seriously wounded partisans and allied airmen who had 'baled out' of their damaged bombers returning from Germany to Italy. There were also 'drops' of stores, some in parachutes – petrol and weapons; the less vulnerable loads, clothing and rations – falling free as bombs at various points in the territory. All this traffic was the business of the Squadron Leader. He fixed the times of the sorties. He guided the machines in. Guy's duty was to transmit reports on the military situation. For these he was entirely dependent on the partisan 'general staff'. This body, together with an old lawyer from Split who bore the title of 'Minister of the Interior', consisted of the General and the Commissar, veterans of the International Brigade in Spain, and a second-in-command who was a regular officer of the Royal Jugoslavian Army. They had their own fluent interpreter, a lecturer in English, he claimed, from Zagreb University. The bulletins dealt only in success; a village had been raided; a fascist supply wagon had been way-laid; mostly they enumerated the partisan bands who had found their way into the Begoy area and put themselves under the command of the 'Army of Croatia'. These were always lacking in essential equipment and Guy was asked to supply them. Thus the General and the Commissar steered a delicate course between the alternating and conflicting claims that the partisans were destitute and that they maintained in the field a large, efficient modern army. The reinforcements excused the demands.

The general staff were nocturnal by habit. All the morning they slept. In the afternoon they ate and smoked and idled; at sunset they came to life. There was a field telephone between them and the airfield. Once or twice a week it would ring and Bakic would announce: 'General wants us right away.' Then he and Guy would stumble along the rutted lane to a conference which took place sometimes by oil-lamp, sometimes under an electric bulb which flickered and expired as often as in the head-quarters at Bari. An exorbitant list of requirements would be presented; sometimes medical stores, the furniture of a whole hospital with detailed lists of drugs and instruments which would take days to encipher and transmit; field artillery; light tanks; typewriters; they particularly wanted an aeroplane of their own. Guy would not attempt to dispute them. He would point out that the allied armies in Italy were themselves engaged in a war. He would promise to transmit their wishes. He would then edit them and ask for what seemed reasonable. The re-sponse would be unpredictable. Sometimes there would be a drop of ancient rifles captured in Abyssinia, sometimes boots for half a company, sometimes there was a jack-pot and the night sky rained machine guns, ammunition, petrol, dehydrated food, socks, and books of popular education. The partisans made a precise account of everything received, which Guy transmitted. Nothing was ever pilfered. The discrepancy be-tween what was asked and what was given deprived Guy of any sense he might have felt of vicarious benefaction. The cor-diality or strict formality of his reception depended on the size of the last drop. Once, after a jack-pot, he was offered a glass of Slivovic.

In mid-April a new element appeared.

Guy had finished breakfast and was attempting to memorize a Serbo-Croat vocabulary with which he had been provided, when Bakic announced:

'Dere's de Jews outside.'

'What Jews?'

'Dey been dere two hour, maybe more. I said to wait.'

'What do they want?'

'Dey're Jews. I reckon dey always want sometin'. Dey want see de British captain. I said to wait.'

'Well, ask them to come in.'

'Dey can't come in. Why, dere's more'n a hundred of dem.'

Guy went out and found the farmyard and the lane beyond thronged. There were some children in the crowd, but most seemed old, too old to be parents, for they were unnaturally aged by their condition. Everyone in Begoy, except the peasant women, was in rags, but the partisans kept regimental barbers and there was a kind of dignity about their tattered uniforms. The Jews were grotesque in their remnants of bourgeois civility. They showed little trace of racial kinship. There were Semites among them, but the majority were fair, snub-nosed, high cheek-boned, the descendants of Slav tribes judaized long after the Dispersal. Few of them, probably, now worshipped the God of Israel in the manner of their ancestors.

A low chatter broke out as Guy appeared. Then three leaders came forward, a youngish woman of better appearance than the rest and two crumpled old men. The woman asked him if he spoke Italian, and when he nodded introduced her companions – a grocer from Mostar, a lawyer from Zagreb – and herself, a woman of Fiume married to a Hungarian engineer.

Here Bakic roughly interrupted in Serbo-Croat and the three fell humbly and hopelessly silent. He said to Guy: 'I tell dese people dey better talk Slav. I will speak for dem.'

The woman said: 'I only speak German and Italian.'

Guy said: 'We will speak Italian. I can't ask you all in. You three had better come and leave the others outside.'

Bakic scowled. A chatter broke out in the crowd. Then the

three with timid little bows crossed the threshold, carefully wiping their dilapidated boots before treading the rough board floor of the interior.

'I shan't want you, Bakic.'

The spy went out to bully the crowd, hustling them out of the farmyard into the lane.

There were only two chairs in Guy's living-room. He took one and invited the woman to use the other. The men huddled behind her and then began to prompt her. They spoke to one another in a mixture of German and Serbo-Croat; the lawyer knew a little Italian; enough to make him listen anxiously to all the woman said, and to interrupt. The grocer gazed steadily at the floor and seemed to take no interest in the proceedings. He was there because he commanded respect and trust among the waiting crowd. He had been in a big way of business with branch stores throughout all the villages of Bosnia.

With a sudden vehemence the woman, Mme Kanyi, shook off her advisers and began her story. The people outside, she explained, were the survivors of an Italian concentration camp on the island of Rab. Most were Jugo-Slav nationals, but some, like herself, were refugees from Central Europe. She and her husband were on their way to Australia in 1939; their papers were in order; he had a job waiting for him in Brisbane. Then they had been caught by the war.

When the King fled, the Ustachi began massacring Jews. The Italians rounded them up and took them to the Adriatic. When Italy surrendered, the partisans for a few weeks held the coast. They brought the Jews to the mainland, conscripted all who seemed capable of useful work, and imprisoned the rest. Her husband had been attached to the army headquarters as electrician. Then the Germans moved in; the partisans fled, taking the Jews with them. And here they were, a hundred and eight of them, half starving in Begoy.

Guy said: 'Well, I congratulate you.'

Mme Kanyi looked up quickly to see if he were mocking her, found that he was not, and continued to regard him now with sad, blank wonder.

'After all,' he continued, 'you're among friends.'

'Yes,' she said, too doleful for irony, 'we heard that the

British and Americans were friends of the partisans. It is true, then?'

'Of course it's true. Why do you suppose I am here?'

'It is not true that the British and Americans are coming to take over the country?'

'First I've heard of it.'

'But it is well known that Churchill is a friend of the Jews.'

'I'm sorry, signora, but I simply do not see what the Jews have got to do with it.'

'But we are Jews. One hundred and eight of us.'

'Well, what do you expect me to do about that?'

'We want to go to Italy. We have relations there, some of us. There is an organization at Bari. My husband and I had our papers to go to Brisbane. Only get us to Italy and we shall be no more trouble. We cannot live as we are here. When winter comes we shall all die. We hear aeroplanes almost every night. Three aeroplanes could take us all. We have no luggage left.'

'Signora, those aeroplanes are carrying essential war equipment, they are taking out wounded and officials. I'm very sorry you are having a hard time, but so are plenty of other people in this country. It won't last long now. We've got the Germans on the run. I hope by Christmas to be in Zagreb.'

'We must say nothing against the partisans?'

'Not to me. Look here, let me give you a cup of cocoa. Then I have work to do.'

He went to the window and called to the orderly for cocoa and biscuits. While it was coming the lawyer said in English: We were better in Rab.' Then suddenly all three broke into a chatter of polyglot complaint, about their house, about their property which had been stolen, about their rations. If Churchill knew he would have them sent to Italy. Guy said: 'If it was not for the partisans you would now be in the hands of the Nazis,' but that word had no terror for them now. They shrugged hopelessly.

One of the widows brought in a tray of cups and a tin of biscuits. 'Help yourselves,' said Guy.

'How many, please, may we take?'

'Oh, two or three.'

With tense self-control each took three biscuits, watching the others to see they did not disgrace the meeting by greed. The grocer whispered to Mme Kanyi and she explained: 'He says will you excuse him if he keeps one for a friend?' The man had tears in his eyes as he snuffed his cocoa; once he had handled sacks of the stuff.

They rose to go. Mme Kanyi made a last attempt to attract his sympathy. 'Will you please come and see the place where they have put us?'

'I am sorry, signora, it simply is not my business. I am a military liaison officer, nothing more.'

They thanked him humbly and profusely for the cocoa and left the house. Guy saw them in the farmyard disputing. The men seemed to think Mme Kanyi had mishandled the affair. Then Bakic hustled them out. Guy saw the crowd close round them and then move off down the lane in a babel of explanation and reproach.

Full summer came in May. Guy took to walking every afternoon in the public gardens. These were quite unscathed. The partisans showed some solicitude for them, perhaps at the instigation of the 'Minister of the Interior', and had cut a new bed in the principal lawn in the shape of a five-pointed star. There were winding paths, specimen trees, statuary, a bandstand, a pond with carp and exotic ducks, the ornamental cages of what had once been a miniature zoo. The gardeners kept rabbits in one, fowls in another, a red squirrel in a third. Guy never saw a partisan there. The ragged, swaggering girls in battle-dress, with their bandages and medals and girdles of hand-grenades, who were everywhere in the streets, arm-in-arm, singing patriotic songs, kept clear of these gardens where not long ago rheumatics crept with their parasols and light romantic novels. Perhaps they were out of bounds.

The only person Guy ever saw was Mme Kanyi whom he saluted and passed by.

'Keep clear of civilians' was one of the precepts of the mission.

Later that month Guy noticed an apprehensive air at head

uarters. General and Commissar were almost ingratiating. He
was told there were no military developments. No demands
were made. On a bonfire in the garden quantities of papers
were being consumed. He was for the second time offered a
glass of slivovic. Guy had not to seek for an explanation of this
new amiability. He had already received news from Bari that
Tito's forces at Dvrar had been dispersed by German parachutists and that he and his staff, the British, American, and
Russian missions had been rescued by aeroplane and taken to
Italy. He wondered whether the General knew that he knew.
A fortnight passed. Tito, he was informed, had set up his headquarters under allied protection on Vis. The General and the
Commissar resumed their former manner. It was during this
period of renewed coldness that he received a signal: *UNRRA
research team requires particulars displaced persons. Report
any your district*. This phrase, which was to be the keywords
of the decade, was as yet unfamiliar.

'What are "displaced persons"?' he asked the Squadron
Leader.

'Aren't we all?'

He replied: *Displaced persons not understood*, and received:
Friendly nationals moved by enemy. He replied: *One hundred
and eight Jews*.

Next day: *Expedite details Jews names nationalities conditions*.

Bakic grudgingly admitted that he knew where they were
quartered, in a school near the ruined Orthodox church. Bakic
led him there. They found the house in half darkness, for the
glass had all gone from the windows and been replaced with
bits of wood and tin collected from other ruins. There was
no furniture. The inmates for the most part lay huddled in little
nests of straw and rags. As Guy and Bakic entered a dozen
or more barely visible figures roused themselves, got to their
feet and retreated towards the walls and darker corners, some
raising their fists in salute, others hugging bundles of small
possessions. Bakic called one of them forward and questioned
him roughly in Serbo-Croat.

'He says de others gone for firewood. Dese one's sick. What
you want me tell em?'

'Say that the Americans in Italy want to help them. I have come to make a report on what they need.'

The announcement brought them volubly to life. They crowded round, were joined by others from other parts of the house until Guy stood surrounded by thirty or more all asking for things, asking frantically for whatever came first to mind – a needle, a lamp, butter, soap, a pillow; for remote dreams – a passage to Tel Aviv, an aeroplane to New York, news of a sister last seen in Bucharest, a bed in a hospital.

'You see dey all want somepin different, and dis isn't a half of dem.'

For twenty minutes or so Guy remained, overpowered, half-suffocated. Then he said: 'Well, I think we've seen enough. I shan't get much further in this crowd. Before we can do anything we've got to get them organized. They must make out their own list. I wish we could find that Hungarian woman who talked Italian. She made some sense.'

Bakic inquired and reported: 'She don't live here. Her husband works on the electric light so dey got a house to demselves in de park.'

'Well, let's get out of here and try to find her.'

They left the house and emerged into the fresh air and sunshine and singing companies of young warriors. Guy breathed gratefully. Very high above them a huge force of minute shining bombers hummed across the sky in perfect formation on its daily route from Foggia to somewhere east of Vienna.

'There they go again,' he said. 'I wouldn't care to be underneath when they unload.'

It was one of his duties to impress the partisans with the might of their allies, with the great destruction and slaughter on distant fields which would one day, somehow, bring happiness here where they seemed forgotten. He delivered a little statistical lecture to Bakic about blockbusters and pattern bombing.

They found the Kanyis' house. It was a former potting-shed hidden by shrubs from the public park. A single room, an earth floor, a bed, a table, a dangling electric globe; compared with the schoolhouse, a place of delicious comfort and privacy

Guy did not see the interior that afternoon for Mme Kanyi was hanging washing on a line outside, and she led him away from the hut, saying that her husband was asleep. 'He was up all night and did not come home until nearly midday. There was a breakdown at the plant.'

'Yes,' said Guy, 'I had to go to bed in the dark at nine.'

'It is always breaking. It is quite worn out. He cannot get the proper fuel. And all the cables are rotten. The General does not understand and blames him for everything. Often he is out all night.'

Guy dismissed Bakic and talked about UNRRA. Mme Kanyi did not react in the same way as the wretches in the schoolhouse; she was younger and better fed and therefore more hopeless. 'What can they do for us?' she asked. 'How can they? Why should they? We are of no importance. You told us so yourself. You must see the Commissar,' she said. 'Otherwise he will think there is some plot going on. We can do nothing, accept nothing, without the Commissar's permission. You will only make more trouble for us.'

'But at least you can produce the list they want in Bari.'

'Yes, if the Commissar says so. Already my husband has been questioned about why I have talked to you. He was very much upset. The General was beginning to trust him. Now they think he is connected with the British, and last night the lights failed when there was an important conference. It is better that you do nothing except through the Commissar. I know these people. My husband works with them.'

'You have rather a privileged position with them.'

'Do you believe that for that reason I do not want to help my people?'

Some such thoughts had passed through Guy's mind. Now he paused, looked at Mme Kanyi and was ashamed. 'No,' he said.

'I suppose it would be natural to think so,' said Mme Kanyi gravely. 'It is not always true that suffering makes people unselfish. But sometimes it is.'

That evening Guy was summoned to general headquarters. A full committee, including even the Minister of the Interior, sat grimly to meet him. Their manner was of a court martial rather than a conference of allies. Bakic stood in the background and the young interpreter took over.

Guy would not have been surprised had they left him standing, but the second-in-command rose, brought his chair round the table for Guy, and himself stood beside the interpreter.

Kanyi's electric plant was again in difficulties. A single pressure-lamp lit the flat faces and round, cropped heads. All three military men were younger than Guy but their skin was weathered by exposure. All smoked captured Macedonian cigarettes and the air was heavy. The second-in-command offered Guy a cigarette which he refused.

The Minister of the Interior had a short white beard and hooded eyes that lacked shrewdness. He did not know why he was there. He did not know why he was in Begoy at all. He had enjoyed a sharp little practice in Split, had meddled before the war in anti-Serbian politics, had found himself in an Italian prison, had been let out when the partisans briefly 'liberated' the coast, had been swept up with them in the retreat. They gave him a room and rations and this odd title 'Minister of the Interior'. Why?

The interpeter spoke. 'The General wishes to know why you went to visit the Jews today?'

'I was acting on orders from my headquarters.'

'The General does not understand how the Jews are the concern of the Military Mission.'

Guy attempted an explanation of the aims and organization of UNRRA. He did not know a great deal about them and had no great respect for the members he had met, but he did his best. General and Commissar conferred: Then: 'The Commissar says if those measures will take place after the war, what are they doing now?'

Guy described the need for planning. UNRRA must know what quantities of seed-corn, bridge-building materials, rolling-stock and so on were needed to put ravaged countries on their feet.

'The Commissar does not understand how this concerns the Jews.'

Guy spoke of the millions of displaced persons all over Europe who must be returned to their homes.

'The Commissar says that is an internal matter.'

'So is bridge-building.'

'The Commissar says bridge-building is a good thing.'

'So is helping displaced persons.'

Commissar and General conferred. 'The General says any questions of internal affairs should be addressed to the Minister of the Interior.'

'Tell him that I am very sorry if I have acted incorrectly. I merely wished to save everyone trouble. I was sent a question by my superiors. I did my best to answer it in the simplest way. May I now request the Minister of the Interior to furnish me with a list of the Jews?'

'The General is glad that you understand that you have acted incorrectly.'

'Will the Minister of the Interior be so kind as to make the list for me?'

'The General does not understand why a list is needed.'

And so it began again. They talked for an hour. At length Guy lost patience and said: 'Very well. Am I to report that you refuse all cooperation with UNRRA?'

'We will cooperate in all necessary matters.'

'But with regard to the Jews?'

'It must be decided by the Central Government whether that is a necessary matter.'

At length they parted. On the way home Bakic said: 'Dey mighty sore with you, captain. What for you make trouble with dese Jews?'

'Orders,' said Guy, and before going to bed drafted a signal:

Jews condition now gravely distressed may become desperate. Local authorities uncooperative. Only hope higher level.

Next morning he received in clear:

P/302/B Personal for Crouchback. Message begins Virginia gave bath son today both well Crouchback message end. Kindly note personal messages of great importance only accepted for transmission Gilpin for brigadier.

'Query "bath",' Guy told his signaller.

Three days later he received:

Personal for Crouchback. Our P/302/B for bath read birch. This not regarded adequate importance priority personal message. See previous signal Gilpin for brigadier.

'Query "birch".'

At length he received: *For birch read birth repeat birth. Congratulations Cape.*

'Send in clear Personal Message Crouchback Bourne Mansions Carlisle Place London Glad both well Crouchback. Message ends Personal to brigadier thank you for congratulations.'

Virginia's son was born on June 4th, the day on which all allied armies entered Rome.

'An omen,' said Uncle Peregrine.

He was talking to his nephew, Arthur Box-Bender, in Bellamy's where he had taken refuge while his flat was overrun by doctor, nurse, and his niece Angela.

The club was rather empty these days. Most of the younger members had moved to the south coast waiting for the day when they would cross the channel. There was no air of heightened expectancy among the older members. They were scarcely aware of the impending invasion. Social convention, stronger than any regulations of 'security', forbade its discussion.

Box-Bender could not regard the birth of a nephew as happy. He had been disconcerted by Guy's marriage. He had counted the months of pregnancy. He regarded the whole thing as a middle-aged aberration for which Guy was paying an unnaturally high price to the eventual detriment of his own children's inheritance. 'Omen of what?' he asked rather crossly. 'Do you expect the boy to become Pope?'

'The idea had not occurred to me. Awfully few of us have become priests in the last generation or two. In any case I should hardly live to see his election. Now you suggest it, though, it is a pleasant speculation – an Englishman and a Crouchback in the chair of Peter – just about at the turn of the century, I suppose.

'Virginia has taken to religion in an extraordinary way

during the last few weeks. Not exactly piety, you know; gossip.
The clergy seem to like her awfully. They keep coming to call
as they never did on me. She makes them laugh. They seem
to prefer that to good works – though, of course, she hasn't
been in a state for them anyway. But she's a much jollier sort
of convert than people like Eloise Plessington.'

'That I can well imagine.'

'Angela has been a great help. Of course you must know all
about child-birth. It has all been rather a surprise to me. I had
never given it much thought but I had supposed that women
just went to bed and that they had a sort of stomach ache and
groaned a bit and that then there was a baby. It isn't at all like
that.'

'I always moved out when Angela had babies.'

'I was awfully interested. I moved out at the end but the
beginning was quite a surprise – almost unnerving.'

'I am sure nothing ever unnerves you, Peregrine.'

'No. Perhaps "unnerving" was not the right word.'

In HOO HQ there was stagnation in the depleted offices.
The more bizarre figures remained – the witch-doctor and the
man who ate grass – but the planners and the combatants had
melted away. In the perspective of 'Overlord', that one huge
hazardous offensive operation on which, it seemed, the fate of
the world depended, smaller adventures receded to infinitesimal
importance.

'Brides in the bath' Whale ordered not a holocaust, but a
relegation to unsounded depths of obscurity in the most secret
archives, of mountains of files, each propounding in detail
some desperate enterprise, each bearing a somewhat whimsical
title, all once hotly debated and amended, all now quite without significance.

Ian Kilbannock, without regret, realized that he had passed
the zenith of his powers and must decline. He was already
negotiating for employment as a special correspondent in
Normandy. That was near home and the centre of interest, but
competition was keen. Ian had his future professional career
to consider. His brief experience as a racing correspondent
seemed irrelevant to the zeitgeist. The time had come, Ian be-

lieved, to establish himself as something more serious. There would be infinite scope, he foresaw, during the whole length of his life, for first-hand war 'revelations'.

The Adriatic was suggested and considered. Burma had been offered and evaded. It was plain from the reports he saw that it was no place for Ian. It might, on the other hand, be just the place for Trimmer.

'All Trimmer reports negative, sir,' Ian reported to General Whale.

'Yes. Where is he now?'

'San Francisco. He's been right across the country. He's flopped everywhere. It isn't really his fault. He went too late. The Americans have heroes of their own now. Besides, you know, they haven't a fully developed consciousness of class. They can't see Trimmer as the proletarian portent. They see him as a typical British officer.'

'Haven't they seen the fellow's hair? I don't mean the way it's cut. The way it grows. *That's* proletarian enough for them, surely?'

'They don't understand that kind of thing. No, sir, he's been a flop in America and he'd be worse in Canada. As I see it we can only keep him moving west. I don't think he ought to come back to the UK at the moment. There are reasons. You might call them compassionate grounds.'

'There's a bigger problem on our hands – General Ritchie-Hook. He's had a blood row with Monty and is out of work and keeps bothering the Chief. I don't quite see why we should be regarded as responsible for him. Ritchie-Hook and Trimmer – why should we be held responsible for them?'

'Do you think they could go as a pair and impress the loyal Indians?'

'No.'

'Nor do I. Not Ritchie-Hook, certainly. They'd soon stop being loyal if he had a go at them.'

'There's Australia.'

'For Trimmer that would be worse than America.'

'Oh, for God's sake settle it yourself. I'm sick of the man.'

General Whale, too, knew he had passed the zenith of his powers and from now on could only decline. There had been a delirious episode when he had helped drive numerous Canadians to their death at Dieppe. He had helped plan greater enterprises which had come to nothing. Now he was where he had started in his country's 'finest hour', with negligible powers of mischief. He occupied the same room, he was served by the same immediate staff as in the years of expansion. But his legions were lost to him.

There was stagnation at Ludovic's station, also. The staff-captain remained. The instructors had been recalled. No new clients appeared for the parachute course. But Ludovic was content.

He employed a typist in Scotland. He had chosen her because she seemed the most remote from enemy action of any of those who offered their services in the *Times Literary Supplement*. Throughout the winter he had sent her a weekly parcel of manuscript and received in return two typed copies in separate envelopes. She acknowledged the receipt of each parcel by postcard but there was a four-day interval during which Ludovic suffered deep qualms of anxiety. Much was pilfered from the railways in those days but not, as things happened, Ludovic's novel. Now at the beginning of June he had it all complete, two piles of laced and paper-bound sections. He ordered Fido to basket and settled down to read the last chapter, not to correct misprints, for he wrote clearly and the typist was competent, not to polish or revise, for the work seemed to him perfect (as in a sense it was), but for the sheer enjoyment of his own performance.

Admirers of his *pensées* (and they were many) would not have recognized the authorship of this book. It was a very gorgeous, almost gaudy, tale of romance and high drama set, as his experience with Sir Ralph Brompton well qualified him to set it, in the diplomatic society of the previous decade. The characters and their equipment were seen as Ludovic in his own ambiguous position had seen them, more brilliant than reality. The plot was Shakespearean in its elaborate improbability. The dialogue could never have issued from human lips, the scenes of passion were capable of bringing a blush to readers of either sex and every age. But it was not an old-fashioned book. Had he known it, half a dozen other English writers, averting themselves sickly from privations of war and apprehensions of the social consequences of the peace, were even then severally and secretly, unknown to one another, to Everard Spruce, to Coney, and to Frankie, composing or preparing to compose books which would turn from the drab alleys of the thirties into the odorous gardens of a recent past transformed and illuminated by disordered memory and imagination. Ludovic in the solitude of his post was in the movement.

Nor was it for all its glitter a cheerful book. Melancholy suffused its pages and deepened towards the close.

So far as any character could be said to have an origin in the world of reality, the heroine was the author. Lady Marmaduke Transept (that was the name which Ludovic had recklessly bestowed on her) was Lord Marmaduke's second wife. He was an ambassador. She was extravagantly beautiful, clever, doomed; passionless only towards Lord Marmaduke; ambitious for everything except his professional success. If the epithet could properly be used of anyone so splendidly caparisoned, Lady Marmaduke was a bitch. Ludovic had known from the start that she must die in the last chapter. He had made no plans. Often in the weeks of composition he had wondered, almost idly, what would be the end of her. He waited to see, as he might have sat in a seat at the theatre watching the antics of players over whom he had no control.

As Ludovic read the last pages he realized that the whole book had been the preparation for Lady Marmaduke's death – a protracted, ceremonious killing like that of a bull in the ring. Except that there was no violence. He had feared sometimes that his heroine might be immured in a cave or left to drift in an open boat. These were chimeras. Lady Marmaduke, in the manner of an earlier and happier age, fell into a decline. Her disease was painless and unspecified. Under Ludovic's heavy arm she languished, grew thinner, transparent, the rings slipped from her fingers among the rich covering of her chaise-longue as the light faded on the distant, delectable mountains. He had hesitated in his choice of title, toying with many recondite allusions from his recent reading. Now with decision

he wrote in large letters at the head of the first page: THE
DEATH WISH.

Fido in his basket discerned his master's emotion, broke
orders to share it, leaped to Ludovic's stout thighs, and remained there unrebuked, gazing up with eyes of adoration that
were paler and more prominent than Ludovic's own.

'What I long to know,' said Kerstie, 'is what went on between Guy and Virginia after she settled in Carlisle Place.
After all there was a good month before her figure began
to go.'

'It's not a thing I should care to ask her,' said Ian.

'I don't think I can now. We made it up all right after our
tiff – it's no good *keeping things up* ever, is it? – but there's
been a coldness.'

'Why are you so keen to know?'

'Aren't you?'

'There's been a coldness between me and Virginia for years.'

'Who was there this evening?'

'Quite a salon. Perdita had brought Everard Spruce. There
was someone I didn't know called Lady Plessington and a
priest. It was all quite gay except for the midwife who kept
trying to show us the baby. Virginia can't bear the sight of it.
In a novel or a film the baby ought to make Virginia a changed
character. It hasn't. Have you noticed that she always calls it
"it", never "he". She calls the midwife "Jenny". It was always
"Sister Jenkins" in the days before the birth. They get on all
right. Old Peregrine speaks of the child as "Gervase". They've
had it christened already, as Catholics do for some reason.
When he asks how Gervase is, Virginia doesn't seem to cotton
on. "Oh, you mean the baby. Ask Jenny." '

When Virginia's baby was ten days old and the news was
all of the Normandy landings, the dingy tranquillity which
enveloped London was disturbed. Flying bombs appeared in
the sky, unseemly little caricatures of aeroplanes, which droned
smokily over the chimney tops, suddenly fell silent, dropped
out of sight and exploded dully. Day and night they came at
frequent irregular intervals, striking at haphazard far and near.

It was something quite other than the battle scene of the blitz with its drama of attack and defence; its earth-shaking concentrations of destruction and roaring furnaces; its respites when the sirens sounded the All Clear. No enemy was risking his own life up there. It was as impersonal as a plague, as though the city were infested with enormous, venomous insects. Spirits in Bellamy's, as elsewhere, had soared in the old days when Turtle's had gone up in flames and Air Marshal Beech had taken cover under the billiard table. Now there were glum faces. The machines could not be heard in the bar but the tall windows of the coffee-room (cross-laced with sticking plaster) fronted St James's Street. All heads were turned towards them and a silence would fall when a motor bicycle passed. Job stood fast at his post in the porter's lodge, but his sang-froid required more frequent stimulation. Members who had no particular duties in London began to disperse. Elderberry and Box-Bender decided it was time they attended to local business in their constituencies.

General Whale made an unprecedented move to the air-raid shelter. It had been constructed at great expense, wired, air-conditioned, and never once used. It had been a convention of HOO HQ that no attention was paid to raid warnings. Now General Whale had a bed made there and spent his nights as well as his days underground.

'If I may say so, sir,' Ian Kilbannock ventured, 'you're not looking at all well.'

'To tell you the truth I don't feel it, Ian. I haven't had a day's leave for two years.'

The man's nerve had gone, Ian decided. He could now safely desert him.

'Sir,' he said, 'with your approval I was thinking of applying for a posting abroad.'

'You, too, Ian? Where? How?'

'Sir Ralph Brompton thinks he could get me sent as war correspondent to the Adriatic.'

'What's it got to do with *him*?' asked General Whale in an access of feeble exasperation. 'How are military postings *his* business?'

'He does seem to have some pull there, sir.'

190

General Whale gazed at Ian despondingly, uncomprehendingly. Three years, two years, even six months ago there would have been a detonation of rage. Now he sighed deeply. He gazed round the rough concrete walls of his shelter, at the silent 'scrambler' telephone on his table. He felt (and had he known the passage might so have expressed it) like a beautiful and ineffectual angel beating in the void his luminous wings in vain.

'What am I doing here?' he asked. 'Why am I taking cover when all I want to do is die?'

'Angela,' Virginia said, 'you'd better go too. I can get on all right now by myself. I don't need Sister Jenny any more really. Couldn't you take that baby down with you? Old Nanny would look after it, surely?'

'She'd probably love to,' said Angela Box-Bender, doubtful but ready to hear reason. 'The trouble is we simply haven't any room for a single other adult.'

'Oh, I don't want to move at all. Peregrine will be quite happy with me and Mrs Corner once the nursery is cleared. Mrs Corner will be over the moon to see the last of it.' (There had been the normal, ineradicable hostility between nursing sister and domestic servant.)

'It's wonderfully unselfish of you, Virginia. If you really think it's the best thing for Gervase . . . ?'

'I really think it's the best thing for – for Gervase.'

So it was arranged and Virginia comfortably recuperated as the bombs chugged overhead and she wondered, as each engine cut out: 'Is that the one that's coming here?'

3

In the world of high politics the English abandonment of their Serbian allies – those who had once been commended by the Prime Minister for having 'found their souls' – was determined and gradually contrived. The king in exile was persuaded to dismiss his advisers and appoint more pliable successors. A British ship brought this new minister to Vis to confer with Tito in his cave. The Russians instructed Tito to make a show

of welcome. Full recognition for the partisans and more substantial help were the inducements offered by the British and
Americans. Meetings 'at the highest level' were suggested for
the near future. And as an undesigned by-product of this
intrigue there resulted one infinitesimal positive good.

Guy had not dismissed the Jews from his mind. The repri-
mand rankled but more than this he felt compassion; something less than he had felt for Virginia and her child but a
similar sense that here again, in a world of hate and waste, he
was being offered the chance of doing a single small act to re-
deem the times. It was, therefore, with joy that he received the
signal: *Central Government approves in principle evacuation
Jews stop Dispatch two repeat two next plane discuss problem
with Unrra.*

He went with it to the Minister of the Interior who was
lying on his bed drinking weak tea.

Bakic explained, 'He's sick and don't know nothing. You
better talk to de Commissar.'

The Commissar confirmed that he too had received similar
instructions.

'I suggest we send the Kanyis,' said Guy.

'He say, why de Kanyis?'

'Because they make most sense.'

'Pardon me.'

'Because they seem the most responsible pair.'

'De Commissar says, responsible for what?'

'They are the best able to put their case sensibly.'

A long discussion followed between the Commissar and
Bakic.

'He won't send de Kanyis.'

'Why not?'

'Kanyi got plenty of work with de dynamo.'

So another pair was chosen and sent to Bari, the grocer and
the lawyer who had first called on him. Guy saw them off.
They seemed stupified and sat huddled among the bundles and
blankets on the airfield during the long wait. Only when the
aeroplane was actually there, illumined by the long line of
bonfires lit to guide it, did they both suddenly break into tears.

But this little kindling of human hope was the least impressive incident on the airfield that evening and it passed quite unnoticed in the solemnity with which the arriving passengers were received.

Guy had not been warned to expect anyone of importance. He realized that something unusual was afoot when in the darkness which preceded the firing of the flare-path, he was aware of a reception party assembling, among whom loomed the figures of the General and the Commissar. When the lights went up, Guy recognized with surprise those rarely glimpsed recluses, the Russian Mission. When the machine came to ground and the doors were open, six figures emerged all in British battle-dress who were at once surrounded by partisans, embraced, and led aside.

The Squadron Leader began supervising the disembarkation of stores. There was no great quantity of them and those mostly for the British Mission – rations, mail, and tin after tin of petrol.

'What am I supposed to do with these?' Guy asked the pilot.

'Wait and see. There's a jeep to come out.'

'For me?'

'Well, for your major.'

'Have I a major?'

'Haven't they told you? They signalled that one was coming. They never tell me anyone's name. He's over there with the gang.'

Strong willing partisans contrived a ramp and carefully lowered the car to earth. Guy stood beside his two Jews watching. Presently an English voice called: 'Guy Crouchback anywhere about?'

Guy knew the voice. 'Frank de Souza.'

'Am I unwelcome? I expect you'll get the warning order on tomorrow's transmission. It was a last-minute decision sending us.'

'Who else?'

'I'll explain later. I'm afraid in the whirligig of war I've now become your commanding officer, uncle. Be a good chap and see to the stores, will you? I've got a night's talking ahead with the general staff and the Praesidium.'

'The what?'

'I thought that might surprise you. I'll tell you all about it tomorrow. Begoy, for your information, is about to become a highly popular resort. We shall make history here, uncle. I must find a present I've got for the general in my valise. It may help cement anti-fascist solidarity.'

He stooped over the small heap of baggage, loosened some straps and stood up with a bottle in each hand. 'Tell someone to do it up, will you? and have it put wherever I'm going to sleep.'

He rejoined the group who were now tramping off the field.

'Right,' said the pilot. 'I'm ready to take on passengers.'

Two wounded partisans were hoisted in; then an American bomber crew who had baled out the week before and been led to the Squadron Leader's headquarters. They were far from being gratified by this speedy return to duty. There was a regulation that if they remained at large in enemy territory for some weeks longer, they could be repatriated to the United States. It was for this that they had made a hazardous parachute jump and destroyed an expensive, very slightly damaged aeroplane.

Last came the Jews. When Guy held out his hand to them, they kissed it.

As always on these night incursions Guy had his sergeant and orderly with him. They were plainly exhilarated by the spectacle of the jeep. He left it and the stores to them and walked back to his quarters. The night of high summer was brilliant with stars and luminous throughout its full firmament. When he reached the farm he told the widows of de Souza's coming. There was an empty room next to his which they immediately began to put in order. It was just midnight but they worked without complaint, eagerly, excited at the prospect of a new arrival.

Soon the jeep drove into the yard. The widows ran to admire it. The soldiers unloaded, putting the rations and tins of petroleum in the store room, de Souza's baggage in the room prepared for him. The Praesidium, whatever that might be, was of no interest to Guy; he was glad de Souza had come; very glad that his two Jews had gone.

'The mail, sir,' reported the orderly.

'Better leave that for Major de Souza in the morning. You know he's taking command here now?'

'Yes, we got the buzz from the air force. Two personal for you, sir.'

Guy took the flimsy air-mail forms that were then the sole means of communication. One, he noted, was from Virginia, the other from Angela.

Virginia's letter was undated but had clearly been written some six weeks ago.

Clever Peregrine tells me he managed to persuade them to accept a telegram for you announcing the Birth. I hope it arrived. You can't trust telegrams any more. Anyway it is born and I am feeling fine and everyone especially Angela is being heavenly. Sister Jennings – Jenny to me – says it is a fine baby. We have rather an embarrassing joke about Jenny and gin and my saying she is like Mrs Gamp – at least it embarrasses other people. I think it quite funny as jokes with nurses go. It's been baptized already. Eloise Plessington who believe it or not is now my great new friend was godmother. I've made a lot of new friends since you went away in fact I'm having a very social time. An intellectual who says he knows you called Everard something brought me a smoked salmon from Ruben's. And a lemon! Where does Ruben get them? Magic. I hope you are enjoying your foreign tour wherever you are and forgetting all the beastliness of London. Ian talks of visiting you. How? Longing for you to be back. V.

Angela's letter was written a month later: *I have dreadful news for you. Perhaps I should have tried to telegraph but Arthur said there was no point as there was nothing you could do. Well, be prepared. Now. Virginia has been killed. Peregrine too and Mrs Corner. One of the new doodle bombs landed on Carlisle Place at ten in the morning yesterday. Gervase is safe with me. They were all killed instantly. All Peregrine's 'collection' destroyed. It was Virginia's idea that I should have Gervase and keep him safe. We think we shall be able to get Virginia and Peregrine taken down to Broome and buried there but it is not easy. I had Mass said for them here this morning. There will be another in London soon for friends. I won't attempt to say what I feel about this except that now more than ever you are in my prayers. You have had a difficult life, Guy, and it seemed things were at last going to come right for you. Anyway you have Gervase. I wish papa had lived to know about him. I wish you had seen Virginia these last weeks. She was*

*still her old sweet gay self of course but there was a difference. I
was getting to understand why you loved her and to love her myself. In the old days I did not understand.*

*As Arthur says there is really nothing for you to do here. I
suppose you could get special leave home but I expect you will
prefer to go on with whatever you are doing.*

The news did not affect Guy greatly; less, indeed, than the
arrival of Frank de Souza and the jeep and the 'Praesidium';
far less than the departure of his two Jewish protégés. The
answer to the question that had agitated Kerstie Kilbannock
(and others of his acquaintance) – what had been his relations
with Virginia during their brief cohabitation in Uncle Peregrine's flat? – was simple enough. Guy had hobbled into the
lift after their return as man and wife from the registrar's
office and had gone back to bed. There Virginia had joined him
and with gentle, almost tender, agility adapted her endearments
to his crippled condition. She was, as always, lavish with what
lay in her gift. Without passion or sentiment but in a friendly,
cosy way they had resumed the pleasures of marriage and in
the weeks while his knee mended the deep old wound in Guy's
heart and pride healed also, as perhaps Virginia had intuitively
known that it might do. January had been a month of content;
a time of completion, not of initiation. When Guy was passed
fit for active service and his move-order was issued, he had felt
as though he were leaving a hospital where he had been skil-
fully treated, a place of grateful memory to which he had no
particular wish to return. He did not mention Virginia's death
to Frank then or later.

Frank came to the farmhouse at dawn, accompanied by two
partisans and talking to them cheerfully in Serbo-Croat. Guy
had waited up for him, but dozed. Now he greeted him and
showed him his quarters. The widows appeared with offers of
food, but Frank said: 'I've had no sleep for thirty-six hours.
When I wake up I've a lot to tell you, uncle,' raised a clenched
fist to the partisans and shut his door.

The sun was up, the farm was alive. The partisan sentries
changed guard. Presently the men of the British Mission stood
in the bright yard shaving. Bakic breakfasted apart on the steps
of the kitchen. The bell in the church tower rang three times,

paused and rang three times again. Guy went there on Sundays, never during the week. Sunday Mass was full of peasants. There was always a half-hour sermon that was unintelligible to Guy whose study of Serbo-Croat had made little progress. When the old priest climbed into the pulpit, Guy wandered outside and the partisan police pressed forward so as not to miss a word. When the liturgy was resumed Guy returned; they retired to the back shunning the mystery.

Now the sacring bell recalled Guy to the duty he owed his wife.

'Sergeant,' he said, 'what rations have we got to spare?'

'Plenty since last night.'

'I thought of taking a small present to someone in the village.'

'Shouldn't we wait and ask the major, sir? There's an order not to give anything to the natives.'

'I suppose you're right.'

He crossed the yard to the Air Force quarters. Things were freer and more easy there. Indeed the Squadron Leader did a modest and ill-concealed barter trade with the peasants and had assembled a little collection of Croatian arts and crafts to take home to his wife.

'Help yourself, old boy.'

Guy put a tin of bully beef and some bars of chocolate into his haversack and walked to the church.

The old priest was back in his presbytery, alone and brushing the bare stone floor with a besom. He knew Guy by sight though they had never attempted to converse. Men in uniform boded no good to the parish.

Guy saluted as he entered, laid his offering on the table. The priest looked at the present with surprise; then broke into thanks in Serbo-Croat. Guy said: 'Facilius loqui latine. Hoc est pro Missa. Uxor mea mortua est.'

The priest nodded. 'Nomen?'

Guy wrote Virginia's name in capitals in his pocket book and tore out the page. The priest put on his spectacles and studied the letters. 'Non es *partisan*?'

'Miles Anglicus sum.'

'Catholicus?'

'Catholicus.'

'Et uxor tua?'

'Catholica.'

It did not sound a likely story. The priest looked again at the food, at the name on the sheet of paper, at Guy's battle-dress which he knew only as the uniform of the partisans. Then: 'Cras. Hora septem.' He held up seven fingers.

'Gratias.'

'Gratias tibi. Dominus tecum.'

When Guy left the presbytery he turned into the adjoining church. It was a building with the air of antiquity which no one but a specialist could hope to date. No doubt there had been a church here from early times. No doubt parts of that structure survived. Meanwhile it had been renovated and re-painted and adorned and despoiled, neglected and cosseted through the centuries. Once when Begoy was a watering place it had enjoyed seasons of moderately rich patronage. Now it had reverted to its former use. There was at that moment a peasant woman in the local antiquated costume, kneeling up-right on the stones before the side altar, her arms extended, making no doubt her thanksgiving for communion. There were a few benches, no chairs. Guy genuflected and then stood to pray asking mercy for Virginia and for himself. Although brought up to it from the nursery, he had never been at ease with the habit of reciting the prayers of the Church for par-ticular intentions. He committed Virginia's soul – 'repose' in-deed, seemed the apt petition – to God in the colloquial monologue he always employed when praying; like an old woman, he sometimes ruefully thought, talking to her cat.

He remained standing with his eyes on the altar for five minutes. When he turned he saw Bakic standing behind him, watching intently. The holy water stoup was dry. Guy genu-flected at the door and went out into the sunlight. Bakic was standing by.

'What do you want?'

'I thought maybe you want to talk to somebody.'

'I don't require an interpreter when I say my prayers,' Guy said. But later he wondered, did he?

The bodies of Virginia, Uncle Peregrine, and Mrs Corner were recovered from the débris of Bourne Mansions intact and recognizable, but the official impediments to removing them to Broome (Mrs Corner, too, came from that village) proved too many for Arthur Box-Bender. He had them buried by the river at Mortlake where there was a plot acquired by one of the family in the last century and never used. It lay in sight of Burton's stucco tent. The requiem was sung a week later in the Cathedral. Everard Spruce did not attend either service but he read the list of mourners aloud to Frankie and Coney.

He had met Virginia only in the last weeks of her life but he had long enjoyed a vicarious acquaintance with her from the newspapers. Like many men of the left he had been an assiduous student of 'society gossip' columns, a taste he excused by saying that it was his business to know the enemy's order of battle. Lately in the decline of social order he had met on friendly terms some of these figures of oppression and frivolity – old Ruby, for instance, at the Dorchester – and many years later, when he came to write his memoirs, he gave the impression that he had frequented their houses in their heyday. Already he was beginning to believe that Virginia was an old and valued friend.

'Who are all these people?' asked Coney. 'What's the point of them? All I know about Mrs Crouchback is that you gave her enough smoked salmon to keep us for a week.'

'Before we'd even had a nibble at it,' said Frankie.

'And a lemon,' said Coney.

The flying bombs had disturbed the good order of the *Survival* office. Two of the secretaries had gone to the country. Frankie and Coney remained but they were less docile than of old. The bombs came from the south-east and were plain in view in the wide open sky of the river. All seemed to be directed at the house in Cheyne Row. They distracted the girls from their duty in serving and revering Spruce. His manner towards them had become increasingly schoolmasterly, the more so as his own nerves were not entirely calm. He was like a schoolmaster who fears that a rag is brewing.

He spoke now with an effort of authority:

'Virginia Troy was the last of twenty years' succession o
heroines,' he said. 'The ghosts of romance who walked betwee
the two wars.'

He took a book from his shelves and read : 'She crossed th
dirty street, placing her feet with a meticulous precision on
after the other in the same straight line as though she wer
treading a knife edge between goodness only knew what in
visible gulf. Floating she seemed to go, with a little spring i
every step and the skirt of her summery dress – white it was
with a florid pattern printed in black all over it – blowing airily
round her swaying march. I bet neither of you know who
wrote that. You'll say Michael Arlen.'

'I won't,' said Coney; 'I've never heard of him.'

'Never heard of Iris Storm "that shameless, shameful lady"
dressed pour le sport? "I am a house of men," she said.
read it at school where it was forbidden. It still touches a nerve
What is adolescence without trash? I dare say you've not hear
of Scott Fitzgerald either.'

'Omar Khayyam?' suggested Frankie.

'No. Anyway the passage I read, believe it or not, is Aldous
Huxley 1922. Mrs Viveash. Hemingway coarsened the image
with his Bret, but the type persisted – in books and in life
Virginia was the last of them – the exquisite, the doomed, and
the damning, with expiring voices – a whole generation younger
We shall never see anyone like her again in literature or in life
and I'm very glad to have known her.'

Coney and Frankie looked at each other with mutiny in
their eyes.

'Perhaps you are going to say "the mould has been broken",
said Coney.

'If I wish to, I shall,' said Spruce petulantly. 'Only the essentially commonplace are afraid of clichés.'

Coney burst into tears at this rebuke. Frankie held her
ground. 'Exquisite, doomed, damning, with an expiring voice,'
she said. 'It sound more like the heroine of Major Ludovic's
dreadful Death Wish.'

Then another bomb droned overhead and they fell silen
until it passed.

The same bomb passed near Eloise Plessington's little house

where she was sitting with Angela Box-Bender. Directly over-head, it seemed, the engine cut out. The two women sat silent until they heard the explosion many streets away.

'It is a terrible thing to admit,' said Eloise, 'but, whenever that happens, I pray, "Please God don't let it fall on me." '

'Who doesn't?'

'But, Angela, that means, "Please God let it fall on someone else." '

'Not necessarily. It might land on Hampstead Heath.'

'One ought to pray, "Please God let it fall on me and no one else." '

'Don't be a goose, Eloise.'

These two women of the same age had known each other since girlhood. Charles Plessington had been one of the young men who seemed suitable for Angela to marry. He came of the same little band of landed recusant families as herself. She, however, had confounded the match-makers of the Wiseman Club by preferring the Protestant and plebeian Box-Bender. Eloise married Charles and became not only a Catholic but a very busy one. Her sons were adult and well married; her only family problem was her daughter, Domenica, now aged 25, who had tried her vocation in a convent, failed, and now drove a tractor on the home farm, an occupation which had changed her appearance and manner. From having been shy and almost excessively feminine, she was now rather boisterous, trousered, and muddied and full of the rough jargon of the stock-yard.

'What were we talking about?'

'Virginia.'

'Of course. I'd got very fond of her this winter and spring but, you know, I can't regard her death as pure tragedy. There's a special providence in the fall of a bomb. God forgive me for thinking so, but I was never quite confident her new disposition would last. She was killed at the one time in her life when she could be sure of heaven – eventually.'

'One couldn't help liking her,' said Angela.

'Will Guy mind awfully?'

'Who can say? The whole thing was very puzzling. She'd begun the baby, you know, before they were re-married.'

'So I supposed.'

'I really know Guy very little. He's been abroad so much. I always imagined he had completely got over her.'

'They seemed happy enough together that last bit.'

'Virginia knew how to make people happy if she wanted to.'

'And what is to become of my godson?'

'What indeed? I suppose I shall have to look after him. Arthur won't like that at all.'

'I've sometimes thought of adopting a baby,' said Eloise, 'a refugee orphan or something like that. You know the empty nurseries seem a reproach when there are so many people homeless. It would be an interest for Domenica, too – take her mind off swill and slag.'

'Are you proposing to adopt Gervase?'

'Well, not *adopt* of course, not legally, not give him our name or anything like that, but just look after him until Guy gets back and can make a home for him. What do you think of the idea?'

'It's wonderfully kind. Arthur would be immensely relieved. I'd have to ask Guy, of course.'

'But there would be no objection to my taking him to visit me while we're waiting for an answer.'

'None that I can see. He's a perfectly nice baby, you know, but Arthur does so hate having him at home.'

'Here comes another of those beastly bombs.'

'Just pray, "Please God let it be a dud and not explode at all." '

It was not a dud. It did explode but far from Westminster in a street already destroyed by earlier bombs and now quite deserted.

'You've read *The Death Wish*?' Spruce asked.

'Bits. It's pure novelette.'

'*Novelette?* It's twice the length of *Ulysses*. Not many publishers have enough paper to print it nowadays. I read a lot of it last night. I can't sleep with those damned bombs. Ludovic's *Death Wish* has *got* something you know.'

'Something very bad.'

'Oh, yes, bad; egregriously bad. I shouldn't be surprised to see it a great success.'

'Hardly what we expected from the author of the aphorisms.'

'It is an interesting thing,' said Spruce, 'but very few of the great masters of trash aimed low to start with. Most of them wrote sonnet sequences in youth. Look at Hall Caine – the protégé of Rossetti – and the young Hugh Walpole emulating Henry James. Dorothy Sayers wrote religious verse. Practically no one ever sets out to write trash. Those that do don't get very far.'

'Another bomb.'

It was the same bomb as had disturbed Angela and Eloise. Spruce and Frankie did not pray. They moved away from the windows.

Frank de Souza kept partisan hours, sleeping all the morning, talking at night. On his first day he appeared at lunch-time.

'Better quarters that I'm used to,' he said. 'Until a few days ago I was living in a cave in Bosnia. But we shall have to do some quick work making them more comfortable. We've got a distinguished party coming to visit us. If I may, I'll leave the arrangements to you. I put the General and the Commissar in the picture last night. You'll find them very ready to help.'

'Perhaps you'd put me in the picture.'

'It's a very pretty picture – an oil painting. Everything is moving our way at last. First, the Praesidium – that's the new government – ministers of education, culture, transport – the whole bag of tricks. Officially, it is temporary, *de facto, ad hoc,* and so forth pending ratification by plebiscite. I don't suppose you saw much of them last night – they're a scratch lot collected from Vis and Montenegro and Bari. Two of them are duds we had to take on as part of the deal with the London Serbs. The real power, of course, will remain with the partisan military leaders. The Praesidium is strictly for foreign consumption. Now I'll tell you something highly confidential. Only the General and the Commissar know. It mustn't get to the ears of the Praesidium for a day or two. Tito's in Italy. He's a guest of honour at allied headquarters in Caserta and from what I picked up from Joe Cattermole I gather it's on the cards he's going to meet Winston. If he does, he'll make rings round him.'

'Who'll make rings round whom?'

'Tito round Winston of course. The old boy is being briefed to meet a Garibaldi. He doesn't know Tito's a highly trained politician.'

'Well, isn't Winston Churchill?'

'He's an orator and a parliamentarian, uncle. Something quite different.

'All we have to do now is to square the Yanks. Some of them are still a bit shy of left-wing parties. Not the President, of course, but the military. But we've persuaded them at this stage of the war the only relevant question is: who is doing the fighting? Mihajlovic's boys were given a test – told to blow a bridge by a certain date. They did nothing. Too squeamish about reprisals. That's never worried our side. The more the Nazis make themselves hated, the better for us. So Mihajlovic is definitely out. But the Yanks don't like taking our intelligence reports on trust. Want to see for themselves. So they're sending a general here to report back how hard the partisans are fighting.'

'As far as I know, they aren't.'

'They will when the Yanks come. Just you wait and see.'

Guy said, 'The thing that's been worrying me most is the refugee problem.'

'Oh yes, the Jews. I saw a file about them.'

'Two went out last night. I hope they get proper attention in Bari.'

'You can be sure they will. The Zionists have their own funds and their own contacts with UNRRA and allied headquarters. It isn't really any business of ours.'

'You talk like a partisan.'

'I am a partisan, uncle. We have more important things to think about than these sectarian troubles. Don't forget, I'm a Jew myself; so are three of the brighter members of the Praesidium. Jews have been valuable anti-fascist propaganda in America. Now's the time to forget we're Jews and simply remember we are anti-fascist. You might just as well start agitating Auchinleck about Scottish nationalism.'

'I can't feel like that about Catholics.'

'Can't you, uncle? Try.'

When Guy went to church next morning at seven there were
two partisans on watch. The priest in his black chasuble was
inaudible at the altar. The partisans watched Guy. When he
went up to communion they followed and stood at the side,
their sten guns slung from their shoulders. When they were sure
that nothing but the host passed between Guy and the priest,
they returned to their places, watched Guy saying his prayers
for Virginia, and followed him back to the mission headquarters.

At luncheon that day de Souza's first words were: 'Uncle,
what's all this about you and the priest?'

'I went to Mass this morning.'

'Did you? That won't be any help. You've upset the Commissar seriously, you know. They made a formal complaint last
night saying you had been guilty of "incorrect" behaviour.
They say you were seen yesterday giving the priest rations.'

'That's quite true.'

'And passing a note.'

'I simply gave him the name of someone who's dead – what
we call a "mass intention".'

'Yes, that's what the priest told them. They've had the priest
up and examined him. The old boy's lucky not to be under
arrest or worse. How could you be such an ass? He produced
a bit of paper he said was your message. It had your name on
it and nothing else.'

'Not mine. Someone in my family.'

'Well you can't expect the Commissar to distinguish, can
you? He naturally thought the priest was trying to put something over on them. They searched the presbytery but couldn't
find anything incriminating, except some chocolate. They confis-
cated that of course. But they're suspicious still. You must have
realized what the situation is here. If it wasn't for our American guests they might have made real trouble. I had to point
out to them that the general was not only going to report back
about the fighting. He would also be asked what Begoy was like
now it's for the moment the capital of the country. If he found
the church shut and cottoned on to the fact that the priest had

just been removed, he might, I told them, just possibly get it
into his noodle that this wasn't exactly the liberal democracy
he's been led to expect. They saw the point in the end, but
they took some persuading. They're serious fellows our comrades. Don't for goodness' sake try anything like that again.
As I said yesterday, this is no time for sectarian loyalties.'

'You wouldn't call communism a sect?'

'No,' said de Souza. He began to say more and then stopped.
All he did was to repeat 'No' with absolute assurance.

The battle prepared for the visiting general was to be an
assault on a little block-house some twenty miles to the west,
the nearest 'enemy' post to Begoy, on a secondary road to the
coast. There were no Germans near. The garrison was a company of Croat nationalists, whose duty it was to send out
patrols along the ill-defined frontiers of the 'liberated' territory
and to find sentries for bridges in that area. They were not the
ferocious *ustachi* but pacific *domobrans*, the local home-guard.
It was in every way a convenient objective for the exercise;
also well placed for spectators, in an open little valley with
wooded slopes on either side.

The General pointed out that frontal assault in daylight was
not normal partisan tactics. 'We shall need air support.'

De Souza composed a long signal on the subject. It was a
measure of the new prestige of the partisans that the RAF
agreed to devote two fighter-bombers to this insignificant
target. Two brigades of the Army of National Liberation were
entrusted with the attack. They numbered a hundred men
each.

'I think,' said de Souza, 'we had better call them companies.
Will the brigadiers mind being reduced to captain for a day or
two?'

'In the Peoples' Forces of Anti-fascism we attach little importance to such things,' said the Commissar.

The General was more doubtful. 'They earned their rank in
the field,' he said. 'It is only because of the great sacrifices we
have made that the brigades have been so reduced in numbers.
Also because the supply of arms from our allies has been so
scanty.'

'Yes,' said de Souza, '*I* understand all that of course but what we have to consider is how it will affect our distinguished observers. They are going to send journalists too. It will be the first eye-witness report of Jugoslavia to appear in the press. It would not read well to say we employed two brigades against one company.'

'That must be considered,' said the Commissar.

'I suggest,' said de Souza, 'the brigadiers should keep their rank and their units be called "a striking force". I think that could be made impressive. "The survivors of the Sixth Offensive".'

De Souza had come with credentials which the General and Commissar recognized. They trusted him and treated his advice with a respect they would not have accorded to Guy or even Brigadier Cape; or for that matter to General Alexander or Mr Winston Churchill.

Guy was never admitted to these conferences which were held in Serbo-Croat without an interpreter. Nor was he informed of the negotiations with Bari. De Souza had all signals brought to him in cipher. The later hours of his mornings in bed were spent reading them and himself enciphering the answers. To Guy were relegated the domestic duties of preparing for the coming visit. As de Souza had predicted he found the partisans unusually amenable. They revealed secret stores of loot taken from the houses of the fugitive bourgeoisie, furniture of monstrous modern German design but solid construction. Sturdy girls bore the loads. The rooms of the farmhouse were transformed in a way which brought deep depression to Guy but exultation to the widows who polished and dusted with the zeal of sacristans. The former Minister of the Interior had been made master of the revels. He proposed a *Vin d'Honneur* and concert.

'He want to know,' explained Bakic, 'English American anti-fascist songs. He want words and music so the girls can learn them.'

'I don't know any,' said Guy.

'He want to know what songs you teach your soldiers?'

'We don't *teach* them any. Sometimes they sing about drink, "Roll out the barrel" and "Show me the way to go home".'

'He says not those songs. We are having such songs also under the fascists. All stopped now. He says Commissar orders American songs to honour American general.'

'American songs are all about love.'

'He says love is not anti-fascist.'

Later de Souza emerged from his bedroom with a sheaf of signals.

'I've a surprise for you, uncle. We are sending a high observing officer too. Apparently it's the rule at Caserta that our VIPs always travel in pairs, the Yank being just one star above his British companion. Just you wait and see who we're getting. I'll keep it as a treat for you, uncle.'

4

IAN KILBANNOCK'S first day in Bari was similar to Guy's. He was briefed by Joe Cattermole and Brigadier Cape. Nothing was said about the impending battle, much about the achievements of the partisans, the failure of Mihajlovic's *cetnics*, the inclusive, national character of the new government, and the personal qualities of Marshal Tito, who was at that moment in Capri awaiting the British Prime Minister.

Ian was the first journalist to be admitted to Jugoslavia. Sir Ralph Brompton had vouched for him to Cattermole, not as one fully committed to the cause, but as a man without prejudice. Cape had an unexpressed, indeed unrecognized, belief that a peer and a member of Bellamy's was likely to be trustworthy. Ian listened to all that was told him, asked a few intelligent questions, and made no comment other than: 'I see this as a job that will take time. Impossible to send spot news. If it suits you, I shall just look about, talk to people, and then return here and write a series of articles.'

He intended to establish himself now and for the future as a political commentator, of the kind who had enjoyed such prestige in the late thirties.

He was taken to dinner at the club by the Halberdier major. More direct than Guy, he said: 'I'm afraid I didn't get your name.'

'Marchpole. Grace-Groundling-Marchpole to be precise. I dare say you know my brother in London. He's a big bug.'

'No.'

'He's a secret big bug. I'm just a cog in the machine. How was London?' Ian described the flying bombs. 'My brother won't like that.'

While they were at dinner, Brigadier Cape came into the room politely propelling a man in the uniform of a major-general, a lean, grey-faced, stiff old man, whose single eye was lustreless, whose maimed hand reached out to a chair-back to steady him as he limped and shuffled to his table.

'Good God,' said Ian, 'a ghost.'

He had sailed with this man to the Isle of Mugg in the yacht *Cleopatra* in December 1941; a man given to ferocious jokes and bloody ambitions, an exultant, unpredictable man whom Ian had taken pains to avoid.

'Ben Ritchie-Hook,' said Major Marchpole, 'one of the great characters of the Corps. He hadn't much use for me though. We parted company.'

'But what's happened to him?'

'He's on the shelf,' said Major Marchpole. 'All they can find for him to do is play second fiddle as an observer. He'll be in your party going across tomorrow night.'

Ostensibly the party which was assembled at the airfield next evening, was paying a call on the new Praesidium. It had grown since the simple project of sending an independent observer had first been raised and accepted.

General Spitz, the American, was still the principal. He had a round stern face under a capacious helmet. He was much harnessed with plastic straps and hung about with weapons and instruments and haversacks. He was attended by an ADC of less militant appearance, who had been chosen for his ability to speak Serbo-Croat, and by his personal photographer, a very young, very lively manikin whom he addressed as 'Mr Sneiffel'. Ritchie-Hook wore shorts, a bush-shirt, and a red-banded forage cap. His Halberdier servant guarded his meagre baggage, the same man, Dawkins, war-worn now like his master, who had served him at Southsands and Penkirk, in

Central Africa and in the desert, wherever Ritchie-Hook's strides had taken him; strides which had grown shorter and slower, faltered and almost come to a halt. Lieutenant Padfield was there with his conductor who, it was thought, might help the partisans with their concert. The Free French had insinuated a representative. Other nondescript figures, American, British, and Jugoslav, made a full complement for the aeroplane. Gilpin was there with a watching brief for Cattermole, and an Air Force observer to report the promised cooperation of the fighter-bombers. He and the two generals specifically, and Gilpin vaguely, were alone in the know about the promised assault.

The Air Commodore in command turned out to see the party on board. The American General instructed Sneiffel to take snapshots of the pair of them. He called Ritchie-Hook to join them. 'Come along, General, just for the record.' Ritchie-Hook looked in a bewildered way at the little figure who squatted with his flash-light apparatus at the General's feet; then with a ghastly grin said: 'Not me. My ugly mug would break the camera.'

Lieutenant Padfield saluted General Spitz and said: 'Sir, I don't think you've met Sir Almeric Griffiths who is coming with us. He is a very prominent orchestral conductor as no doubt you know.'

'Bring him up. Bring him in,' said the General. 'Come, Griffiths, stand with me.'

The bulb flashed.

Gilpin said: 'He ought to get security clearance before taking photographs on our airfield.'

Ian resolved to make himself agreeable to this photographer and get prints of all his films. They might serve to illustrate a book.

As the last glow of sunset faded they boarded the aeroplane in inverse order of seniority beginning with the Halberdier servant and ending after some lingering exchanges of politeness with General Spitz. A machine had been provided that was luxurious for these parts, fitted with seats as though for paying passengers in peace-time. Little lights glowed along the roof. The doors were shut. The lights went out. It was completely

dark. What had once been windows were painted out. The roar
of the engines imposed silence on the party. Ian, who had put
himself next to Sneiffel, longed for a forbidden cigarette and
tried to compose himself for sleep. It was far from his normal
bedtime. He had worn the same shirt all day without a chance
of changing. In the hot afternoon it had been damp with sweat.
Now in the chill upper air it clung to him and set him shiver-
ing. It had not occurred to him to bring his greatcoat. It had
been an unsatisfactory day. He had wandered about the streets
of the old town with Lieutenant Padfield and Griffiths. They
had lunched at the club and had been ordered to report at the
airfield two hours before they were needed. He had not dined
and saw no hope of doing so. He sat in black boredom and
discomfort until, after an hour, sleep came.

The aeroplane flew high over the Adriatic and the lightless,
enemy-held coast of Dalmatia. All the passengers were sleeping when at last the little lights went up and the American
General who had been travelling in the cockpit returned to his
place in the tail saying: 'All right, fellows. We're there.' Everyone began groping for equipment. The photographer next to
Ian tenderly nursed his camera. Ian heard the change of speed
in the engines and felt the rapid descent, the list as they banked,
then straightened for the run-in. Then unexpectedly the engines
burst up in full throat; the machine suddenly rose precipitously,
throwing the passengers hard back in their seats; then as suddenly dived, throwing them violently forward. The last thing
Ian heard was a yelp of alarm from Sneiffel. Then a great door
slammed in his mind.

He was standing in the open beside a fire. London, he
thought; Turtle's Club going up in flames. But why was maize
growing in St James's Street? Other figures were moving
around him, unrecognizable against the fierce light. One
seemed familiar. 'Loot,' he said, 'what are *you* doing here?'
and then added: 'Job says the gutters are running with
wine.'

Always polite Lieutenant Padfield said: 'Is that so?'

A more distinctly American, more authoritative voice was
shouting: 'Is everyone out?'

Another familiar figure came close to him. A single eye glittered terribly in the flames. 'You there,' said Ritchie-Hook, 'were you driving that thing?'

As though coming round from gas in the dentist's chair Ian saw that 'that thing' was an aeroplane, shorn of its under-carriage, part buried in the great furrow it had ploughed for itself, burning furiously in the bows, with flames trickling back along the fuselage like the wines of Turtle's. Ian remembered he had left Bari in an aeroplane and that he had been bound for Jugoslavia.

Then he was aware of the gaunt figure confronting him and of a single eye which caught the blaze. 'Are you the pilot?' demanded Ritchie-Hook. 'Pure bad driving. Why can't you look where you're going.' The concussion which had dazed his companions had momentarily awakened Ritchie-Hook. 'You're under arrest,' he roared above the sound of the fire.

'Who's missing?' demanded the American General.

Ian then saw a man leave the group and trot to the pyre and deliberately climb back through the escape-hatch.

'What the devil does that idiot think he's doing?' cried Ritchie-Hook. 'Come back. You're under arrest.'

Ian's senses were clearer now. He still seemed to be in a dream but in a very vivid one. 'It's like the croquet match in *Alice in Wonderland*,' he heard himself say to Lieutenant Padfield.

'That's a very, very gallant act,' said the Lieutenant.

The figure emerged again in the aperture, jumped, and dragged out behind him not, as first appeared, an insensible fellow passenger but, it transpired, a bulky cylindrical object; he staggered clear with it and then proceeded to roll on the ground.

'Good God, it's Dawkins,' said Ritchie-Hook. 'What the devil are you doing?'

'Trousers on fire, sir,' said Dawkins. 'Permission to take them off, sir?' Without waiting for orders he did so, pulling them down, then with difficulty unfastening his anklets and kicking the smouldering garment clear of his burden. He stood thus in shirt, tunic, and boots gazing curiously at his bare legs. 'Fair roasted,' he said.

The American General asked: 'Were there any men left inside?'

'Yes, sir. I think there was, sir. They didn't look like moving. Too hot to stay and talk. Had to get the General's valise out.'

'Are you hurt.'

'Yes, sir. I think so, sir. But I don't seem to feel it.'

'Shock,' said the General. 'You will later.'

The flames had now taken hold of the tail. 'No one is to attempt any further rescue operations.' No one had shown any inclination to do so. 'Who's missing?' he said to his aide. 'Count and find out.'

'I don't see Almeric,' said Lieutenant Padfield.

'How did any of us get out?' Ian asked.

'The General, our General Spitz. He got both the hatches open before anyone else moved.'

'Something to be said for technological training.'

Gilpin was loudly complaining of burned fingers. No one heeded him. The little group was behaving in an orderly, mechanical manner. They spoke at random and did not listen. Each seemed alone, isolated by his recent shock. Someone said: 'I wonder where the hell we are.' No one answered. Ritchie-Hook said to Ian: 'You were not in any way responsible for that intolerable exhibition of incompetence?'

'I'm a press-officer, sir.'

'Oh, I thought you were the pilot. You need not consider yourself under arrest. But be careful in future. This is the second time this has happened to me. They tried it on before in Africa.'

The two generals stood side by side. 'Neat trick of yours that,' Ritchie-Hook conceded, 'getting the door open. I was slow off the mark. Didn't really know what was happening for a moment. Might have been in there still.'

The aide came to report to General Spitz: 'All the crew are missing.'

'Ha,' said Ritchie-Hook. 'The dog it was that died.'

'And six from the rest of the party. I'm afraid Sneiffel is one of them.'

'Too bad, too bad,' said General Spitz; 'he was a fine boy.'

'And the civilian musician.'

'Too bad.'

'And the French liaison officer.'

General Spitz was not listening to the casualty list. An epoch seemed to have passed since the disaster. General Spitz looked at his watch. 'Eight minutes,' he said. 'Someone ought to be here soon.'

The place where the aeroplane had fallen was pasture. The maize field lay astern of it, tall, ripe for reaping, glowing golden in the firelight. These stalks now parted and through them came running the first of the reception party from the airfield, partisans and the British Mission. There were greetings and anxious inquiries. Ian lost all interest in the scene. He found himself uncontrollably yawning and sat on the ground with his head on his knees while behind him the chatter of solicitude and translation faded to silence.

Another great space of time, two minutes by a watch, was broken by someone saying: 'Are you hurt?'

'I don't think so.'

'Can you walk?'

'I suppose so. I'd sooner stay here.'

'Come on, it's not far.'

Someone helped him to his feet. He noticed without surprise that it was Guy. Guy, he remembered, was an inhabitant of this strange land. There was something he ought to say to Guy. It came to him. 'Very sorry about Virginia,' he said.

'Thank you. Have you got any belongings?'

'Burned. Damn fool thing to have happened. I never trusted the Air Force ever since they accepted *me*. Must be something wrong with people who'd accept *me*.'

'Are you sure nothing hit you on the head in that crash?' said Guy.

'Not sure. I think I'm just sleepy.'

A partisan doctor went round the survivors. No one except Halberdier Dawkins and Gilpin had any visible injuries; the doctor made light of Gilpin's burnt fingers. Dawkins was suffering from surface burns which had rapidly swelled into enormous blisters covering his legs and thighs. He prodded them with detached curiosity. 'It's a rum go,' he said; 'spill a kettle on your toe and you're fair dancing. Boil you in oil like a heathen and you don't feel a thing.'

The doctor gave him morphia and two partisan girls bore him off on a stretcher.

The unsteady little procession followed the path the rescuers had trodden through the maize. The flames cast deep shadows before their feet. At the edge of the field grew a big chestnut. 'Do you see what I see?' asked Ian. Something like a monkey was perched in the branches gibbering at them. It was Sneiffel with his camera.

'Lovely pictures,' he said. 'Sensational if they come out.'

When Ian woke next morning it was as though from a debauch; all the symptoms of alcoholic hangover, such as he had not experienced since adolescence, overwhelmed him. As in those days, he had no memory of going to bed. As in those days, he received an early call from the man who had put him there.

'How are you?' asked Guy.

'Awful.'

'There's a doctor going the rounds. Do you want to see him?'

'No.'

'Do you want any breakfast?'

'No.'

He was left alone. The room was shuttered. The only light came in narrow strips between the hinges. Outside poultry was cackling. Ian lay still. The door opened again; someone stamped into the room and opened shutters and windows revealing herself, in the brief moment before Ian shut his eyes and turned them from the light, as a female in man's uniform, wearing a red cross brassard and carrying a box of objects which clinked and rattled. She began stripping Ian of his blanket and pulling at his arm.

'What the devil are you doing?'

The woman flourished a syringe.

'Get out,' cried Ian.

She jabbed at him. He knocked the instrument from her

hand. She called: 'Bakic. Bakic,' and was joined by a man to whom she talked excitedly in a foreign tongue. 'She's de nurse,' said Bakic. 'She's got an injection for you.'

'What on earth for?'

'She says tetanus. She says she always injects tetanus for everyone.'

'Tell her to get out.'

'She says are you frightened of a needle? She says partisans are never frightened.'

'Turn her out.'

So far as anything so feminine could be ascribed to this visitant, she exhibited pique. So far as it was possible to flounce in tight battle-dress, she flounced as she left her patient. Guy returned.

'I say I'm sorry about that. I've been keeping her out all the morning. She got through while I was with the General.'

'Did you put me to bed last night?'

'I helped. You seemed all right. In fact in fine form.'

'It's worn off,' said Ian.

'You'd just like to be left alone?'

'Yes.'

But it was not to be. He had closed his eyes and lapsed into a state approaching sleep when something not very heavy depressed his feet, as though a dog or a cat had landed there. He looked and saw Sneiffel.

'Well, well, well, so you're a newspaper man? My, but you've got a story. I've been down to the wreck. It's still too hot to get near it. They reckon there's five stiffs in there besides the crew. Lieutenant Padfield is het up about some British musician he's lost. What the Hell? There isn't going to be any concert now. So what? There'll be an elegant funeral when they get the bodies out. Everyone seems kinda het up today. Not me though. Maybe it's being light I don't shock so easy. The partisans were for putting off the battle but General Spitz works to a schedule. He's got to have the battle on the day it was planned and then get out his report and I've got to have the pictures to go with it. So the battle's tomorrow as per schedule. What say you come round with me and talk to some of these partisans? I've got the General's interpreter. He's not

feeling too bright this morning but I reckon he can still hear
and speak.'

So Ian gingerly set foot to the floor, dressed and began his
work as a war correspondent.

No one could give a technical explanation of the night's
mishap. Guy had stood at his usual post on the edge of the
airfield. He had heard the Squadron Leader talking his peculiar
jargon into his wireless set, had seen the girls run from tar-
barrel to barrel lighting the path for the incoming aeroplane,
had watched it come down as he had watched many others,
had seen it overrun its objective, rocket suddenly up like a
driven pheasant and fall as though shot half a mile away. He
had heard de Souza say: 'That's the end of *them*,' had seen
the flames kindle and spread and then had seen one after another a few dark, unrecognizable, apparently quite lethargic
figures emerge from the hatches and stand near the wreck. He
had joined in the rush to the scene. After that he had been
busy with his duties as host in getting the survivors to their
beds and finding in the store replacements for their lost equipment.

The partisans were inured to disaster. They had a certain
relish for it. They did not neglect to mention that this was an
entirely Anglo-American failure, but they did so with a rare
cordiality. They had never been convinced that the allies were
taking the war seriously. This unsolicited burnt-offering seemed
in some way to appease them.

De Souza was very busy with his tear-off cipher-pads and it
devolved on Guy to arrange the day of the newcomers. General
Spitz's aide had been struck with a delayed stammer by his
fall and complained of pains in his back. Gilpin now had both
hands bandaged and useless. The two generals were the fittest
of the party; General Spitz brisk and business-like, Ritchie-
Hook reanimated. Guy had not seen him in his decline. He was
now as he had always been in Guy's experience.

Halberdier Dawkins said: 'It's been a fair treat for the
General. He's his old self. Come in this morning and gave me
rocket for disobeying orders getting his gear out.'

Dawkins was a stretcher case, and after arduous years in

Ritchie-Hook's service not sorry to be honourably at ease. He submitted without complaint to his tetanus injections and basked in the hospitality of the Mission sergeant who brought him whisky and cigarettes and gossip.

The former Minister of the Interior reluctantly cancelled the *Vin d'Honneur* and the concert but there were sociable meetings between the general staff and their guests, the observers, at which the plans for the little battle were discussed. It was after one of these that Ritchie-Hook took Guy aside and said: 'I'd like you to arrange for me to have a quiet talk with the fellow whose name ends in "itch".'

'All their names end like that, sir.'

'I mean the decent young fellow. They call him a brigadier. The fellow who's going to lead the assault.'

Guy identified him as a ferocious young Montenegran who had a certain affinity to Ritchie-Hook in that he, too, lacked an eye and a large part of one hand.

Guy arranged a meeting and left the two warriors with the Commissar's interpreter. Ritchie-Hook returned in high good humour. 'Rattling good fellow that Itch,' he said. 'No flannel or ormolu about him. D'you suppose all his stories are true?'

'No, sir.'

'Nor do I. I pulled his leg a bit but I am not sure that interpreter quite twigged. Anyway, we had a perfectly foul drink together – *that* ended in itch too – extraordinary language – and we parted friends. I've attached myself to him for tomorrow. Don't tell the others. Itch hasn't room for more than one tourist in his car. We're driving out tonight to make a recce and get the men in place for the attack.'

'You know, sir,' Guy said, 'there's a certain amount of humbug about this attack. It's being laid on for General Spitz.'

'Don't try and teach your grandmother to suck eggs,' said Ritchie-Hook. 'Of course I twigged all that from the word "go". Itch and I understand one another. It's a demonstration. Sort of thing we did in training. But we enjoyed that, didn't we?'

Guy thought of those long chilly exercises in 'biffing' at Southsands, Penkirk, and Hoy. 'Yes, sir,' he said, 'those were good days.'

'And between you and me I reckon it's the last chance I have
f hearing a shot fired in anger. If there's any fun going, Itch
ill be in it.'

At eight next morning General Spitz and his aide, the
ritish Mission, the partisan general staff, Ian and Sneiffel
ssembled beside the line of miscellaneous cars which the Jugo-
lavs had all the summer kept secreted, with so much else, in
he forest. Guy made Ritchie-Hook's excuses to General Spitz
vho merely said: 'Well, there's plenty of us without him.'

The convoy set out through a terrain of rustic enchantment,
s through a water-colour painting of the last century. Strings
f brilliant peppers hung from the eaves of the cottages. The
vomen at work in the fields sometimes waved a greeting, some-
imes hid their faces. There was no visible difference between
liberated' territory and that groaning under foreign oppression.
an was unaware when they passed the vague frontier.

'It's like driving to a meet,' he said, 'when the horses have
one on ahead.'

In less than an hour they were in sight of the block-house.
A place had been chosen 500 yards from it, well screened by
oliage, where the observers could await events in comfort and
afety. The partisans had moved out in the darkness and should
ave been in position surrounding their objective in the near-
st cover.

'I'm going down to look for them,' said Sneiffel.

'I shall stay here,' said Ian. He was still feeling debauched by
hock.

General Spitz studied the scene through very large binoculars.
Block-house' had been a slightly deceptive term. What he saw
vas a very solid little fort built more than a century earlier,
art of the defensive line of Christendom against the Turk. 'I
ppreciate now why they want air support,' said General
Spitz. 'Can't see anyone moving. Anyway we've achieved
urprise.'

'As a matter of fact,' said de Souza aside to Guy, 'things have
ot gone quite right. One of the brigades lost its way in the
pproach-march. They may turn up in time. Don't let on to
ur allies.'

'You'd think there would be more sign of life from a German post,' said General Spitz. 'Everyone seems asleep.'

'These are *domobrans*,' said the Commissar's interpreter 'They are lazy people.'

'How's that again?'

'Fascist collaborators.'

'Oh. I got the idea in Bari we were going to fight Germans I suppose it's all the same thing.'

The sun rose high but it was cool in the shade of the observation post. The air support was timed to begin at ten o'clock. That was to be the signal for the infantry to come into the open.

At half-past nine rifle-fire broke out below them. The partisan general looked vexed.

'What are they up to?' asked General Spitz.

A partisan runner was sent down to inquire. Before he returned the firing ceased. When he reported, the interpreter said to General Spitz 'It is nothing, it was a mistake.'

'It's lost us surprise.'

De Souza, who had heard and understood the runner's report, said to Guy: 'That was the second brigade turning up. The first thought they were enemy and started pooping off. No one's been hit but, as our ally remarks, we have "lost surprise".'

There was no longer peace in the valley. For the next quarter of an hour occasional shots came, at random it seemed, some from the parapet of the block-house, some from the surrounding cover; then sharp at ten, just as on General Spitz's elaborate watch the minute hand touched its zenith, there came screaming out of the blue sky the two aeroplanes. They swooped down one behind the other. The first shot fired simultaneously two rockets which just missed their target and exploded in the woods beyond, where part of the attacking force was now grouped. The second shot straighter. Both his rockets landed square on the masonry, raising a cloud of flying rubble. Then the machines climbed and circled. Guy, remembering the dive-bombers in Crete relentlessly tracking and pounding the troops on the ground, waited for their return. Instead they dwindled from sight and hearing.

The airman who had been sent to observe them, stood near.
'Lovely job,' he said, 'right on time, right on target.'

'Is that all?' asked Guy.

'That's all. Now the soldiers can do some work.'

Silence had fallen in the valley. Everyone, friend and enemy
alike, expected the return of the aeroplanes. The dust cleared
revealing to those on the hillside equipped with binoculars two
distinct patches of dilapidation in the massive walls of the
block-house. Some of the partisans began discharging their
weapons. None came into view. The Air Force observer began
to explain to General Spitz the complexity of the task which
he had seen successfully executed. The Commissar and the
partisan General spoke earnestly and crossly in their own language. A runner from below came to report to them. 'It
appears,' the interpreter explained to General Spitz, 'that the
attack must be postponed. A German armoured column has
been warned and is on its way here.'

'What do your men do about that?'

'Before a German armoured column they disperse. That is
the secret of our great and many victories.'

'Well, uncle,' said de Souza to Guy, 'we had better begin
thinking of luncheon for our visitors. They've seen all the sport
we have to offer here.'

But he was wrong. Just as the observers were turning towards their cars, Ian said: 'Look.'

Two figures had emerged from the scrub near the block-
house walls and were advancing across the open ground. Guy
remembered the precept of his musketry instructor: 'At 200
yards all parts of the body are distinctly seen. At 300 the out-
line of the face is blurred. At 400 no face. At 600 the head is
a dot and the body tapers.' He raised his binoculars and recognized the incongruous pair, the first was Ritchie-Hook. He was
signalling fiercely, summoning to the advance the men behind
him, who were already slinking away; he went forward at a
slow and clumsy trot towards the place where the rocket-bombs
had disturbed the stones. He did not look back to see if he was
being followed. He did not know that he was followed, by one
man, Sneiffel, who like a terrier, like the pet dwarf privileged
to tumble about the heels of a prince of the Renaissance, was

gambolling round him with his camera, crouching and skipping, so small and agile as to elude the snipers on the walls. A first bullet hit Ritchie-Hook when he was some 20 yards from the walls. He spun completely round, then fell forwards on his knees, rose again and limped slowly on. He was touching the walls, feeling for a hand-hold, when a volley from above caught him and flung him down dead. Sneiffel paused long enough to record his last posture, then bolted, and the defenders were so much surprised by the whole incident that they withheld their fire until he had plunged into the ranks of the retreating partisans.

The German patrol – not, as the partisan scouts had reported an armoured column, but two scout cars summoned by telephone when the first shots were fired – arrived at the block-house to find the scars of the rockets and the body of Ritchie-Hook. They did not move from the road. A section of *domobrans* investigated the wood where the first aeroplane had misplaced its missiles. They found some smouldering timber and the bodies of four partisans. A puzzled German captain composed his report of the incident which circulated through appropriate files of the Intelligence Service attracting incredulous minutes as long as the Balkan branch continued to function. The single-handed attack on a fortified position by a British major-general, attended in one account by a small boy, in another by a midget, had no precedent in Clausewitz. There must be some deep underlying motive, German Intelligence agreed, which was obscure to them. Perhaps the body was not really Ritchie-Hook's – they had his full biography – but that of a sacrificial victim. Ritchie-Hook was being preserved for some secret enterprise. Warning orders were issued throughout the whole 'Fortress of Europe' to be vigilant for one-eyed men.

Lieutenant Padfield had not spent an agreeable morning in Begoy. His only company had been Gilpin and he had been troubled by a deputation of Jews who, hearing that an American was among them, had come to inquire about the arrangement UNRRA was making for their relief. The Lieutenant was no linguist. Bakic was surly. The conversation had been a train on his spirits already subdued by the aeroplane crash. It was with great pleasure that, earlier than expected, the observers came driving into the town.

The death of Ritchie-Hook had changed the events of the day from fiasco to tragic drama. There was ample material for recriminations but in the face of this death even the Commissar was constrained to silence.

Sneiffel was jubilant. He had secured a scoop which would fill half a dozen pages of an illustrated weekly, the full photographic record of a unique event.

Ian was soberly confident. 'You didn't miss much, Loot,' he said, 'but the object of the exercise has been attained. General Spitz is satisfied that the partisans mean business and are skilled in guerrilla tactics. He was rather sceptical at one moment but Ritchie-Hook changed all that. A decision of the heart rather than of the head perhaps.

'It's an odd thing. In all this war I've only twice had any part in an operation. Both have afforded classic stories of heroism. You wouldn't have thought, would you, that Trimmer and Ritchie-Hook had a great deal in common?'

Guy took it on himself to inform Halberdier Dawkins of his master's death.

The much blistered man displayed no extremity of bereavement. 'So that's how it was,' he said and added with awe at the benevolent operation of Providence: 'Hadn't been for going sick, like enough I'd be with him. He's led me into some sticky places I can tell you, sir, these last three years. He was fair asking to cop one. As you'll remember, sir, he always spoke very straight and more than once he's said to me right out: "Dawkins, I wish those bastards would shoot better. I don't want to go home." One thing for him; different for me that's got a wife and kids and was twenty years younger. Of course I'd go anywhere with the General. Had to really, and he was a fine man, no getting away from that. So it's turned out the best for both parties the way things are. I don't know how I'll do about his gear. Ought to ship it back to the base. Maybe your orderly would lend a hand when they send to fetch us. It's a shame we couldn't bury him proper, but you can trust the jerries to do what's right, he always said. He wasn't a strictly religious man. Just so as he has his grave marked, he wouldn't want more.'

The partisans dug a deep common grave for the bodies in the aeroplane. They, too, were anxious to do what was right and offered the services of the village priest but since little was known about the beliefs of any of the dead, except Sir Almeric Griffiths who, Lieutenant Padfield said, was of Wesleyan origin and sceptical temper, a firing-party and a bugler performed the last office.

Later the Air Force made a daylight sortie with fighter cover to collect General Spitz and the remnants of his party. When Guy and de Souza returned from the airfield to their quarters they found the partisan girls already removing the bourgeois furniture.

'The captains and the kings depart,' said de Souza. 'What do we do now, uncle, to keep ourselves amused?'

There was not work for two liaison officers. There was barely enough for one. As the result of General Spitz's recommendations supplies came almost nightly in great profusion. The Squadron Leader arranged for them, the partisans collected them, Guy and de Souza were spectators. Throughout the last weeks of August and the first weeks of September the Commissar and the General were uncomplaining, even comradely. De Souza drove Guy in the jeep round the 'liberated' area visiting partisan camps.

'It seems to me,' said Guy, 'that they've got all they can use at the moment. If they're going to mount a summer offensive they'd better get on with it.'

'There's not going to be a summer offensive here in Croatia,' said de Souza. 'You might have noticed that we're moving troops out, as soon as they're equipped. They're going into Montenegro and Bosnia. They'll keep on the heels of the Germans and move into Serbia before the *cetnics* can take over. That's the important thing now. Begoy has served its purpose. They'll just leave enough men to deal with the local fascists. I have the feeling I shan't be staying long myself. Can you face the winter alone, uncle? Once the snow comes the landing strip will be out of service, you know.'

'I'd like to do something about the Jews.'

'Oh, yes. Your Jews. I'll make a signal.'

He got in reply: *Plans well advanced evacuation all Jews your area before snow.*

'I hope that's cheered you up, uncle.'

That was in the middle of the third week in September. In the middle of the fourth week de Souza came into their common-room with his file of signals and said: 'I shall be leaving you tonight, uncle. I've been recalled to Bari. Let me know if there's anything I can do for you there.'

'Remind them about the Jews.'

'You know, uncle, I'm beginning to doubt if you're fit to be left. You've an *idée fixe*. I hope you aren't going to become a psychiatrist's case like your predecessor here.'

It was not until dinner that de Souza said: 'I dare say you ought to know what's happening. Tito has left Vis and gone to join the Russians. He might have done it more politely. He never said a word to anyone. Just took off while everyone was asleep. Some of our chaps are rather annoyed about it, I gather. I bet Winston is. I told you he'd make rings round the old boy. Winston imagined he'd worked the same big magic with Tito he did with the British Labour leaders in 1940. There were to be British landings in Dalmatia and a nice coalition government set up in Belgrade. That's what Winston thought. From now on any help Tito needs is coming from Russia and Bulgaria.'

'Bulgaria? The Jugoslavs hate their guts.'

'Not any more, uncle. You don't follow modern politics any more than poor Winston does. The Bulgarians have, as our Prime Minister might have put it, "found their souls".'

'I don't think you'll have a very busy winter. There won't be so much Anglo-American interest as there's been in the last few months. In fact they might close this Mission down before Christmas.'

'Any suggestion of how we're supposed to get out?'

'I'll leave you the jeep, uncle. You might get through to Split.'

It seemed to Guy then that he had never really liked Frank de Souza.

The officer in Bari who distributed educational matter had sent a huge bundle of illustrated American magazines, mostly of distant date. In the long hours of early October Guy read them, slowly, straight through, like a Protestant nanny with her Bible.

Days passed without his receiving any summons to general headquarters. Bakic did not like walking. Guy got some pleasure from tramping the autumnal countryside with the spy limping behind him. The church was locked up; the priest had left. Three members of the Praesidium were installed in the presbytery.

'What's become of him?' Guy asked Bakic.

'He gone some other place. Little village more quiet than here. He was old. Too big a house for one old man.'

On Guy's 41st birthday he received a present; a signal reading: *Receive special flight four Dakotas tomorrow night 29th dispatch all Jews.*

He went joyfully to the Commissar, who, as before, had received confirmation from his own source of authority, and coldly gave his assent to the proposal.

It seemed to Guy, in the fanciful mood that his lonely state engendered, that he was playing an ancient, historic role as he went with Bakic to inform the Jews of their approaching exodus. He was Moses leading a people out of captivity.

He was not well versed in Old Testament history. The bullrushes, the burning bush, the plagues of Egypt belonged in his mind to very early memories, barely distinguishable from Grimm and Hans Andersen, but the image of Moses stood plain before his eyes, preposterously striking water from rock near the Grand Hotel in Rome, majestically laying down the law in St Peter-in-Chains. That day Guy's cuckold's horns shone like the patriarch's, when he came down from the awful cloud on Sinai.

But there was no divine intervention to help the Jews of Begoy, no opening of the sea, no inundation of chariots. Guy was informed that no further assistance was required from him. A partisan security company was detailed to muster the refugees and examine their scant baggage. At dusk they were marched out of their ghetto along the road to the airfield. Guy

saw them pass from the corner of the lane. It was the season of
mists and Guy felt the chill of anticipated failure. Silent and
shadowy the procession trailed past him. One or two had somehow borrowed peasants' hand carts. The oldest and feeblest
rode in them. Most were on foot bowed under their shabby
little bundles.

At ten o'clock when Guy and the Squadron Leader went out
the ground-mist was so thick that they could hardly find the
familiar way. The Jews were huddled on the embankment,
mostly sleeping.

Guy said to the Squadron Leader: 'Is this going to lift?'

'It's been getting thicker for the last two hours.'

'Will they be able to land?'

'Not a chance. I'm just sending the cancellation order now.'

Guy could not bear to wait. He walked back alone but could
not rest; hours later, he went out and waited in the mist at the
junction of lane and road until the weary people hobbled past
into the town.

Twice in the next three weeks the grim scene was repeated.
On the second occasion the fires were lit, the aeroplanes were
overhead and could be heard circling, recircling, and at length
heading west again. That evening Guy prayed: 'Please God
make it all right. You've done things like that before. Just send
a wind. Please God send a wind.' But the sound of the engines
dwindled and died away, and the hopeless Jews stirred themselves and set off again on the way they had come.

That week there was the first heavy fall of snow. There
would be no more landing until the Spring.

Guy despaired, but powerful forces were at work in Bari. He
soon received a signal: *Expect special drop shortly relief supplies for Jews stop Explain partisan HQ these supplies only
repeat only for distribution Jews.*

He called on the General with this communication.

'What supplies?'

'I presume food and clothing and medicine.'

'For three months I have been asking for these things for my
men. The Third Corps have no boots. In the hospital they are
operating without anaesthetics. Last week we had to withdraw
from two forward positions because there were no rations.'

'I know. I have signalled about it repeatedly.'

'Why is there food and clothes for the Jews and not for my men?'

'I cannot explain. All I have come to ask is whether you can guarantee distribution.'

'I will see.'

Guy signalled: *Respectfully submit most injudicious discriminate in favour of Jews stop Will endeavour secure proportionate share for them of general relief supplies*, and received in answer: *Three aircraft will drop Jewish supplies point C 1130 hrs 21st stop. These supplies from private source not military stop Distribute according previous signal.*

On the afternoon of the 21st the Squadron Leader came to see Guy.

'What's the idea?' he said. 'I've just been having the hell of a schemozzle with the Air Liaison comrade about tonight's drop. He wants the stuff put in bond or something till he gets orders from higher up. He's a reasonable sort of chap usually. I've never seen him on such a high horse. Wanted everything checked in the presence of the Minister of the Interior and put under joint guard. Never heard of such a lot of rot. I suppose someone at Bari has been playing politics as usual.'

That night the air was full of parachutes and of 'free-drops' whistling down like bombs. The anti-fascist youth retrieved them. They were loaded on carts, taken to a barn near the General's headquarters and formally impounded.

Belgrade fell to the Russians, Bulgarians, and partisans. A day of rejoicing was declared in Begoy by the Praesidium. The concert and the *Vin d'Honneur*, postponed in mourning, were held in triumph. On order from high authority a *Te Deum* was sung in the church, re-opened for that day and served by a new priest whom the partisans had collected during their expansion into Dalmatia. At nightfall the anti-fascist choir sang. The anti-fascist theatre group staged a kind of pageant of liberation. Wine and slivovic were copiously drunk and Guy through the interpreter made a formal little acknowledgement of the toast to Winston Churchill. And next day, perhaps, as part of the celebrations – Guy could never discern by what process the partisans from time to time were moved to acts of generosity – the Jews received their supplies.

Bakic greeted him with: 'De Jews again,' and going into the yard he found it full of his former visitors, but now transformed into a kind of farcical army. All of them, men and women, wore military greatcoats, Balaclava helmets, and knitted woollen gloves. Orders had been received from Belgrade, and distribution of the stores had suddenly taken place, and here were the recipients to thank him. The spokesmen were different on this occasion. The grocer and lawyer had gone ahead into the promised land. Madame Kanyi kept away for reasons of her own; an old man made a longish speech which Bakic rendered 'Dis guy say dey's all very happy.'

For the next few days a deplorable kind of ostentation seemed to possess the Jews. A curse seemed to have been lifted. They appeared everywhere, trailing the skirts of their greatcoats in the snow, stamping their huge news boots, gesticulating with their gloved hands. Their faces shone with soap, they were full of Spam and dehydrated fruits. They were a living psalm. And then, as suddenly, they disappeared.

'What has happened to them?'

'I guess dey been moved some other place,' said Bakic.

'Why?'

'People make trouble for them.'

'Who?'

'Partisan people dat hadn't got no coats and boots. Dey make trouble wid de Commissar so de Commissar move dem on last night.'

Guy had business that day with the Commissar. When it was ended Guy said: 'I see the Jews have moved.'

Without consulting his chief the intellectual young interpreter answered: 'Their house was required for the Ministry of Rural Economy. New quarters have been found for them a few miles away.'

The Commissar asked what was being said, grunted, and rose. Guy saluted and the interview was at an end. On the steps the interpreter joined him.

'The question of the Jews, Captain Crouchback. It was necessary for them to go. Our people could not understand why they should have special treatment. We have partisan women who work all day and have no boots or overcoats. How are we to explain that these old people who are doing nothing for our cause, should have such things?'

'Perhaps by saying that they *are* old and *have* no cause. Their need is greater than a young enthusiast's.'

'Besides, Captain Crouchback, they were trying to make business. They were bartering the things they had been given. My parents are Jewish and I understand these people. They want always to make some trade.'

'Well, what's wrong with that?'

'War is not a time for trade.'

'Well, anyway, I hope they have decent quarters.'

'They have what is suitable.'

The gardens in winter seemed smaller than in full leaf. From fence to fence the snow-obliterated lawns and beds lay open; the paths were only traceable by boot-prints. Guy daily took a handful of broken biscuits to the squirrel and fed him through the bars. One day while he was thus engaged, watching the little creature go through the motions of concealment, cautiously return, grasp the food, jump away, and once more perform the mime of digging and covering, he saw Mme Kanyi approach down the path. She was carrying a load of brushwood, stooping under it, so that she did not see him until she was quite close.

Guy had just received a signal for recall. The force was being renamed and re-organized. He was to report as soon as feasible to Bari. Word had gone to Belgrade, he supposed, that he was no longer *persona grata*.

He greeted Mme Kanyi with warm pleasure. 'Let me carry that.'

'No, please. It is better not.'

'I insist.'

Mme Kanyi looked about her. No one was in sight. She let him take the load and carry it towards her hut.

'You have not gone with the others?'

'No, my husband is needed.'

'And you don't wear your greatcoat.'

'Not out of doors. I wear it at night in the hut. The coats and boots make everyone hate us, even those who had been kind before.'

'But partisan discipline is so firm. Surely there was no danger of violence?'

'No, that was not the trouble. It was the peasants. The partisans are frightened of the peasants. They will settle with them later, but at present they are dependent on them for food. Our people began to exchange things with the peasants. They would give needles and thread, razors, things no one can get, for turkeys and apples. No one wants money. The peasants preferred bartering with our people to taking the partisans' bank-notes. That was what made the trouble.'

'Where have the others gone?'

She spoke a name which meant nothing to Guy. 'You have not heard of that place? It is twenty miles away. It is not a place of good repute. It is where the Germans and Ustachi made a camp. They kept the Jews and gypsies and communists and royalists there, to work on the canal. Before they left they killed what were left of the prisoners – not many. Now the partisans have found new inhabitants for it.'

They had reached the hut and Guy entered to place his load in a corner near the little stove. It was the first and last time he crossed the threshold. He had a brief impression of orderly poverty and then was outside in the snow. 'Listen, Signora,' he said. 'Don't lose heart. I am being recalled to Bari. As soon as the road is clear I shall be leaving. When I get there I promise I'll raise Cain about this. You've plenty of friends there and I'll explain the whole situation to them. We'll get you all out, I promise.'

As they stood on the little patch before the door which Mme Kanyi had cleared of snow they saw through the leafless shrubs the lurking figure of Bakic.

'You see you have been followed here.'

'He can't make any trouble.'

'Not for you, perhaps. You are leaving. There was a time when I thought that all I needed for happiness was to leave. Our people feel that. They must move away from evil. Some hope to find homes in Palestine. Most look no further than Italy – just to cross the water, like crossing the Red Sea.

'Is there any place that is free from evil? It is too simple to say that only the Nazis wanted war. These communists wanted it too. It was the only way in which they could come to power. Many of my people wanted it, to be revenged on the Germans, to hasten the creation of the national state. It seems to me there was a will to war, a death wish, everywhere. Even good men thought their private honour would be satisfied by war. They could assert their manhood by killing and being killed. They would accept hardships in recompense for having been selfish and lazy. Danger justified privilege. I knew Italians – not very many perhaps – who felt this. Were there none in England?'

'God forgive me,' said Guy. 'I was one of them.'

5

GUY had come to the end of the crusade to which he had devoted himself on the tomb of Sir Roger. His life as a Halberdier was over. All the stamping of the barrack square and the biffing of imaginary strongholds were finding their consummation in one frustrated act of mercy. He left Begoy without valediction save for the formal application at general headquarters for leave to travel. He took his small staff with him. His last act was to send by the hand of his orderly the pile of illustrated magazines to Madame Kanyi. He gave the widows such remains of his stores as the Squadron Leader did not require. The widows wept. The Squadron Leader expressed the hope that he, too, would soon get an order of recall.

The road to the coast was free of enemy and passable by jeep. It led through the desolate Lika where every village was ravaged and roofless, down into the clement coast of the Adriatic. Forty-eight hours after leaving Begoy Guy and his men were under the walls of Diocletian at Split, where they found an English cruiser in harbour, whose company were forbidden to land. Partisans had the shore batteries trained on her. This, more than anything he had seen in Jugoslavia, impressed the sergeant. 'Who'd have thought the Navy would stand for that, sir? It's politics, that's what it is.'

There was a British liaison officer at Split who gave him an order that had come, to drive on to Dubrovnik where a small British force, mostly of field artillery, had been landed and then held impotent. He was posted there as liaison officer between this force and the partisans.

His task was to hear from the partisan commander allegations of 'incorrect behaviour' by the British troops and convey them to the puzzled brigadier in command who had come under the supposition that he was a welcome ally; also to hear demands for supplies – the contrast between the fully equipped invaders and the ragged partisans was remarked by the townspeople – and to receive clandestine visits from civilians of various nationalities who wished to enrol themselves as displaced persons. On his first day he made a signal: *Situation of displaced persons in Begoy area desperate*, and received in answer: *Appropriate authority informed*, but his further lists of exiles received no acknowledgement.

At length, in mid-February the British force withdrew. Guy with the advance-party. He was set ashore at Brindisi and drove up to Bari just a year after he had first gone there. The almond was again in flower. He reported to Major Marchpole. He dined at the club.

'Everything is packing up here,' said the Major. 'I shall stay on as long as I can. The Brigadier has gone already. Joe Cattermole is in charge. You'll be returning to UK as soon as you want.'

It was from Cattermole that he learned that the Jews of Begoy had escaped. A private charitable organization in America had provided a convoy of new Ford trucks, shipped them to Trieste, driven through the snow of Croatia, and, leaving the trucks as a tip for the partisans, brought the exiles to Italy. It was indeed as though the Red Sea had miraculously drawn asunder and left a dry passage between walls of water.

Guy got permission to visit them. They were back behind barbed wire in a stony valley near Lecce. With them were four or five hundred others collected from various prisons and hiding places, all old and all baffled, all in army greatcoats and Balaclava helmets.

'I can't see the point of their being here,' said the Commandant. 'We feed them and doctor them and house them. That's all we can do. No one wants them. The Zionists are only interested in the young. I suppose they'll just sit here till they die.'

'Are they happy?'

'They complain the hell of a lot but then they've the hell of a lot to complain about. It's a lousy place to be stuck in.'

'I'm particularly interested in a pair called Kanyi.'

The Commandant looked down his list. 'Not here,' he said.

'Good. That probably means they got off to Australia all right.'

'Not from here, old man. I've been here all along. No one has ever left.'

'Could you make sure? Anyone in the Begoy draft would know about them.'

The Commandant sent his interpreter to inquire while he took Guy into the shed he called his mess, and gave him a drink. Presently the man returned. 'All correct, sir. The Kanyis never left Begoy. They got into some kind of trouble there and were jugged.'

'May I go with the interpreter and ask about it?'

'By all means, old man. But aren't you making rather heavy weather of it? What do two more or less matter?'

Guy went into the compound with the interpreter. Some of the Jews recognized him and crowded round him with complaints and petitions. All he could learn about the Kanyis was that they had been taken off the truck by the partisan police just as it was about to start.

He took the question to Major Marchpole.

'We don't really want to bother the Jugs any more. They really cooperated very well about the whole business. Besides the war's over now in that part. There's no particular point in moving people out. We're busy at the moment moving people in.' This man was in fact at that moment busy dispatching royalist officers – though he did not know it – to certain execution.

Guy spent his last days in Bari revisiting the offices where by signal he had begun his work of liberation. But this time he received little sympathy. The Jewish office showed little interest in him when they understood that he had not come to sell them illicit arms. They showed no interest in the Kanyis when they learned they were bound for Australia and not for Zion. 'We must first set up the State,' they said. 'Then it will be a refuge for all. First things first.'

An old Air Force acquaintance from Alexandrian days had a flat in Posillipo and asked Guy to stay. For a journey such as his it was a matter of being fitted into an aeroplane at the last moment when someone more important failed.

On the day before he was due to leave for Naples, he was accosted by Gilpin who said: 'Before you leave I shall want your security pass back.'

'I'm afraid I've lost it.'

'That will be very awkward.'

'Not for me,' said Guy. 'I have a friend in Air Priorities.'

Gilpin scowled. 'I hear you've been making inquiries about a couple named Kanyi.'

'Yes, I'm interested in them.'

'I thought you might be. It didn't sound like Frank de Souza exactly.'

'What didn't?'

'The confidential report. The woman was the mistress of a British Liaison Officer.'

'Nonsense.'

'He was seen leaving her home when her husband was away on duty. They were a thoroughly shady couple. The husband was guilty of sabotaging the electric light plant. A whole heap of American counter-revolutionary propaganda was found in their room. The whole association was most compromising to the Mission. It's lucky Cape had handed over to Joe before we got the report. You might have found yourself on a charge. But Joe's not vindictive. He just moved you where you couldn't do any harm. Though I may say that some of the names you sent us as displaced persons at Dubrovnik are on the black list.'

'What happened to the Kanyis?'

'What do you suppose? They were tried by a Peoples' Court. You may be sure justice was done.'

Once before in his military career Guy had been tempted to strike a brother officer – Trimmer at Southsands. The temptation was stronger now, but before he had done more than clench his fist, before he had raised it, the sense of futility intervened. He turned and left the office.

Next day he settled in Posillipo.

'For a chap who's on his way home you don't seem very cheerful,' said his host and then changed the subject, for he had had many men through his hands who were returning to problems more acute than any they had faced on active service.

Festival of Britain

In 1951, to celebrate the opening of a happier decade, the government decreed a Festival. Monstrous constructions appeared on the south bank of the Thames, the foundation stone was solemnly laid for a National Theatre, but there was little popular exuberance among the straitened people and dollar-bearing tourists curtailed their visits and sped to the countries of the Continent where, however precarious their condition, they ordered things better.

There were few private parties. Two of these were held in London on the same June evening.

Tommy Blackhouse had returned to England in May. He was retiring from the army with many decorations, a new, pretty wife, and the rank of major-general. In the last years he had advanced far beyond his commando into posts of greater and greater eminence and responsibility, never seeming to seek promotion, never leaving rancour behind him among those he surpassed; but his first command lay closest to his heart. Meeting Bertie in Bellamy's he had suggested a reunion dinner. Bertie agreed that it would be agreeable. 'It would mean an awful lot of organizing though,' said this one-time adjutant. It was left for Tommy, as always, to do the work.

The officers who had assembled at Mugg were not so scattered as those of other war-time units. Most of them had been together in prison. Luxmore had made an escape. Ivor Claire had spent six months in Burma with the Chindits, had done well, collected a DSO and an honourably incapacitating wound. He was often in Bellamy's now. His brief period of disgrace was set aside and almost forgotten.

'You're going to invite everyone?' asked Bertie.

'Everyone I can find. What was the name of that old Halberdier? Jumbo someone? We'll ask the sea-weed eater. I don't somehow think he'll come. Guy Crouchback of course.'

'Trimmer?'

'Certainly.'

But Trimmer had disappeared. All Tommy's adroit inquiries failed to find any trace of him. Some said he had jumped ship in South Africa. Nothing was known certainly. Fifteen men eventually assembled including Guy.

The second, concurrent festivity was given in part by Arthur Box-Bender. He had lost his seat in parliament in 1945. He rarely came to London in the succeeding years but that June evening he was induced to pay his half share in a small dance given in an hotel for his eighteen-year-old daughter and a friend of hers. For an hour or two he stood with Angela greeting the ill-conditioned young people who were his guests. Some of the men wore hired evening-dress; others impudently presented themselves in dinner-jackets and soft shirts. He and his fellow-host had been at pains to find the cheapest fizzy wine in the market. Feeling thirsty, he sauntered down Piccadilly and turned into St James's. Bellamy's alone retained some traces of happier days.

Elderberry was alone in the middle hall reading Air Marshal Beech's reminiscences. He, also, had lost his seat. His successful opponent, Gilpin, was not popular in the House but he was making his mark and had lately become an under-secretary. Elderberry had no habitation outside London. He had no occupation there. Most of his days and evenings were passed alone in this same armchair in Bellamy's.

He looked disapprovingly at Box-Bender's starched front.

'You still go out?'

'I had to give a party tonight for my daughter.'

'Ah, something you had to pay for? That's different. It's being *asked* I like. I'm never asked anywhere now.'

'I don't think you would have liked this party.'

'No, no, of course not. But I used to get asked to dinners – embassies and that kind of thing. Well, so did you. There was a lot of rot talked but it did get one through the evening. Everything's very quiet here now.'

This judgement was immediately rebutted by the descent of the Commando dinner party who stumbled noisily down the staircase and into the billiard room.

Guy paused to greet his brother-in-law.

'I didn't ask you to our dance,' said Box-Bender. 'It is very